ANGELS
to the
RESCUE

ANGELS
to the
RESCUE

a novel

DAN YATES

Covenant Communications, Inc.

Covenant

Published by Covenant Communications, Inc.
American Fork, Utah

Printed in the United States of America
First Printing: October 1997

04 03 02 01 00 99 98 97   10 9 8 7 6 5 4 3 2 1

ISBN 1-57734-210-0

PROLOGUE

When she was a child, Samantha had always wanted a sister. She loved her brother, Michael, who was two years younger than she was, but he wasn't the same as a sister. When Samantha was six years old, her cousin Lisa had come into the family. As far as Samantha was concerned, she had her sister. And she had a second sister two years later when her cousin Julie was born.

As the years passed, Samantha was always there for her cousins, at first as a baby-sitter when Lisa and Julie were small. As the two girls grew into young womanhood, Sam became more of a friend and confidante. Samantha loved Lisa's even-tempered mildness, although she loved Julie equally for her quick wit and easy laughter. The girls' mother, Sam's Aunt Katherine, often said Julie was another Samantha; she was just wrapped in a different package.

J.T.—as everyone but Samantha called her Uncle Mac—adored his wife, Katherine, and his two daughters, and spent every free minute with them. True, in those days he was never able to give his family much in the way of material things. It never seemed to matter much, though. They were an exceptionally happy family, and Katherine often remarked how rich they were in the important things life had to offer.

Samantha had heard rumors of Aunt Katherine giving up a life of great wealth to marry Uncle Mac. According to the rumors, she had had another suitor who was very rich. But Samantha never got the whole story out of either Katherine or her Uncle Mac. Katherine just smiled peacefully when Samantha asked her, and her Uncle Mac scowled at her, a look he wore more and more when Katherine was hospitalized for cancer.

It was barely six months after Katherine's death when J.T. came into the first stages of his own wealth. It happened when a real estate scheme he had been investing in for more than five years took a sudden upward turn. Despite his new financial success, however, he became even more withdrawn. Samantha hated seeing her beloved uncle sink into this gloom, and she understood that not only was he grieving for the loss of his wife, he was overcome with guilt. Guilt that his wealth had come too late to be shared with his beloved Katherine.

J.T. continued to grow harder and colder as his assets swelled to enormous size. A cynical frown replaced the smile he used to wear almost continually before Katherine's death. His face withered into a mass of wrinkles, and he took on the look of a man much older than his years. Worst of all, he became so protective of his daughters that he suspected everyone of befriending them just to get at his money. This was one side of J.T. that Samantha refused to tolerate lightly. She spoke out on Lisa and Julie's behalf, often standing between them and one of J.T.'s outlandish restrictions. Time and again she managed to overrule him, allowing the girls to attend a party or some outside school function he had heatedly forbidden.

Leaving Lisa and Julie behind, to fend for themselves with Uncle Mac, had been one of the hardest parts of Samantha's decision to cross the line into the far side of forever. But when she realized it was either that or give up Jason Hackett, her choice was clear and certain. She chose to be with Jason. Even now, she had to smile when she remembered the early days of their courtship, and the first day Jason had suddenly appeared in her apartment declaring his undying love for her. He had been insulted when she had called him a ghost. "I'm an angel," he had corrected her.

As Samantha stood in shock, unable to understand how Jason had managed to get into her apartment, Jason had tried to explain. "We have a special contract that ties our destinies together, but because my friend Gus made a typo on my contract, I was born in 1926 when I should have been born in 1962. And because I didn't live at my appointed time, the contract is in jeopardy of being annulled unless I can convince you to help me salvage it."

But, even after Samantha had started to believe the crazy story Jason was telling her, it didn't change the fact that she was engaged to Bruce Vincent. And even though Jason finally managed to win her heart, that didn't change the fact that as an angel, he lived in a completely different dimension than Samantha, who was very much alive. So, facing the facts, Samantha had finally decided to go ahead with her marriage to Bruce. Fortunately, Gus had stepped in at the last moment with a plan that had allowed Samantha to join Jason on the far side of forever, and both were extremely happy together.

* * *

Nine months had now passed since the day Samantha made her decision. Much had happened in those months, and Samantha was pleased that her former fiancé, Bruce, was now happily engaged to her best friend, Arline Wilson—with Samantha's help, of course. Even though she would be unseen, Samantha vowed to be at their upcoming wedding to watch her two friends begin a contract of their own. A contract like the one she shared with her dear Jason.

Samantha had enjoyed getting Bruce and Arline together, and she hadn't minded her mortal jaunt at all. Now it looked like she might be needed once again. Samantha knew her Uncle Mac had been ornery ever since her Aunt Katherine died, but who would have ever guessed he would pull a stunt like this last one? Everyone seemed to agree that the old rascal had finally gone too far when he . . . Well, maybe it would be better if you turned the page and read about it for yourself.

CHAPTER 1

A gentle breeze pressed its crisp autumn chill against Samantha's cheeks as she stood looking out over the still waters of Dove Park Lake. Memories flooded her mind of the many happy hours she had spent here in the final days of her life on this side of forever. It had been in this very place that Jason had appeared to her when she was feeding the ducks. She had been pretty embarrassed when she realized some boys playing nearby thought she was carrying on a one-sided conversation with herself. Until that moment, she had had no idea she was the only one who could see or hear Jason.

So much had happened since that day. Samantha smiled with contentment at the thought that she too was a angel now. A very happy angel, she might add.

Why did Gus ask to meet me here in this park? she wondered. *Why didn't he just ask me to drop by his office? We could have even met at my house.* Samantha didn't have to ponder the question long. As was his habit, Gus suddenly appeared out of nowhere. "Hi ya, Sam," he said with an overly cheerful ring in his voice that left Samantha even more curious what he was up to. "Yer lookin' sharp this mornin'. Life with old Jase must be agreein' with ya."

Samantha couldn't help but laugh at him. She'd known Gus forever it seemed, but still his remark was flattering. "Good morning, Gus. Living with 'old Jase', as you put it, does agree with me. I shudder to think where I might be right now if you hadn't talked me out of marrying Bruce. I owe you a big one, Gus. But don't go getting too puffed up. If you hadn't made the typo in the first place, you wouldn't have had to talk me out of marrying Bruce—would you?"

"Drat you, Sam," Gus grumbled. "Are ya ever gonna let me live that one down?"

"Not in this eternity," she teased. "But I do forgive you. That's something, isn't it? I mean, after all, everything did turn up roses in the end. I have my cute little ghost, Jason, and I love the mountain home you had built for me. I know that Bruce and Arline are together, and I still get to teach the children whenever they need a substitute. What more could I ask for, Gus? I guess the effects of your typo are all pretty much history now."

Gus nervously shifted his weight from one leg to the other. "Not exactly, Sam," he hesitantly admitted. "We've . . . uh . . . sorta got ourselves another little problem, it seems."

Looking more closely into Gus' eyes, Samantha saw something there she hadn't noticed earlier. "Something's bothering you, isn't it, Gus?" she asked pointedly. "What do you mean we have another problem?"

"That's why I asked ya ta meet me here this mornin', Sam. We need ta talk, and I thought this would be a better spot than my office. Ya see, the typo isn't exactly history yet. It's sorta come back ta haunt us again. The higher authorities have just informed me there's another glitch in the works, and we hafta stop it."

"Another glitch?" Samantha frowned. "Gus Winklebury, don't you dare tell me my contract with Jason is in jeopardy again. I don't want to hear it. Enough is enough."

"Not to worry, Sam!" Gus quickly assured her. "Yer contract with Jason is caked in stone, ya have my word on it."

"That's 'cast in stone,' Gus. And if that's true, then why are you telling me there's another glitch to deal with?"

Gus removed the golf cap he was wearing and wiped his brow with the back of his hand. "The glitch I'm referring to concerns some of yer family, Sam."

A wrinkle creased Samantha's forehead. True, she did leave family on this side when she crossed the line to be with Jason. There were her parents, who were living in Europe where her father, a captain in the Air Force, was stationed. But she had checked on them only a couple of days earlier and they were doing fine. She also had a younger brother, Michael, who worked as a security guard at the local city museum, but things seemed to be going well for him, too.

"How can my family be affected by your typo?" she said, after a moment's thought. "I thought that concerned no one but Jason and me—and Bruce, of course, but he and Arline are doing just fine."

Gus fidgeted with the hat he was holding. "The people I'm talking about weren't directly affected by the typo," he explained. "They were sorta what ya might call secondhand victims."

Samantha was confused. "'Secondhand victims'?" she repeated. "You're not making any sense, Gus."

Gus put the cap back on his head and took a moment to straighten it. Then, reaching into his jacket pocket, he retrieved an envelope that he held in such a way that Samantha could see it. But he didn't offer it to her just yet. "The problem," he went on to explain, "lies with yer cousins, Lisa and Julie MacGregor. They're in a bit of a pickle, I'd say. Especially Lisa."

Samantha felt her pulse quicken at the mention of her cousins' names. Since she had wanted but had never had sisters of her own, she had been thrilled when Lisa and Julie had joined the family. In her eyes, the two girls could do no wrong. They were as close to perfect as two young ladies could be. Well—there was one thing. Julie and Lisa both had long, shiny hair. Not that Samantha was jealous or anything. But still, there were times when she wished her hair was as long as theirs. Many times, as a matter of fact.

"Are the girls all right?" she quickly asked. "They're not in any serious trouble, I hope."

"They're all right fer now, Sam. But they won't be if that ornery old J.T. has his way. That man has slipped more than a few cogs on his thinkin' apparatus. I think ya better read this copy of the report that came down from the higher authorities. It'll tell the story better than I can."

Gus handed the envelope to Samantha. She took it from him, opened it cautiously, and for the next several minutes studied the contents thoroughly. At last she lowered the papers and looked back to Gus.

"You say this came down from the higher authorities?" she asked.

Gus nodded. "Just this mornin', Sam," he replied.

Samantha felt a large knot form in the pit of her stomach. "You're right, Gus," she replied. "The effects of the typo aren't dead.

It's obvious I have my work cut out for me. I think I'd better get started right away, don't you agree?"

Gus stopped smiling. "Now wait a minute, Sam," he began. "I know how ya must feel. But ya hafta let me handle this problem my way. What do ya say we take ourselves a walk along the lake? It might make what I have ta say a little easier.

"Ya see, Sam," he began. "When I made the mistake that brought old Jase here more than thirty years too soon, the higher authorities were pertty understandin' and all, but they refused ta fix the problem. They said since I brought it on myself, I could just figure out how to fix it myself. When I approached them with the idea of havin' you cut yer stay in mortality short in order to be with Jason, they gave me the green light. I just naturally supposed that would be the end of the problem."

Gus let out a very loud sigh before continuing. "As you can tell from the report ya just read, I was wrong. That wasn't the end of the problem. Now I find myself faced with a foul-up almost as big as gettin' you and Jason together in the first place. Bottom line—I need Jason's help. And ta tell ya the truth, I'm not too keen on the idea of facin' him with the prospect of his comin' back here again."

Samantha stopped short in her tracks. "That's it, Gus?" she asked. "You want to use Jason to straighten out this mess, and you're afraid to approach him with the idea yourself. That's what you're up to, isn't it? You just wanted me to do the asking for you."

"Take it easy, Sam," Gus pleaded. "Don't go gettin' all riled up. You know darn well Jason will listen ta you. And since the problem concerns part of yer family, I thought—"

"Hold it right there, Gus. You said it yourself, the problem is with *my* family. *I'm* the one you should be considering here. If anyone's going to play ghost, it's going to be me, not Jason."

Gus shook his head. "Uh-uh," he asserted. "You're too close ta the problem on this one. And besides, Jason has years of experience in these things. He's the natural one for the project. All we gotta do is convince him of that."

"*I'm* too close to the problem?" Samantha countered indignantly. "And just what is that supposed to mean, Gus?"

"It should be obvious, Sam. You read the report. It's yer uncle that's interferin' with destiny, here. Use yer head, Sam. There's no way that ornery old man would be frightened of yer ghost. Fer one thing, yer just too close to him. And fer another, yer too darned pertty ta be scary. Jason, on the other hand, could really scare the pants off the old coot."

Samantha narrowed her eyes. "Wait a minute. I agree that Uncle Mac wouldn't be afraid of me, but what difference does that make? The report says I'm the one who would have been instrumental in influencing Uncle Mac if I were still alive. What makes you think I can't be just as effective as a ghost?"

"Now, Sam, you can't—" Gus stuttered nervously.

Putting her hands on her hips, Samantha glared at Gus. "You know how angry it makes me when someone tells me I *can't* do something, don't you, Gus?"

Gus put up his hands as if to fend her off. "I know, Sam. Believe me, I know. And I'm not sayin' ya *couldn't* do it. I'm only sayin' Jason is the one with the experience, so he stands a better chance of gettin' the job done faster. And of course, I'd be workin' with him."

Samantha rolled her eyes. "If you'll remember, it was *my* plan that got Arline and Bruce together after you and Jason nearly blew it."

Gus shrugged. "Okay, so ya did help out a little on that one, but Jason and I had everythin' under control the whole time. We would have got the job done on our own, if ya'd let us."

"Listen," Samantha said persuasively, "you needed me on that project, and you need me on this one—because this project definitely needs a woman's touch. And if it's experience you're worried about, I'll talk Jason into giving me a hand."

Gus shook his head. "The higher authorities are *not* gonna like this," he huffed. "They like ta keep these projects on a less personal level."

Samantha smiled. "You're not kidding me for one minute, Gus. With all your connections, you can have me cleared for the project before I can get dressed for my first appearance to Uncle Mac. Now, if you're finished giving me a hard time, I'd really like to get started."

Gus stood looking at her for what seemed a very long time. "Okay, Sam," he agreed at last. "But I want yer word you'll talk to Jason about helpin' out with the project."

"You have my word, Gus," Samantha agreed cheerfully. "Now with your permission, I'd like to pay a visit to my favorite uncle."

"Not just yet, Sam," Gus responded. "First I hafta fill ya in on a few things pertinent ta the case. Because of the special nature of this assignment, the higher authorities have cleared me ta use something very special—a selected event shown by holographically enhanced regeneration."

Sam stared at Gus. "A selected what?"

Gus laughed. "Gotcha there, didn't I? You've never seen one of these things, Sam, but lemme tell ya, it's the next best thing ta bein' there when the event happened in the first place. Hold on ta yer horses and I'll show ya what I mean."

Samantha didn't quite know what Gus was talking about, but she knew him well enough to understand that when he said hold on, she'd better do just that. This was no exception. In one split second the two of them were no longer in Dove Park. Instead, they were in some sort of a large gymnasium filled with people and music. It took only a moment for Samantha to realize they were at a dance, and from the signs and posters strategically placed throughout the room, she surmised it was a political fund-raising event of some sort.

As soon as her head cleared, she spoke. "Okay, Gus, I give up. Why have you brought me to a dance?"

"In the first place, Sam, yer not really *at* the dance. Ya just *feel* like yer at the dance. Not only can ya see the people yer interested in, ya can feel what they were feelin', and even know what they were thinkin'. That's why it takes special permission from the higher authorities ta use a holographically enhanced regeneration. If it was ta be misused, it would be sorta like an invasion of privacy, if ya get my drift."

Samantha gave Gus a suspicious look. "Did you ever use one of these things to put me under your microscope? Because if you did—"

"Put yer mind at ease, Sam. I didn't have to. I was workin' with Jason before you were even born. I saw all I needed ta see of yer story firsthand."

"That's bad enough," Samantha responded. "And I'm not too sure I like the idea of spying on these people like this. Is it really necessary?"

"Yer the one who pushed me fer this case, Sam. If ya want ta change yer mind . . ."

Samantha shook her head. "Forget it, Gus. You're not getting rid of me, so let's just get on with your little show, whatever it is."

Gus gave an exasperated sigh before continuing his explanation. "The reason I wanted ya ta see this is because it depicts the event in time where the problem we're dealin' with first got started. Take a look right over there." He pointed to a couple on the dance floor. "I think yer gonna see what I mean."

Samantha looked. "It's Cousin Lisa!" she cried out. "But who's that guy she's dancing with? I don't remember him."

"The guy's name is Greg Reeves. His dad is one of yer Uncle Mac's recent business associates. And that's another big problem yer gonna hafta deal with. Fer now I want ya ta pay particular attention to the guy playin' lead guitar in the band. He's the fella ya read about in the report from the higher authorities. You know, the one old Mac ran off."

"I know him, sort of," Samantha said. "That's Rob Jensen. Rob went to high school with Lisa, but the two of them were never friends or anything. They just saw each other around at school or basketball games, stuff like that."

"Ya got that right, Sam. But the story goes a little deeper than that. Ya see, Lisa and Rob have a contract with each other, just like you and Jason. They were destined ta meet and fall in love in high school, but because of yer Uncle Mac's influence Lisa didn't listen to her heart. I had ta take special steps ta get the two of them together, and that's what this dance was all about. I'm the one who got them both here."

"Lisa and Rob are contracted? So why is Lisa dancing with Greg Reeves?"

"Lisa and Rob haven't got together yet, Sam. I told ya, that's why I cooked up this dance. I knew Rob would be with the band, and it was easy gettin' Lisa here with Greg since he's the only one she ever dates these days. Not that she wouldn't like ta date others—but since old Mac likes Greg, it's easier for her to date him than face one of the old boy's lectures."

Gus blew on his knuckles and rubbed them against his shirt. "You like ta think of yerself as quite a cupid, Sam. Well ever' now and then I make a pertty good Cupid myself."

Samantha couldn't help laughing at Gus just a little. "I'll agree with you on this one," she admitted. "But how will you—or I guess that should be how *did* you—get the two of them together when Lisa was here with Greg, and Rob was on the stage performing with the band?"

Gus laughed. "That, Sam, is one of the advantages of bein' in my position. I have celestial technology at my disposal, which in this case means Maggie's computer. All she had ta do was program one tiny moment where Lisa's eyes met Rob's, then . . . *magic!*"

Samantha was disbelieving. "That's it?" she asked. "Why wasn't it that easy for Jason and me?"

Gus shrugged again. "What can I say, Sam? You're a lot more stubborn than Lisa ever was. Although that Julie—now she's a feisty one. She sorta reminds me of a certain stubborn angel I know."

"Why, thank you, Gus," Samantha smiled. "Now, tell me, what else do I need to know about Lisa and Rob, and this Greg character?"

* * *

Lisa had to admit that Greg was a good dancer. And he had other good points, as well. But somehow she knew he would never be the man she had dreamed of as a girl, the prince who would ride up on his white stallion and whisk her away to his castle in a land of eternal flowers and sunshine. No matter how hard her father tried to make her care for his business partner's son, it just wasn't there.

As Lisa danced, she suddenly realized the song Rob Jensen was singing was one he had composed while the two of them were still in high school. It was a really great song with a catchy beat. She remembered that he had sung it in a school assembly. Following an impulse, she turned to look at Rob only to discover that his eyes were on her, too. In that instant a strange thing happened. It wasn't easy to explain, but it felt like a warm flame passing completely through her. In less than a heartbeat, their eyes broke contact and the feeling was gone. But its memory remained, filling her with an overpowering desire to pursue it further. Crazy as it seemed, she wanted to see Rob again, to get to know him better. And even crazier, she felt he did, too.

As the evening drew on, Lisa couldn't keep her eyes off Rob. She knew he was looking at her, too. Their chance came during intermission, when Greg stepped away to make a phone call. They only said a few words, but that was all it took for her to accept a date to the movies with him.

What have you done, Lisa MacGregor? she asked herself as she watched Rob walk back to the stage. *Father will be furious. You'll just have to call Rob and tell him the date is off.* But by the time the next dance number had started, she knew she wouldn't cancel their date. She couldn't explain how she knew, but she realized a prince had just ridden into her life. She'd just have to find a way to keep father from knowing. That shouldn't be too hard, she thought Her sister Julie would help. Julie was always there for her. And since Julie had little use for Greg Reeves, she would be more than willing to help Lisa get away with dating someone like Rob Jensen without their father knowing about it.

* * *

"Wow, Gus," Samantha exclaimed. "You were right. I not only saw what happened between Lisa and Rob, I really did feel her emotions. I even knew her thoughts. That's incredible. How does it work?"

"Beats me. All I know is it works. You should count yerself lucky—most angels never get the chance ta see one of these things, and you've been cleared ta do more than that, Sam. You actually get ta use a couple of them yerself, later on. With yer Uncle Mac, I mean."

"Are you kidding me? I get to use this with Uncle Mac? But how? I have no idea how to make one work."

"No problem, Sam. It's as easy as cake. You'll figure it out when the time comes. Fer now, I got something else I want ya ta see."

In an instant, the scene changed. Samantha and Gus were no longer at the dance, but were now inside J.T. MacGregor's magnificent home. Samantha recognized it instantly, having been there many times over the years. "What are we doing here?" she asked.

"I'm just tryin' ta give ya some background information on the problem at hand," he explained. "What yer gonna see now happened about a month and a half after the dance where Lisa and Rob met. They've been spendin' more time together than Snow White spent fixin' breakfast fer her ugly stepsisters."

"That was Cinderella, Gus. Snow White didn't have ugly step-sisters."

"Yeah, well be that as it may," Gus said loftily, "Lisa and Rob are pertty much hung on each other by this time. Anyway, this is where Lisa finally bites the bullet and introduces Rob ta yer Uncle Mac. I'm sure ya can imagine what yer about ta see happen here."

Samantha understood perfectly. "Poor Lisa. I wish I could be—uh, I mean—*could have been* here to help her through this one. This is all so real I keep forgetting it's already happened. So, where is everyone?"

"Rob and Lisa aren't here yet. Julie and yer uncle are in the family room. Would ya like ta join 'em?"

"*Would I like ta join 'em?*" Samantha asked, using her best Gus impersonation. "Are you kidding? Come on, pal, let's go."

* * *

"I don't want to wear a tie, Julie," J.T. grumbled. "Why should I make myself uncomfortable to meet some young pup I know I'm not going to like even before I see him?"

"Will you hold still, Dad?" Julie retorted. "I can't get this knot straight with you squirming around like this. And don't be so fast to put the man down just because he's a musician. You should trust Lisa's judgment. She's an intelligent woman, you know."

A muffled growl escaped J.T.'s throat as he reluctantly submitted to her tying his tie. "Lisa has no business fooling around with some two-bit singer when she has Greg. He's the right one for her, and you know it, Julie MacGregor."

Finished with the knot, Julie stepped back to examine her efforts. "Yeah," she chuckled, giving her father's tie one last little twist, "Greg and all his father's money, you mean. That's what makes him the right man for Lisa in your book, Dad. You're not fooling me for one minute."

"Hogwash! That's not the only reason I want Greg for my son-in-law. He's an upstanding man with a good head on his shoulders—and he loves your sister. You're the one who's always lecturing me on the importance of loving someone."

"Love is a two-way street, Dad," Julie reminded her father. "Lisa doesn't love Greg and she never will. And as far as that goes, I doubt Greg loves her, either. I don't think Greg could love anyone but himself."

J.T. opened his mouth to respond, but before he could get the words out, the sound of the front door opening caught his attention. "Come on, Dad," Julie said, taking him by the arm and leading him toward the living room where she knew they'd find her sister and Rob. "And straighten up! You're slumping again. You look ten years older when you slump like that."

"Humph," J.T. snorted, deliberately loosening the knot on his tie. "Anyone would think you were my mother instead of my daughter."

A moment later, J.T. MacGregor approached a smiling Lisa, who stood with her arm linked through Rob's. "Father, this is Rob. He sings and plays lead guitar in a great band. And he's going to school to earn a business degree. He only has three more semesters to go. Rob, this is my father."

"Happy to meet you, sir," Rob said, extending his hand in J.T.'s direction. "Lisa's told me so much about you."

"I'll bet she has, young man," J.T. responded coldly, ignoring Rob's hand. "You do know she's practically engaged to Greg Reeves, don't you?"

Lisa looked startled. "Father! I am *not* practically engaged to Greg. We're just friends, and that's all."

Not knowing what else to do with his hand, Rob pulled it back and shoved it into his front pants pocket. "We've talked about Greg, sir," he stammered. "But Lisa has never mentioned being almost engaged."

Julie elbowed her father out of the way and stepped up to Rob. "Don't mind him, Rob," she said. "He's been in a cantankerous mood all day. I think he must have eaten Mexican food for lunch again. Mexican food always does this to him. You want a soda, or something?"

"Some lemonade would be nice," Lisa said, trying to lighten the tension in the room.

"You got it," Julie responded, motioning for Lisa to get Rob seated on the sofa a few feet away, while she nudged J.T. to the recliner near where he was standing. "I'll bring you some milk, Dad. I wouldn't want your ulcer aggravated any more than it already is." Julie left for the kitchen while the others sat down.

"Rob's just written a new song," Lisa said, trying to sound upbeat. "I bet it will be on the top ten in no time—that is, if he can get someone to record it and get it on the market."

J.T. showed no signs of being impressed. "Top ten?" he huffed. "Whose top ten? Our local radio station's? Does that mean you'll only lose an arm, instead of an arm and a leg, like I'm sure most aspiring young musicians lose when they try to make it in the big league?"

Lisa flushed. "Father!"

"Speaking of losing a leg," J.T. said, with a sharp look at Rob, "isn't your father the one who lost both legs from the knees down in a gas explosion?"

"Yes, sir. That was my dad." After a brief pause, Rob asked, "How did you know that, sir?"

"I read about him in the paper. The accident was a couple of years ago, if I remember right."

Rob's voice was firm. "Two and a half years, to be exact. I'm very proud of my dad. He needed gas, so he pulled into the Texaco station on Rand Boulevard. He was filling his tank when a vanload of teenagers came barreling into the station. I guess the kids had been out partying, and the driver was just drunk enough to think he was in control. The van hit one of the pumps. Gas flew everywhere and was instantly ignited by sparks from the crash. Everyone but the driver got out, but he was either too drunk or too stunned by the impact to move. My dad rushed in and pulled him out. He was carrying the kid away from the fire when the whole thing exploded. The kid made it fine, but my dad wasn't so lucky. He was hit by a piece of jagged metal that nearly severed both legs. They had to be amputated."

"Yes, I'm aware of the amputation," J.T. acknowledged stiffly. "You might as well know, son, when I learned you were dating my daughter, I had you and your family checked out."

Lisa groaned. "Father, you didn't. How could you do such a thing?"

Rob took her hand. "It's all right," he said. "If your father wants to check up on my family, let him."

J.T. went on, "Your father was quite a hero, Rob, but what did it get him? He didn't even have the good sense to sue Texaco. He could easily have gotten a million or two out of them."

Rob stood up, and facing J.T. said, "I'll tell you this much, sir, we have nothing to hide. My dad has too much integrity to do as you suggested. It wasn't Texaco's fault those kids ran into one of their pumps. And the kids themselves were driving without insurance, so there was no recourse in that direction, either. But you know what? Dad didn't just lay down and die. He's a salesman and a good one, too. Sure, he makes fewer sales from his wheelchair than he used to make when he had two good legs, but in my family we know that money isn't everything. He and Mom have learned to live on less, but I've never seen them happier."

J.T. grunted. "Hogwash! Happiness never came from being poor. Your father's integrity, as you call it, is nothing more than stubborn pride. I don't want any young fool with those kinds of notions in his head hanging around my daughter. And that, son, is exactly where you stand in my book."

Lisa was in tears as she stood and led Rob toward the door. "I can't believe you said that, Father. And I can't believe you actually checked up on Rob's family. Sometimes I think you're despicable." She slammed the door as they left.

"Well," Julie said as she returned with a tray loaded with drinks. "That certainly went well. Lisa's right, you know, Dad. You can be pretty despicable at times. And that's usually on one of your good days."

J.T. didn't answer. He was used to Julie speaking her mind. The main thing was that he didn't let his girls make the same mistake his wife had.

CHAPTER 2

Samantha was a little surprised to learn their next destination was Dove Park.

"Now this took place just six months ago," Gus said, nodding toward the opposite side of the lake where the boat rental shed stood. It was now early evening and the cool breeze across the lake felt good on Samantha's face.

"Six months ago?" she frowned in concentration. "That's about the time I was working with Bruce and Arline. Do you mean to tell me I was that close when my uncle pulled this little stunt, and I didn't know it was happening? I could have been there . . ." Her words trailed off as she noticed a young couple preparing to get into a canoe. Looking closer, she recognized them as Rob and Lisa, although Lisa looked out of place in her lovely satin appliqué dress.

"What's going on, Gus?" she asked. "They're not planning on going out on the lake in that little canoe with Lisa dressed like that, are they?"

Gus nodded a yes. "Rob pulled an old switcheroo on her, Sam. He took her out for dinner, and she thought they were goin' to a party afterward. He had somethin' else in mind, though. Just keep watchin'. I think yer gonna like what ya see."

The two of them moved in a little closer so they could hear what Lisa was saying to Rob.

* * *

"You can't be serious, Rob Jensen. You want to get me out on the lake in this little canoe? The electric boats seem much safer to me."

Rob smiled mischievously. "Forget the electric boat, that's for kids. Canoeing is more fun. Don't tell me you've never tried it."

Lisa pulled a face. "I'll probably get seasick or something."

"Hey! You finally got used to riding around in my old Chevy, didn't you? You always said nothing could be worse than riding in that."

Lisa thought affectionately of Rob's old Chevy. She'd given Rob a hard time about his car from the first time they'd gone out, but now she was thinking she'd choose the Chevy over this canoe any day.

When Lisa didn't speak, Rob said persuasively, "Look at that full moon. You want to waste it?"

But Lisa ignored the moon and stared at the canoe. Even though Rob didn't know it, she had never been in a canoe. On a couple of occasions, Julie had tried to get her in one, but she flatly refused. She didn't trust canoes. They looked so unstable, as if they might roll over any second, treating their occupants to a watery surprise. She bit her lip and gathered up her courage. "All right, I'll get in your canoe. But you'd better take it easy with me."

Rob smiled as he picked out an oar from the rack. "You can trust me," he promised.

"Yeah, like when you told me we were going to a party, right?"

"Just get in the canoe!"

Very cautiously she eased herself into one end of the canoe and sat down. Rob dropped a small box he had brought along into the other end, then got in himself.

Lisa looked on curiously. "What's in the box?" she asked.

"It's a surprise. I'll show you later."

"I hate your surprises, Rob Jensen," Lisa complained. "Tell me what's in the box."

"What's in the box is for me to know and for you to find out later, Miss MacGregor." He pushed off from the dock and began rowing out onto the lake.

Lisa held her breath and tried not to listen to the pounding of her own heart. "Okay," she said, after they had moved a short distance through the still, dark water. "I did it. Can we go back now?"

Laughing, Rob shook his head. "Sure, go ahead. You'll have to swim, though. There's no way I'm docking the canoe now. We came out here for a boat ride, and we're going to have our boat ride."

Lisa settled back and tried to relax while Rob rowed smoothly out onto the lake. It didn't take long for her to see that the canoe wasn't going to tip over, and within a few minutes she realized she was actually enjoying the ride. Light from the full moon filled the night with a brilliant luster, and the young couple was completely alone on the lake—unless you counted the four ducks swimming through the nearby lily pads.

Rob lifted the oar out of the water and laid it in the canoe. Opening the box, he removed—of all things—a toy ukelele, which he began to play.

"We were sailing along on Moonlight Bay . . ." he sang, and Lisa recognized the song as one her father sometimes played from his cherished collection of old 78 rpm records.

Although Lisa ordinarily enjoyed Rob's music, she squealed and put a finger in each ear.

Rob forced a hurt look. "Some people pay to hear me, you know. Just last week a guy with a white cane and tin cup tossed me a quarter. Now here you are getting a free concert and what do you do? You interrupt and complain. I thought most girls like to be serenaded."

He began strumming one more time. "Just the two of us together—now don't go away . . ."

Lisa started to laugh and Rob lowered the ukelele. "It's rude of you to laugh at my love song, you know," he said.

"Love song?" Lisa asked, still laughing. "Is that what it was? Oh my, I am sorry. I thought you were trying to call those ducks over to the boat."

Rob immediately tossed the ukelele over the side of the boat. "You've done it now. My feelings are shattered."

Lisa couldn't believe her eyes although ever since she'd begun dating Rob, he was always pulling some off-the-wall stunt. She never knew what to expect next. "You know what you are, Rob Jensen?" she asked. "You're crazy, that's what. You're about the craziest human being I've ever met."

"I'm supposed to be crazy," he argued. "I'm a musician. All musicians are crazy. Go ahead, deny it, that's the biggest reason you fell in love with me."

"In love with you?" Lisa raised her eyebrows. "Is that what you think, that I'm in love with you?"

"Well, of course you're in love with me," Rob said reasonably. "In fact, you're madly in love with me. It's written all over your face, especially in those big, beautiful, blue eyes. Who knows, you might even love me as much as I love you. Hey! That would make a great opening line for my next song." He hummed a few notes, as if testing out a new song.

"You're—in love with me?" Lisa could barely speak.

"Yeah, I am," Rob answered casually. "Have been for weeks now, just never found the right time or way of telling you." He gave a deep sigh. "And when I decide to do it in song, this is your reaction."

Lisa's mind whirled in confusion. Lisa had never been in love, and she had no idea how it felt. But as she thought about it, it began to make sense. How else could she explain the funny little tricks her heart had been playing on her lately? And why else hadn't she been able to get Rob off her mind? If this wasn't love, it still felt pretty darn wonderful.

Rob moved to the center of the canoe and reached out for her. "Give me your hand," he said.

"What are you up to, Mr. Jensen?" she giggled.

"Your hand," he said again. "Give me your hand."

Slowly she extended her hand, which he held in both of his own. "There's something I've been meaning to bring up for some time now. I think you're much too special to go through life without me, Lisa. So I picked up a little something for you."

As she looked on in amazement, he slid a small diamond ring on her finger.

Lisa thought her heart would explode. "What are you saying, Rob? Are you . . . ?"

"I'm asking you to marry me, Lisa. A simple 'yes' will do nicely. And you have to kiss me, of course."

"Are you serious?" she gasped.

"I've never been more serious in my life. I love you and I want to marry you. I'll have my degree in business management in about a year, and I can always get a fill-in job at the post office where my uncle works if I need to. You'll have to keep teaching for a couple of years, you know, just until I get a handle on things. I admit I can't give you what your father thinks you deserve in a the way of material things, but I can give you a heart full of love. We'll be a long way from the welfare rolls, and don't forget my Chevy is paid for. Half of it will be yours," he promised solemnly.

Lisa swallowed hard and pulled her hand back to look at the ring in the light of the moon. "How ever did you pay for this, Rob?" she asked.

"Don't you worry how I paid for it. Just say you'll marry me."

"But—what about your music? And what about my father? You know how he feels about you, Rob."

Rob reached out and took her hand again. "Lisa," he said earnestly, "I've never been naive enough to think I could support myself and a family with my music. I've always figured business management would be my career, and music would be my passion. If a big break comes, so be it. And as for your father—he'll get over it. Maybe I'll even write a song about him, or something. That should soften him up some. Now are you going to give me that yes, or do I have to go find that ukelele and start all over again?"

Lisa didn't answer right away. Even though there was a 'yes' crying from her heart, she couldn't get it past her lips.

Rob watched her carefully, then a crafty smile crept across his face. "All right, that's it. Answer me now, or else I'll tip over this canoe." He grabbed the sides of the craft with both hands and began to rock it back and forth.

"Stop that!" she screamed. "I have on my best dress!"

"Will you marry me?" he asked again, rocking the canoe even harder.

"Yes! Just stop rocking the boat."

He stopped and stared at her. "You will?" he asked at last.

"I said 'yes,' didn't I?"

The sound of Rob's loud *Ya-hoooo* replaced the silence of the night for as far as the ear could hear.

* * *

Samantha wiped the moisture from her eyes as the scene drew to a close. "I like Rob Jensen," she said thoughtfully. "He's definitely the right guy for my cousin Lisa. A little further out in the fast lane than I thought she'd be happy with, but who knows, that might be the best thing that ever happened to her. Although I would have enjoyed this tender moment more if I hadn't already read the report from the higher authorities on what lies ahead for these two."

"Yeah," Gus snorted. "It does sorta take the wind out of your shells. Are ya up ta watchin' one more little piece of history, Sam?"

Samantha nodded. "I guess the more I know about how things happened, the better prepared I'll be to set this whole matter straight. So how did Uncle Mac manage to get rid of Rob? I find it hard to believe Rob's the sort that could be bought off."

"Ya hit that one on the head, Sam. That old Mac is a smart one; he knew exactly what ta do. He not only figured how ta get to Rob, he figured it so he'd be gettin' ta Lisa, too. And darned if it didn't work." Gus sighed loudly. "Just once I'd like ta have it easy gettin' destiny back on track. I don't think I'll ever get rid of all the wrinkles my typo caused."

Samantha smiled sympathetically. "Hey, Gus, hang in there. You have Jason and me on your side. And don't forget Maggie's computer. There aren't many wrinkles her computer can't iron out."

Gus smiled proudly. "Yeah, she can make miracles on the same computer I made a mess with. Where's the justice? What do ya say we pay a little visit ta the doctor's office so ya can get on with puttin' destiny back in place?"

"Doctor's office?" Samantha asked nervously. "Don't tell me Uncle Mac shot Rob?"

"Nah—even yer hardheaded uncle wouldn't go so far as ta shoot the young fella. The doctor we're about ta visit is Howard Kemp. I'm sure ya've heard of him."

"Howard Kemp," Samantha echoed. "The noted orthopedist?"

"One and the same, Sam."

"How in the world does an orthopedist fit into this picture?"

"Sounds crazy, don't it? But I told ya Mac was a smart one. Come on, Sam. Let's pay a visit ta that doctor's office and ya'll see fer yerself."

The scene shifted, and Samantha found herself inside Dr. Kemp's office. Glancing at Gus who was right beside her, she asked, "What ever happened to those fancy tunnels of light you used to take me through when we moved through time and space? You know, like the time you took me from the elevator in my apartment building to your office to rework the contract between Jason and me."

"I just threw that in fer effect," he admitted. "You had my back ta the wall and I needed all the help I could get. I figured takin' ya on that little trip might impress yer mind with how skilled I was and you'd keep yer demands down some. I guess we both know it didn't work, don't we?"

Samantha punched Gus lightly in the shoulder. "Gus Winkelbury, are you still brooding over the contract I negotiated back then? You got off easy and you know it. If I hadn't signed that contract, think where you'd be now. I'm sure the higher authorities would have had something extra special in store for you. And besides, your trip through the light display didn't scare me one bit. I loved it. And if I get to use one of those with Uncle Mac, you can be sure he'll get the full treatment."

Gus shook his head. "In a way I almost feel sorry for old Mac," he said. "Goin' up against you is like goin' up against a tornado, Sam. I love ya, but boy do I hate doin' business with ya. You even put yer old grandaddy ta shame, and take it from me, that's goin' some."

Samantha gave a well-satisfied smile as she turned her attention to the scene in front of her. Lisa was there with Rob, and of all things Uncle Mac was there, too. She listened carefully to their conversation.

* * *

"I've gone over your father's medical records quite thoroughly, young man," the doctor said. "And I can say without qualification that he can be fitted with prostheses with a one hundred percent chance of success. There's no reason he can't walk again—or even run, for that matter—if he wishes. I've handled dozens of cases worse than your father's. Of course, this sort of thing is very expensive, and there's no way your father can qualify for government help."

"The cost is no problem," J.T. broke in. "I'll take care of whatever it amounts to. I want to be sure the man gets the best of everything."

Rob squirmed in his chair. "Look, J.T., I know there has to be a catch to all this. I mean, we both know you don't like me that much. If you help my father with these prosthetic devices, what's in it for you?"

"That's a fair question, my boy," J.T. answered. "Doctor, would you mind leaving the three of us alone to talk for a few minutes?" The doctor nodded and left them alone. When he was gone, J.T. leaned back and put his fingertips together.

"It's not that I don't like you, Rob," he began. "I'm sure you're a fine young man. You even remind me a lot of myself when I was your age. But I don't think you're right for my daughter."

"Father—" Lisa spoke up.

"Stay out of this, Lisa," J.T. said, laying a hand on her arm. "I'm only doing what I must to assure that you have the time necessary to reason this out before jumping into a marriage I know you'll regret." He turned his attention back to Rob. "You say you love my daughter, and maybe you do. I'm not one to judge what's in your heart. But I'll give you the benefit of the doubt. Let's say you do love her. That being the case, I want you to listen to what I have to say. For most her life, Lisa has lived under the umbrella of my fortune. She's used to the finer things—beautiful clothes, expensive cars, not to mention the home she lives in. Have you any idea how difficult it would be for her to give all this up?"

Rob was silent for a moment before he said, "So what you're asking is that I step out of her life, is that right? All I have to do is agree never to see her again, and you give my father back his legs."

"No, son. I'm not asking you to step out of her life. Not forever, anyway. I'm asking for one year. I'll need your word, and Lisa's, that the two of you will have no contact whatsoever for that year. No phone calls, no letters, no contact at all. And yes, I will do everything in my power to persuade her to forget you during that year. But on the off chance I don't succeed, then at the end of the year you can marry with my blessing. And your father will have the benefit of being able to walk again."

"Father," Lisa said tearfully, "this isn't fair. Rob loves me, and I love him. I can't stand the thought of not seeing him for a year. I can't believe you could be so cruel."

"I don't consider it being cruel," J.T. responded. "I'm only looking out for your welfare. Someday you'll thank me for doing this. And Rob will thank me, too. I'm sure he'll find someone else in time."

J.T. stood and walked to the door. There he paused to say, "The two of you have tonight to decide. You can let me know your answer tomorrow morning. If you decide to take my offer, I'll have an open-ended check in Dr. Kemp's hands before noon."

J.T.'s voice grew softer as he added, "I want you to know I'm not ignorant to the hurt I'm putting the two of you through, and I am sorry. But I feel I must do this. I could never forgive myself if I didn't.

"Oh and one last thing. Lisa is not to wear your ring during the year, Rob. In fact, I think I should keep the ring for you, Lisa. That way you won't be tempted to wear it when you think I wouldn't know. You can give it to me in the morning, Lisa."

Having said this, he slipped out of the doctor's office and closed the door behind him.

"Those poor kids," Samantha said as the young couple left the doctor's office together. "You just wait until I get a word with that hardheaded uncle of mine."

* * *

Never had a goodbye been so painful for Lisa as the one said on her front doorstep that night. Looking into Rob's eyes, she tried to speak but the words refused to come. Very gently Rob lifted her hand to his lips and kissed it. "There was a full moon in the sky the night I placed this ring on your finger," he whispered, "just like the one up there tonight."

A sob escaped Lisa's lips as she felt him remove the ring, place it in her palm, and wrap her fingers around it. She closed her eyes, squeezing back the tears. When she opened them again, it was to see Rob removing the gold chain from around his neck. "This was my mother's," he said, his voice quivering noticeably. "She gave it to me before she died. She wanted me to have it so that my memory of her would never fade. I've worn it ever since. It always makes me feel as if she's very nearby."

With loving hands, Rob slid the chain around Lisa's neck and fastened it in place. "Your father forbids you to wear my ring, Lisa," he choked, "but I want you to wear this chain so your memory of me will never fade. And I hope it will keep the nearness of my love ever with you, as it kept my mother close to me."

Lisa was crying openly by now She raised a hand to feel the chain and vowed never to remove it until she was in Rob's arms once again. Then, just as in the time-honored story of Cinderella the stroke of midnight sounded its cruel chime. One final kiss and her carriage became pumpkin. As Rob walked out of her night, Lisa knew it would be a long lonesome wait before her glass slippers would ever dance to his music again. That night was the first she would cry herself to sleep but it wouldn't be the last.

* * *

In the time it would take to snap her fingers, Samantha was back at Dove Park, where it was morning again. Everything she had seen and heard had taken not so much as one tick off the clock. That sort of thing always amazed Samantha.

"Now that ya've seen what yer up against," Gus asked. "Are ya sure ya wouldn't like ta reconsider lettin' ole Jase take charge of this one?"

"Not in this eternity," Samantha was quick to answer. "Now if you haven't any objections, I'd like to pay a visit to my favorite uncle."

CHAPTER 3

J.T. MacGregor rubbed his eyes wearily. This real estate deal was one of the hardest he had ever tackled but it was worth every minute he spent on it. This one would earn him profits like nothing he had ever done before. To think that Edward "Big Ed" Reeves had sought him out for this deal . . .

That was certainly a stroke of luck when Greg Reeves began dating Lisa, J.T. thought with satisfaction. *Not only is Greg the exact sort of man I'd like Lisa to marry, but I have Greg to thank for opening up the way for this deal with his father.* As J.T. contemplated the closing of the deal, he thought he might take Lisa and Julie to Europe before school started again in the fall. He could even invite Greg along. Who knew what good might come from Greg and Lisa being together in some romantic setting in Italy or France?

J.T. and Katherine had often dreamed of going to Europe someday. But like so many other somedays, theirs never came. Katherine had died, leaving him with two young daughters to raise alone. He didn't know how he had done it. The years seemed to have passed in a blur of pain and struggle. He had thrown himself into his work, and it had paid off. He had large trust funds for his daughters and was able to pay for their educations. Lisa was now an elementary school teacher. She had always admired her cousin Samantha, and wanted to follow in her footsteps. Julie had already been accepted to law school and would start in the fall.

Reaching for the picture of Katherine he kept on his desk, J.T. held it close where he could see every little detail of her lovely face. Closing his eyes, he leaned back in his chair. "How I wish you were

here to see them," he said aloud, as if she could hear him. "You'd be
so proud."

"She is proud—very proud," a voice said clearly.

After a moment of stunned silence, J.T. opened his eyes to the
greatest shock of his life. She stood just on the other side of his desk.
"Sam?!" he gasped in utter amazement. "What is this?! You can't be
here. You're . . ."

"The word you're looking for is 'dead,' Uncle, Mac" Samantha
finished his sentence. "Don't be afraid to use the word. So I'm dead.
So what, everybody dies. It's no big deal."

J.T. rubbed his eyes and looked back to see her still standing
there, wearing that same mischievous smile he had grown to know so
well over the years. "No," he reasoned aloud. "This just isn't possible.
Things like this don't happen."

"Oh, but they do," Samantha was quick to respond, her eyes
sparkling mischievously. "When there's a reason for it, that is. And
no, you're not dreaming. That was going to be your next question,
wasn't it?"

J.T. rubbed his eyes again. Even though this woman looked and
sounded like Samantha, he knew that was impossible. "Who are you
really?" he managed to ask, still searching for a logical explanation.
"How—did you get in my study through that locked door? What do
you want with me?"

Samantha laughed sympathetically. "I can understand your
confusion. It is a little shocking to have someone show up from out of
nowhere. I remember very well the first time Jason pulled this on me."

J.T.'s mind whirled with questions. Who was Jason? And how
did this woman know about his niece, Samantha, who had died
nearly a year ago? How had she managed to get into his office when
he had locked the door, and most of all, what did she want? A bolt of
apprehension shot through him as he thought about the project he
was working on. Without a doubt, this mall deal was the biggest and
most important undertaking he had ever tackled. Could this woman
be here in an attempt to undermine the project? The thought caused
him to shudder. A leak on this deal could be costly. So costly he had
even taken the precaution to lock the door before examining the
documents, something he seldom bothered to do.

"I'll ask you once more," he demanded, "how did you get in here through that locked door?"

Samantha just smiled. "You're lucky I didn't walk through the door the way Jason did when I first met him, although I may try it sometime just for laughs." Looking at her uncle, she couldn't restrain a small giggle. "I wish you could see the look on your face, Uncle Mac. I had no idea playing ghost could be this much fun."

J.T. narrowed his eyes. "You keep calling me Uncle Mac. No one but the real Samantha ever called me that. You're clever, I'll give you that much. But not clever enough to convince me you're anything but a spy." Hurriedly, he scooped up the papers from off his desk.

"I couldn't care less about your silly project, Uncle Mac," Samantha said impatiently. "I'm here for a much more important reason than checking on your plans to invest in a new mall. I have to admit, there was a time when the thought of all those new shopping places would have sent chills through me. But where I live now, we have malls that put the dinky little thing you're planning to shame."

J.T. was more confused than ever. His heart told him this was the Samantha he had known and loved from the moment he first saw her as an infant in the arms of Katherine's sister-in-law, Wilma. But his businessman's cold logic told him this was impossible. Although there was a time when his heart would have spoken the loudest, the man he had now become was more accustomed to listening to his head.

"I like what you've done to your study," Samantha said, looking around the room. "You've completely redone it since the last time I was here. And speaking of your study, do your remember how the girls and I used to visit you in your makeshift office at the old house? You were fun back then, Uncle Mac. You'd always pull out little butterscotch candies for us. I'll never forget how good they tasted."

J.T.'s mouth fell open, but he recovered quickly. "I don't know where you got your information, but it won't work. I wasn't born yesterday, you know."

Samantha became more serious. "Look at me, Uncle Mac," she pleaded. "It's me, Sam. I'm real and I'm not here to spy on you. I'm here to prevent you from making the greatest mistake of your life. And even if it kills you, I'm going to keep you from making that mistake." Her grin returned. "Maybe killing you isn't such a bad idea at that. It worked pretty well in my case."

Shocked as he was, J.T. was getting tired of this bewildering exchange. "You must be insane, woman! What are you talking about?"

"Listen, Uncle Mac," she said sternly, "I'm here to salvage three very important contracts, one of which is between you and Aunt Katie. I would think you'd care about that."

At the mention of the word "contract," J.T. heard no more. She was, he assumed, referring to his contract negotiations with Edward Reeves for the mall, and his suspicions mounted. Samantha was quick to read his thoughts from the look in his eyes.

"Big Ed is another big problem we're going to have to deal with sometime," she said soberly. "Let me ask you a question, Uncle Mac. Why would a money lord like Edward Reeves want to do business with a little fish like you? Now, let me answer my own question. He's out to get you, that's why. And if I didn't plan on saving your neck, he'd have it on the block with the ax in his hand before you had time to count the change in your pocket."

At her words J.T. jumped up from his chair.. "How dare you call me a little fish? I'll match my bank account with yours any time Miss—Miss—whoever in thunder you are. Regardless of how rich Edward Reeves might be, he's always open to a deal that will bring him more. He came to me, I didn't go to him. Big Ed knows what a shrewd businessman I am, and he wants to capitalize on my skills."

Samantha folded her arms and shook her head. "You may think Big Ed, as he's called, has confidence in you—but I know something you don't know. And I'm in a position to know, Uncle Mac, because I'm an angel. Not that I particularly like being called an angel, mind you. I rather like the idea of being thought of as a ghost. Being a ghost has always seemed like more fun than being an angel. But since the higher authorities like the word 'angel,' I'm more or less stuck with it. That, by the way, is how I came through your door. Locks don't mean much to us angels."

J.T. shoved the papers into an open safe behind him. One snap, and it was locked. "An angel indeed," he said, facing her again. "More like a spy and an imposter. You have just ten seconds to get out of my study, young woman, before I pick up this phone and call the police."

Samantha sighed. "Go ahead, try to use the phone if you like. But I'll tell you up front it won't work. I had my friend Maggie disable it ten minutes ago."

J.T. grabbed the phone and pressed it to his ear. She was right, it was dead. He clicked the receiver several times, but it made no difference. Dropping the phone back to the hook, he glared at her. "You're not in this alone, are you?" he snapped. "You mentioned a Jason, and now a Maggie. I'd like to know who you're working for."

"Who am I working for?" she laughed. "You'll figure that one out for yourself when the time comes. For now it's enough to say I'm an angel here to save you from yourself. Offhand, I'd say the two of us are in for a pretty tough tussle before we're through. But when it's over, I'm planning on being the winner. Which means that you and your daughters will also be winners."

Samantha paused to look around his study. "You've come a long way since that little place you lived in when Aunt Katie was alive, haven't you?"

J.T.'s face paled. "What do you know about Katherine?" he choked, unable to hide the emotion in his voice.

"What do I know about Katherine?" Samantha countered. "I practically grew up in your home, Uncle Mac. And by the way, I talked to her only this morning. Boy, has she had it with you. That thing you pulled on Lisa and Rob ruffled her feathers good. You're lucky it's me you're facing right now, and not her. Talk about having a tiger by the tail. You'd think you were in a cage full of them if she were here."

J.T. fell limp to his chair and his eyes shone with unshed tears. "You couldn't have talked to Katie," he whispered. "She's been gone more than ten years."

"I told you, I'm an angel. Talking to Aunt Katie is perfectly natural for me. In fact, it's a lot more natural than talking to you these days. But since I have the approval of the higher authorities, here I am. Like it or not, you're stuck with this angel, Uncle Mac. At least until I can force some sense into that thick head of yours."

"You know there's no such thing as angels!" J.T. fumed. "Admit it! You're just a spy who's come here to learn what you can about my mall deal."

Exasperated, Samantha folded her arms. "I already know every-thing there is to know. For instance, I know you just opened a dedi-cated account and transferred two million dollars into it. Big deal. Where I live now two million dollars wouldn't be worth a good lick on a root-beer lollipop. And you might as well get this through your head, Uncle Mac—until our business is finished, you can figure I'll be closer than your own shadow.

"And now, you're about to see a demonstration to prove my point." Samantha's eyes sparkled with glee as she described what was about to take place. "You and I are going on a little trip down the dusty road of your past, Uncle Mac. The higher authorities have approved me using a selected event shown by holographically enhanced regeneration," she said smugly, "and that, my dear uncle, is something even my cute little Jason never got to use."

Before J.T. even had time to consider a response, he found himself in the midst of an experience much stranger than merely seeing an angel. Suddenly, he was no longer standing in his study. He wasn't standing anywhere, exactly. He was more or less—flying. Not like flying in an airplane, mind you. More like flying through some strange passageway of brilliantly colored lights at a speed that left him feeling he must have been shot from a cannon. Stripped of his wits, J.T. could only remain in helpless submission to whatever power had seized control over him.

Just as suddenly as the whole thing had started, it was over. At least the tunnel of light, that is. The ordeal itself had only begun. Still too frightened for words, J.T. found himself floating, as it were, in mid-air over what appeared to be city lights below. It was much like looking out from a Goodyear blimp—only without the blimp. The strange woman who called herself Samantha was still with him—smiling like a cat about to pounce on a ball of yarn. "What's happening to me?" he asked with uncharacteristic meekness.

Samantha laughed. "Neat, huh, Uncle Mac? I remember the first time something like this happened to me. I was in an elevator at the Anderson Apartment Building where I used to live, remember? Gus—I'll have to tell you about him sometime—took me through one of these travel ducts to his office. That's when I negotiated the contract that set Jason's destiny and mine back on track. But that's another story. I never thought back then that I'd ever be the one escorting someone else on a trip like this. All I can say is *wow!* What a kick!"

"Help me!" J.T. begged, seeing the unnatural position he was in. "Please, don't let me fall!"

"You're not going to fall," Samantha reassured him. "Just relax and enjoy yourself. After all, it's not every day you get the chance to have an experience like this."

"But—what's keeping me up here? I'm standing on air."

"It's the higher authorities, Uncle Mac. They can do anything they like. Temporarily overruling gravity is child's play for them. Now get a hold of yourself so we can get on with the show."

It took only a few moments for J.T. to realize Samantha was telling the truth. He wasn't falling. Even though logic told him it was impossible, he remained suspended a few hundred feet above the city below. "How is all this happening?" he gasped. "You really are some sort of angel, aren't you?"

"Yes, Uncle Mac. I am an angel. And I am your niece, Sam. The sooner you admit that the better off we'll both be."

J.T. had always prided himself on being able to adapt to any situation, and to remain in control at all times. Even though he had never encountered a situation quite like this, he refused to let it get the best of him. Gathering his courage, he mounted an offense. "Angel or no angel," he grumbled. "You have no right to put me through this. I insist you take me back to my office and haunt me no longer."

"I'll take you back to your office when *I* decide it's time, Uncle Mac. For now, I want you to look at that building down there and tell me if you recognize it."

In disgust, J.T. looked in the direction she was pointing. What he saw left him dumbfounded. "This is impossible," he snapped. "That looks like the old Clifton Hotel, but it can't be. That hotel was destroyed in a fire more than twenty years ago."

"That's right," Samantha nodded approvingly. "Now take a closer look, and tell me who the man is standing near the front of the hotel."

As J.T. strained to see the man Samantha was pointing to, he realized he was slowly descending. In only a few seconds he felt his feet touch down on the concrete sidewalk not far from the entrance of the hotel.

J.T. swallowed hard. "It all looks so real," he said, looking around him slowly. "I assume the man is supposed to be me, when I was much younger, of course. Let's see, this would have been the year 1972. I would have been twenty-three at the time. I worked as a valet here at this hotel. This would probably be the night I first met Katie, right?"

"Very good," Samantha beamed, the school teacher in her showing itself. "Now tell me about what's going on here. Where is Aunt Katie now?"

"She's—inside the hotel with . . . *him.*" J.T. stared at himself as a young man, then at the entrance to the hotel, and finally at Samantha. "As long as we're here," he asked, with his first hint of submissive interest. "I don't suppose I could take a peek inside?"

Samantha shook her head no. "I know what you want, Uncle Mac," she apologized. "And I'd like to oblige. But the higher authorities have set restrictions on this particular replay. You're only allowed to see those things you actually saw the day they happened."

Disappointment filled J.T.'s eyes. "I don't even know what he looked like; all I know is that Katie's in there with the man she's engaged to marry. They're having a fight right about now. I don't know what the fight was about. She never told me."

"That's right," Samantha agreed. "And I know how curious you've always been about the man she's with. I really do wish I could let you have a look at him, but rules are rules."

J.T.'s voice was full of regret. "I know he had the approval of Katie's mother and father," he said. "That's something I never had the privilege of enjoying. They didn't approve of me from the day Katie and I married, and they never changed their minds. They both went to their graves disliking me."

"Yeah, I know," Samantha said, betraying a hint of sadness in her voice. "They are my father's parents, you know. They were mixed-up while they were here on this side, and I'm sorry to say they're still mixed-up. We've all been working with them on my side, but we haven't had much luck. It's funny how little difference it makes in people's thinking when they cross to my side of forever. The person they are here is the person they are there, too." She forced her smile to return. "But we won't give up on them, Uncle. You can bet on that."

J.T. stared at her. "Are you trying to say that Katie's parents are angels, too?"

Samantha nodded. "Yes, they are. But they live in a different area than Aunt Katie and the rest of our family. I'm not allowed to say much more about that, so why don't you tell me everything you do know about the man she's inside the hotel with?"

J.T. turned his attention back to the hotel entrance. "I know little about him other than that he was very wealthy. That's why Katie's parents approved of him." After a deep sigh and a long thoughtful pause, he asked, "These rules of yours, do they give me the right to change the way things happened that night?"

Samantha smiled and again shook her head no.

"If only I could do something to prevent what's about to happen. I'd give away everything I own if I could make that young fool turn and run as fast as his—that is, as fast as *my* legs would carry me."

"You wouldn't really want to do that, Uncle Mac. If you did that, you'd never have Lisa or Julie as your daughters."

By this time all signs of anger were missing from J.T.'s voice. "Yes," he responded. "But perhaps Lisa and Julie could have had a better father. And Katie—well, Katie might still be alive to give them the mother's love I deprived them of."

"That sort of thinking," Samantha flatly stated, "is exactly why you're being shown this replay. You've allowed your thinking to get all twisted around. Unless you seriously rearrange your priorities, your future with Aunt Katie is in danger of being lost forever."

"My future with Katie? It's too late for any future between the two of us. Katie's dead and buried. That, young woman, is the cold hard fact."

"My name is Sam, Uncle Mac. I hate it when you call me '*young woman.*'"

Just then a thought occurred to her that she hadn't fully understood before. "You know what? I think I'm beginning to realize how important it is to hear ourselves called by our own name. When Jason was courting me as an angel, I refused to call him by his name because at first I just thought of him as a pesky ghost. Until now, I had no idea why that bothered him so much." She paused thoughtfully, before remembering her present purpose. "I guess you wouldn't know about that would you, Uncle Mac? No matter, let's get back to Aunt Katie. You're off base assuming she's gone from you. She's only a heartbeat away, on the other side of forever from where you are right now. She's as alive as I am, and the sooner you get that through your thick skull the better off we'll all be. Now you'd better get a grip on it because you're about to watch yourself meet Aunt Katie all over again. Just the way it happened back in 1972."

J.T.'s eyes shifted to the hotel entrance. "I'm going to see Katie?" he gulped.

"Just keep looking at the door, Uncle Mac. The fight inside has climaxed and she's on her way out even as we speak."

A second later, as he looked on in astonishment, his beloved Katherine stormed through the revolving doors. Just as before, she ran into the young J.T. and sent him sprawling to the sidewalk.

"She's so beautiful," J.T. murmured. "I'd forgotten just how beautiful she really was."

"She is beautiful," Samantha agreed. "And I love her dress. I hope it comes back in style in the next century or two. Although I think green is more my color. The blue looks great on her, mind you, but I do better in green. What do you think, Uncle Mac? Wouldn't that dress look good on me?"

"Yes, yes," J.T. muttered, not really hearing her. "Look, Katie's bending over me to see if I'm all right. I can't believe this. It's so real," J.T. said, his eyes still glued to the scene before him. "I just realized something, too. I've always known Lisa resembled her mother, but I never realized just how much. Don't you think she looks like Lisa, Sam?"

Startled, Samantha turned to look at her uncle. "You called me Sam. All right, Uncle Mac!"

But he was too absorbed in the scene before him to reply. "Look, I'm getting up and brushing myself off. I'm about to—yes— I'm asking if I can take her home." He sighed happily. "I hate to brag, but when I was that age I was quite popular with the ladies. Not that her anger at her date didn't have something to do with her decision to say yes—but whatever her reason, I had my foot in the door."

"And you weren't about to back away easily," Samantha added. "Once you learned where Aunt Katie lived, you kept after her until she gave in and went out with you. Over the next few months, the two of you carried on a secret friendship that eventually grew into a lasting love."

"That's the way it all happened," J.T. agreed. "I can't believe how much I've forgotten about this night, or the months that followed. I do remember the way I hated slipping around to see Katie. She didn't dare let her parents or her 'boyfriend' find out about me. I tried to convince her to confront the bunch of them, but she refused. Back then I had the idea that love could conquer all. You know, like so many young folks believe today. I know now, of course, that her parents were right, Sam. And I refuse to let either of my daughters make the same mistake Katie made."

"I know," Samantha nodded. "That's why you pulled the stunt you did on Rob, to get him out of the picture."

"Yes!" J.T. growled. "I did find a way to get Rob out of the picture, for a year at least. And, by thunder, I'm going to find a way to keep him out of the picture forever. Otherwise, he could ruin Lisa's chances at happiness, just as I ruined Katie's."

"You are a stubborn one, Uncle Mac. I expected what you just saw would soften you up at least a little."

J.T. gazed lovingly on the scene once again. "I loved Katie," he admitted. "I loved her more than my own life. But I had no right to deprive her of the finer things by forcing myself on her. Not only did I cheat her out of a more comfortable life, I sent her to an early grave."

"Oh please," Samantha groaned. "Don't ever get the idea you're the one who decided when Aunt Katie would cross the line to the far side of forever. Only the higher authorities have that right. And believe me, Uncle Mac, you aren't one of them. You may think of yourself as a kingpin, but where I come from you wouldn't make a wave the size of a marble tossed into the Pacific Ocean. Aunt Katie was called home because she was needed at the time, Uncle Mac. That's it, cut and dried."

J.T. was shaken by Samantha's remarks. The firm belief that he alone was responsible for Katherine's death was embedded deeply in his mind. Samantha's arguments did little more than fan the flame of his already burning guilt. "Take me home, Sam," he cried. "I beg of you, take me home. I can't bear looking at any more of this. Beautiful as Katie is, I just can't bear it."

"All right," Samantha frowned. "If that's what you want, I'll take you home. But I hope you've learned something from my first visit."

J.T. shot a piercing glance Samantha's way. "First visit," he gulped. "There's more?"

Samantha smiled complacently. "Oh yes, Uncle Mac. Like I said, you and I have some business to attend to, and until you come around, you're stuck with me."

Just to give J.T. a little shake, Samantha made the trip home in the fastest mode possible, leaving J.T. completely breathless. In one instant, he was in the year 1972. In the next he was back in his office. It took several seconds for him to recover his senses. "I don't know how you did that, Sam," he said in wonder. "But I have to admit, it was some trip." Glancing over his shoulder, he discovered he was talking to himself. "Where are you, Sam?" he called out. There was no answer.

Crossing the room to his desk, he took a seat and stared at the picture of Katherine there. It took several minutes for him to sort out everything in his mind, but once he did, he decided the whole thing was a trick of his imagination, the result of the enormous stress he was under with his current land deal. Sam's visit had never really happened at all. It couldn't have happened, there were no such things as angels, and his niece, Sam, had been gone nearly a year.

He stared next at the phone. The last time he had tried to use it—or at least thought he had tried to use it—it was dead. He picked it up and listened for the dial tone. It was there, adding strength to his belief that the whole thing had occurred in his mind. Or perhaps he had fallen asleep and dreamed of it all. He punched a number into the phone. That number, known by only a select few, would put him directly through to one of the most powerful men in the city. The phone on the opposite end rang twice before being picked up. "Reeves here," a voice said.

"Big Ed," J.T. spoke into the phone. "This is J.T. MacGregor. When would you like to get together to go over the final details of our deal?"

CHAPTER 4

Samantha loved her majestic mountain home on the far side of forever. It was the home she had negotiated with Gus before she would sign his revised contract between her and Jason. Gus had not been happy at her insistence that he include the home in the contract. She had to admit, though, he did a great job filling his part of the bargain. And, he was a good sport about it.

Samantha stepped into her sparkling kitchen to find Jason there tinkering with a new recipe he wanted to perfect before using it at the Paradise Palace, where he was head chef. Jason knew Samantha had had an appointment in Dove Park that morning with Gus, and this was the first time he had seen her since.

She came to him with a kiss. Then, stroking her fingers through his thick hair, she made her case. "Want to know what Gus had in mind?" she asked seductively.

Jason returned her kiss. "I'm not sure," he said with a chuckle. "A meeting with Gus usually means trouble. What was on his mind this time, trying to get out of more typing lessons?" Jason was referring to the typing lessons Samantha had been giving Gus ever since she came to this side. That was part of the renegotiated contract, too. Samantha was determined to prevent Gus from making any more typos like the one that caused Jason to be born thirty years too soon.

Samantha smiled. "Gus had more on his mind than typing, I'm afraid. He wanted me to talk you into another assignment."

"What!" Jason shouted. "Gus wants me back down there again? And he has the gall to use you to persuade me? This has to be an all-time low, even for him. I won't do it, Sam. I hope you told him that."

Samantha dipped her finger into the mix Jason was working on. "Umm, that's good," she said, after a quick taste. "What is it?"

"It's a new dessert made from some Jeremiah berries I had shipped in from the far South Galaxy. But what about Gus? You did tell him I wouldn't take the assignment, didn't you, Sam?"

"Yeah, sorta," Samantha said, taking a second taste of Jason's dessert. "I think a bit more tangerine would set this off just right. What do you think?"

"Sam! It has all the tangerine it needs. What do you mean 'sorta'? Either you told Gus I wouldn't take the assignment, or you didn't. Which is it?"

"Settle down, Jason," Samantha soothed. "There's no reason for you to get upset with me, because I talked Gus into using *me* for the assignment instead. I think it will be great fun."

Jason was flabbergasted. "You talked him into what?!" he gasped.

Sam was still licking her lips thoughtfully. "I'm sure just a touch more tangerine would bring out the flavor you're looking for here."

"Darn it, Sam! Stick to the subject! How could you possibly let Gus trick you into one of his hair-brained schemes?"

"He didn't trick me," Samantha said bluntly. "I went to great lengths to persuade him to use me in your place, and he didn't take to the idea easily. Besides, what's the big deal anyway? It's not like I'm committing some heaven-shattering event here. It's just a one-time assignment that won't take more than a few weeks at most."

"For crying out loud, Sam. Didn't you get your fill of that sort of thing working with Arline and Bruce?"

"No, I didn't get my fill working with Arline and Bruce. Just because you think playing ghost is such a pain, it doesn't mean everyone feels that way," Samantha said reasonably. "And you have to admit, if it hadn't been for my help with Arline and Bruce, things would never have come together so smoothly. You and Gus certainly didn't have the situation in hand."

"I'll give you that much, Sam," Jason was forced to admit. "But Arline and Bruce were a far cry from my first experience. I hung around for more than twenty years searching for a way to make you fall in love with me."

Samantha slipped an arm through Jason's and gave him another kiss, this time on his cheek. "Was courting me really all that bad?" she asked sweetly.

"Well, you have to admit you didn't exactly make my courting easy," Jason grumbled.

"Nothing worthwhile ever comes easy," she quipped. "And you have to admit I was worth it—don't you?"

Not answering right away, Jason deliberately scrunched up his face into an expression of serious contemplation.

"Jason Hackett!" Samantha yelled, ready to let him have it good. She would have, too, if his kiss hadn't cut her short.

"Of course you're worth it, you little tease," he reassured her. "You're the best thing that's ever happened to me."

Samantha poked a playful finger to the tip of Jason's nose. "You'd better believe it, my crazy ghost. And it's useless for you to try and talk me out of this assignment. Especially since it concerns my cousins Lisa and Julie."

Jason was aghast. "Your cousins? What are you saying, Sam? Surely Gus didn't give you an assignment working with your own family. That sort of thing just isn't done."

Samantha laughed. "It took some persuasiveness on my part, but I finally got Gus to bend the rule just a bit. He's good at that, you know."

"Yeah, and I also know how good you are at convincing him to do just that, if it's for something you want. This whole thing is crazy, Sam. Let me talk to Gus. I'm sure I can get you out of the deal if we act fast. Once you've let Lisa or Julie see you, it'll be too late."

"All right," Samantha grinned. "If you want to talk to Gus, be my guest. But before you do, you should know it's already too late."

"Oh no," Jason said, laying his head in one hand. "You've already shown yourself, haven't you?"

"Uh-huh," Samantha replied, as her smile grew even wider.

Jason released a very loud sigh. "Well then, I guess that's it, but don't forget I warned you. Which one did you choose to work with, Lisa or Julie?"

"Neither," she shrugged. "I'll be working with Uncle Mac. He's the one causing the problem I need to solve."

"You're working with J.T.? This gets worse by the minute. That guy has a harder head than Gus." For an instant, Jason was sympathetic. "Sam, Sam, Sam," he said, shaking his head. "I'm afraid you've bitten off more than you can chew on this one."

"Jason Hackett," Samantha said, putting her hands to her hips. "Are you implying I'm not tough enough to handle Uncle Mac? You had better take that one back, buster, or you'll be wearing that new dessert of yours for a halo."

Now it was Jason's turn to laugh. "You're cute when you get angry, you know that, Sam. And now that I think about it, I'd definitely say J.T. is the one in trouble here. From what you say, I assume you've already shown yourself to him."

Samantha relaxed her arms. "I popped in on him a couple of hours ago," she responded. "The darn guy refused to believe me at first. He thought I was a spy after his plans to build a silly old mall."

"Yep, that sounds just like J.T., all right. I don't envy you, Sam, but if this is really what you want, you have my blessings. I think you're making a mistake, but you still have my blessings."

Samantha pushed Jason into a chair near the dining table, and she slid onto his lap. "I need a bit more than your blessings," she murmured, as she nuzzled him on the ear. "I need your help with my assignment."

Jason groaned. "Sam, no. Please don't ask that of me."

"But I do need you, Jason," Samantha insisted. "For one thing, Gus only let me have the assignment on the condition I would get your help. But more important, I want you working with me. Think how much I'll learn watching an old pro like you at work—especially since I'm sort of in love with this old pro."

"Cut it out, Sam," Jason pleaded. "You know I can't resist you when you approach me like this, but I don't want to play ghost again. I'll talk to Gus, if it will help. But please, don't drag me back down there again. Twenty years was enough."

Samantha was adamant. "No deal, my handsome ghost. We're in this one together, and that's that. Of course you have to understand I'm the one in charge. Your job is to assist me when I need you. Come on, admit it. Working with me will be fun. I'll even wash and press your old Casper outfit for you."

"Sam," Jason began, "I—"

Samantha put her hand over his mouth. "Tut, tut. No more excuses. My mind is made up, and you should know what that means."

"Okay," he said reluctantly. "But there's one thing I want to know. If you're working with J.T., who do you have in mind for me?"

That question was all it took for Samantha to know she had him on the line. Throwing both arms around his neck, she gave him a tight squeeze. "I'll fill you in on everything when the time comes," she said. "But for now I want you to pay a visit to Maggie. There's a certain computer that I need her to make fail come next Monday morning."

"You want me to get Maggie's help?" Jason asked. "What about Gus? Shouldn't I be working with him, instead of Maggie?"

"Not if you want the job done right, you shouldn't. Just do as I say, and ask Maggie. I'll take care of facing Gus when the time comes. Now if you'll excuse me, I need to get back on the job. I have a couple of cousins waiting for my help. Oh, and you really ought to put a little more tangerine in your dessert while you're at it, okay?"

CHAPTER 5

A smile formed on J.T.'s lips as he hung up the phone. Doing business with Ed Reeves was a pleasure almost beyond description. Just hearing Big Ed's voice was enough to bring J.T. back to reality after his strange dream about his dead niece. After all, that's what it had to be—a dream. He had been tired after pouring over those documents for two solid hours. He remembered closing his eyes and leaning back in his chair. That's when it must have happened. His exhausted mind had slipped into a nap that had culminated in the dream. He nearly had himself convinced when his eyes chanced upon Katherine's picture. As he started to wonder, his thoughts were interrupted by the sound of someone at the front door.

After taking time to return Katherine's picture to its honored place in the center of his desk, J.T. made his way to the living room where he answered the door. It was Greg.

"Good morning, son. Are you here to pick up Lisa?"

"Yeah," Greg said carelessly, stepping inside without waiting to be invited. "We have a tennis date this morning."

J.T. closed the door. "I was just talking to your father. I made an appointment with him for next week to go over the papers on the super mall we have pending."

Greg smiled, but it was one of those mechanical smiles that come more as a duty than as a sincere expression. "I'll be glad when the two of you get this mall thing behind you," he said sourly. "Ed's been driving me up the wall. I can't remember when he's been this concerned over a business deal, and for the life of me I can't understand why. So he's putting in a mall, big deal. This is two-bit child's play alongside most of his encounters."

"'Two-bit child's play?'" J.T. said in a strangled voice. "Maybe for your father, but certainly not for me. This is a major undertaking in my book. I'll say this much, working with your father has been an exciting prospect for me. The man's a financial genius. Grab a seat in the living room, son, while I tell Lisa you're here. I think the girls are out by the pool."

Greg made his way to the living room where he flopped down on a sofa while J.T. stepped through the sliding glass doors onto the patio. Outside, he spotted his daughters basking in lounge chairs near the pool's edge. He couldn't help thinking how beautiful they looked, so much like their mother. And after the strange dream, or whatever it was, J.T. had a sudden consciousness of how close they had been to their cousin Samantha.

"Greg's here for you, Lisa," he called out as he approached.

Lisa glanced at her wristwatch. "Oh no," she grimaced. "Is it that time already? Please, Father, can't you tell him I have a headache, or something? Anything to get me out of this date. I'm in absolutely no mood for Greg at the moment."

J.T. shook his head in a definite no. "I've already told him you're here, Lisa. You're not getting off the hook that easily. Don't you think it's about time you stop playing games, and start thinking a little more seriously about setting a date to marry the man? It's been three months since you stopped seeing that musician."

Lisa removed her sunglasses and laid them on the table next to her chair. Slowly she stood and walked over to where J.T. was standing. "I've told you, Father, I have no intention of marrying Greg. I thought by this time you'd understand that. Rob and I vowed to wait for each other, and I intend to do just that."

"Hogwash," J.T. grumped. "Your musician has flown the coop on you, and you know it. He left town not three weeks after our deal, and he's not been heard from since."

"He's on tour with a group, Father. I've been reading about them in the papers. He's doing very well for someone just starting out."

"What do you mean you've been reading about him in the papers? We have a deal, young woman, and don't you forget it."

"C'mon, Dad," Julie interrupted. "If my sister wants to read about Rob in the newspapers, that's not the same as seeing him and you know it."

J.T. shook a finger at Julie. "You stay out of this, young lady. This is between your sister and me. I'll not have her drooling over this worthless fool when Greg Reeves has made it plain he has plans for her future."

Julie gave a cynical laugh. "You're so lucky, big sister. I sure do wish Dad would pick out some rich guy he wanted me to marry, and start cramming him down my throat like he crams Greg down yours."

Lisa was not amused. "That's not funny, Julie. And unless I miss my guess, your day is coming. Probably sooner than you think."

A heavy frown wrinkled J.T.'s face. "I'd like you to tell me what's so wrong with my wanting you to marry a man who can offer you the sort of life you deserve? This Rob fellow wants you around to support him so he can run off on some musical tour every month or so. What kind of marriage would that be? I want you to forget him, Lisa. I don't ever want to hear his name mentioned in this house again."

As she turned toward the house, Lisa said clearly, "I know what you want, Father. And I've promised to give Greg a fair chance. But so far he's not making many points with me."

J.T. stepped in front of her. "Believe me, my dear, you're much better off without Rob. Greg can afford to give you the life your mother deserved—I mean, you deserve." He put an arm around her as he spoke and drew her head close to his chest. But Lisa tensed and pulled away, leaving J.T. with the disappointing knowledge he was failing to reach her. Still, he loved her too much to stand by and do nothing while she threw away her best chance at happiness.

"Well," he said awkwardly, "run along now and enjoy your game of tennis. In time you'll forget about that musician. And when you do, Greg will start to look better to you, I promise."

As Julie and J.T. watched Lisa entered the house, J.T. sighed, "I'd give anything if your sister had never met Rob Jensen. All he did was confuse her. She was doing so well with Greg before he came along. There's something I want you to promise me, Julie. Give me your word you'll never let some young fool turn your head, like that singer did with your sister."

Julie didn't hesitate. "Not on your life," she spoke definitely. "When it comes to the guys in my life, I can find my own without your help. You might be able to bully Lisa into going out with Greg, but don't you ever try pushing some loser like him off on me."

J.T. shook his head wearily. "You always were the strong-willed one, Julie. When will you ever learn that I only want what's best for you and Lisa?"

"No, Dad," Julie corrected him. "You want what you *think* is best for us. But we're not your little girls anymore. We've grown up and we have minds of our own. And you might as well know this right now—when I find my Mr. Right, you'll be the last one to ever know. In fact," Julie smiled mischievously, "I may not even invite you to the wedding. Now what do you think of that, huh, Dad?"

J.T. glared suspiciously at his daughter. "Are you telling me you have taken up with some fellow?" he pressed.

"Got you wondering, don't I?" Julie teased, then added, "What if I am seeing someone? Just for the sake of argument, what you would do about it?"

J.T. removed a handkerchief from his pocket and wiped his brow. "You wouldn't do that to me, Julie—would you? I mean, if you are seeing someone, as your father I have the right to meet him."

"I don't think so," Julie shook her head. "Why would I do a thing like that? So you could run him off, like you did Rob?"

J.T. gently stroked back his daughter's long beautiful hair. "Please, Julie," he said pleadingly. "Don't do this to your father. Tell me the truth—are you seeing someone?"

"I know you think you know what's best for us," Julie said, stepping back from her father and looking him squarely in the eye. "But you're offering up my sister on an auction block like some old cow ready for market. 'How much can you bid, Rob?' 'Sorry, my boy, not enough.' 'And how much can you bid, Greg Reeves?' 'Ah—now that's impressive. I'll order up Lisa's wedding dress first thing in the morning.' You can forget about putting me on that auction block. I'm not interested. And you can just keep on wondering if I'm seeing someone—because I'm not telling you."

Julie's sharp words cut J.T. to the quick. Every since she was a little girl, Julie had shown herself to be emotionally stronger and more independent than Lisa, and he had always known that she would be more difficult to influence when it came to courtship and marriage. But never had she been this blunt. The hurt in his eyes must have shown more than he realized. It took Julie only a moment to notice.

"Darn you, Dad," she said regretfully. "Darn you for being so hardheaded and so blind to the truth." Taking a step forward, she slid both arms around his neck and lay her face against his rough cheek. "I love you," she said. "You know I love you. But don't think that gives you a green light to throw me in the path of some rich suitor you think would make a good son-in-law. Get that through your head right now."

J.T. pulled his daughter close to his chest. "You know I love you, Julie. You know I will always want what's best for you. Why don't we talk about this another time, all right?" And in the meantime, he hoped law school would keep her too busy to bother with a boyfriend.

* * *

Samantha stared at the young man on the sofa with his face buried in a finance magazine. *So you're Greg Reeves,* she thought. *You're the one Uncle Mac has picked out for Cousin Lisa. From the magazine you're reading, I can guess why. I mean, other than already having your pockets full of your father's money, you obviously think like my uncle. I'll bet you're the kind who'd sell your own mother a piece of worthless swamp land if it meant making a buck on the deal. You're darn lucky I'm not assigned to you, buster. If you could hear me, I'd let you know in no uncertain terms what I think about you monopolizing my cousin.*

Samantha smiled to herself when she thought about what she had planned. She remembered very well how furious she had been when she learned that Jason had secretly stolen along on her early dates with Bruce. That was before she could see him, of course. It was months after the fact when she learned what he had done. If it weren't for the fact he was already a ghost, she could have killed him. How different it all seemed now that the halo was on her head—so to speak.

Samantha glanced up just in time to see Lisa slip into the room. Quietly, she folded her arms and watched from her invisible perch as the scene unfolded.

Greg hadn't noticed Lisa come in. Nor did he notice when she stood in front of the sofa looking down at him for several seconds. When at last he did notice, he stood abruptly and dropped the magazine to the chair. Leaning forward, he kissed her on the cheek.

"You look lovely, sweetheart," he said approvingly.

"Oh sure," Lisa said with a laugh. "I know how lovely I look dressed for tennis."

"And speaking of one's dress," Samantha said, looking over Greg, "you should take a look at yourself, Greg old boy. What kind of guy wears a sweatshirt with the picture of an oversized hundred dollar bill on it? It's obvious your favorite color is money green."

Not that Greg wasn't handsome in his own way, Samantha had to admit, with his curly jet black hair, dark penetrating eyes, and sharp cheekbones. But his long narrow chin reminded Samantha of the exaggerated caricatures for sale by carnival artists.

"We'd better hurry," Greg pressed, glancing nervously at his watch. "We're scheduled to meet the others at the club in twenty minutes." Having said this, he headed for the door, leaving Lisa to follow. By the time she caught up, he had already crossed the lawn to the circular driveway and was standing near the back of his green Porsche convertible.

"Look," he said, pointing to the rear license plate. "It came only this morning, and I had my mechanic install it right away. I was anxious for you to see it. What do you think?"

Lisa glanced at the plate to see her own name on it. "A personalized plate," she remarked. "How—nice."

"Nice?" Greg queried. "That's it? Just nice?"

Lisa shrugged. "What can I say? I'm flattered."

Greg stared at her, obviously disappointed at her lack of response. "Well, let's go," he said over his shoulder as he hurried to the car and opened his door. "Time's burning on us."

"Where did this guy learn his manners?" Samantha groaned. "If he's a gentleman, I'm a Sumo wrestler."

Even before Lisa had time to fasten her seat belt, the car lurched forward and shot out of the driveway with the tires squealing loud enough to set a dozen or so nearby pigeons to flight. Fortunately Samantha, being the angel she was, had little trouble getting to the back seat.

With all the road noise in the speeding convertible, conversation was minimal. Samantha was sure this didn't bother Lisa, who was obviously lost in her own thoughts. *She's probably thinking of Rob,* Samantha surmised.

Twenty or so minutes later, Greg brought the convertible to an abrupt stop in the parking lot of the Pinetop Club tennis courts. "I wonder why they call this place 'Pinetop,'" she mused. "There's not a pine tree within miles of here."

Greg shrugged. "What difference does that make? It's only a name."

"Sure it's only a name," Lisa responded. "But it's a name that implies the place is something it's obviously not."

Greg looked bored with the conversation. "Who cares? Let's play tennis."

This place reminds me a lot of you, Greg Reeves, Samantha said to herself as she watched Greg hurry toward another couple who had evidently been waiting for them. *You have a way of representing yourself as something you're not, too.*

Barbara and Al were already on the court. Stepping from the car, Lisa followed Greg across the recently trimmed lawn to the courts.

After two sets of doubles, it was obvious that Lisa's heart wasn't in the game.

"Why don't you and Barbara take a break?" Greg suggested. "I want to play some serious tennis with Al."

The two women walked to a nearby table where they each opened a bottle of Evian water and sat in the shade to relax.

"That Greg is some catch," Barbara said, wiping her face with a dry towel. "I envy you, Lisa."

"You envy me?" Lisa asked, surprised.

Watching Greg successfully return a ball from deep in his own court, Barbara sighed. "You're darn right I do. I'd trade you Al for him any day. Al is all right, but he lacks at least one of Greg's finer qualities—his bottomless checkbook. You know how flattering that characteristic can be in a man."

"You sound like my father," Lisa said dryly. "Are you sure he didn't hire you to sell me on Greg?"

This time it was Barbara's turned to be surprised. "Are you kidding? If I tried to sell you on anything, it would be getting you to step out of the picture. Then I could go after Greg myself."

"If you have eyes for the man," Lisa waved her hand toward Greg, "he's all yours. I don't own him." After a pause, she added, "He doesn't own me, either."

"I certainly hope you're not serious," Barbara quipped. "If you are, then you must be crazy."

Lisa shrugged. "Maybe I am crazy. Who knows?"

Barbara set her bottle of water on the table and bounced to her feet. "Save my seat for me," she said, starting off in the direction of the clubhouse. "I have to powder my nose."

Samantha watched Barbara walk away and shook her head. "I wish you could hear me, Lisa," she said to her cousin. "I'd tell you not to worry. You deserve better than Greg, and you're going to get it, I promise." She glanced back to the court where the men were playing and snorted in disgust. "Uncle Mac, how could you be so blind? You'd run off a man like Rob for this weasel? You and I have some serious work ahead of us."

Before she knew it, Samantha was lost in her thoughts, remembering the things Gus had shown her. So deeply was she contemplating how she would approach this particular problem that she failed to realize Greg had walked up until she heard his voice.

"Lisa, sweetheart, I asked you a question. Didn't you hear me?"

Apparently Samantha wasn't the only one lost in her thoughts. Greg had slipped up without either of them noticing, and was completely offended at Lisa's lack of attention.

"Lisa!" he said again, sharply.

"Oh!" Lisa gasped. "I'm sorry, I must have been thinking of someone—uh . . . that is, something else. What was it you asked?"

"I asked if you'd like to play another set of tennis," Greg repeated himself impatiently. "Or would you rather call it quits for today?"

"I'd really like to call it quits, if you don't mind. My heart's just not in it."

"That's obvious," he said. "How about if we stop by the club-house for a couple of drinks?"

Lisa wrinkled her nose. "Do you still have to ask that question?" she asked. "You know perfectly well I don't drink."

"Yes, I know that," Greg said with more than a touch of irritation in his voice, "but you can have a soda while I have a few. Maybe we can even get up a game of poker or something, while we cool off."

"Greg, you know how I feel about riding in the car with you after you've been drinking," Lisa said quietly.

Greg rolled his eyes. "Oh brother," he said, laying a hand to his brow. "I can see I have my work cut out for me after we're married. You've got to get with the times, lady. Loosen up and learn to relax. Put a little fun in your life once in a while."

Lisa shook her head. "The problem is, what you call fun and what I call fun are two different things."

Greg snorted. "The problem is, what you call fun, everyone else calls *boring.*"

Lisa tossed her empty water bottle into a container next to the bench. "Why don't you take me home," she said, moving briskly in the direction of Greg's car. "Then you can return and have all your kind of fun you like."

Greg sighed and followed her to the car. "Get in," he agreed. "I'll take you home."

As they drove, Samantha noticed that Greg kept looking at Lisa. Lisa must have noticed, too, because she made it a point not to look his way. Finally, just before they reached the turnoff to her father's home, he spoke. "I need a favor, Lisa."

Lisa looked at him suspiciously. "What sort of favor?"

"Well," he began, "I have a slight problem. You know I'll be away on business all next week. The problem is my secretary, Becky, is getting married this weekend. She'll be off on her honeymoon at the same time I'm gone, which means leaving no one to watch the office. I just need someone to answer the phone and set future appointments. And since your teaching job is on temporary hold for summer break, I was wondering . . ." His voice trailed off.

Lisa didn't make it easy for him. "Yes?"

Greg had hoped that Lisa would understand without his having to actually ask her. "Well, I'm in a bit of a lurch here, Lisa," he said. "I need someone dependable, someone I can trust to handle my personal affairs. I'm anticipating calls from some very influential people. I haven't talked much to you about my plans to run for state senate in the next election, but the idea is on tap. This information, of course, isn't to be made public just yet. Any leak could severely damage my chances. I'm sure you can see that hiring a temporary secretary under the circumstances is out of the question. What do you say? Will you do it for me, Lisa?"

"I don't know, Greg," she replied hesitantly. "It's not something I'd really enjoy doing."

"You have to do this for me, Lisa," Greg insisted. "I've already told everyone that my fiancée would be taking care of my office while I'm away. After we're married you'll be helping with all my political campaigns, so watching my office will give you some good experience."

Lisa's eyes widened in surprise. "You told these people I'm your fiancée?" she asked abruptly. "What right did you have to do that, Greg Reeves? I've never agreed to marry you."

Greg sighed. "Lisa, for crying out loud. You know you'll marry me when the time comes. Why are you being so stubborn?"

From the back seat, Samantha nearly choked at Greg's easy assurance that Lisa found him so irresistible. Even though she knew Lisa couldn't hear her, she leaned forward. "If I were you, Lisa, I'd shove that tennis racket you're holding up his nose. But as much as I hate to see this jerk get his way, your taking the job at his office is a part of the plan to get destiny back on track."

Lisa was speaking, unable to hide the emotion in her voice. "I know we've been seeing a lot of each other lately, Greg, but I for one haven't considered marriage."

Greg shot an angry glance at her. "You're not still pining over that two-bit musician who left you high and dry, are you? For heaven's sake, Lisa, forget him. I'm ten times—twenty times—no, for crying out loud, I'm a hundred times better man than he is. I can offer you an exciting life and the security every woman wants. And you offer me exactly what an aggressive politician needs in a wife. You're beautiful, intelligent, a wonderful conversationalist, and you have no ambitions of your own to get in the way of mine."

Greg smiled smugly. "Every politician needs a good woman behind him, and you're the right woman to be behind me, Lisa. I plan on being governor of this state within ten years. Think of the prestige that will be yours when that happens. How does that compare to a life sitting at home while your worthless husband chases all over the country singing in dives and bars?"

Lisa turned away to hide the tears in her eyes, and Greg mistook her failure to respond as her acknowledgment that he was right. Bringing the Porsche to a stop in front of J.T.'s house, he watched as Lisa got out and closed the door behind her. Reaching under the seat, he pulled out a small package and handed it to her.

"What is it?" she asked, looking at the package but not taking it from him just yet.

"It's your name tag," he said. "You know, to put on your desk while you fill in for Becky. I had it made just for this occasion. Here, take it."

Lisa took the package and unwrapped it. She had to admit, the name tag was nicely done. It held only her first name, which was done in gold letters on a pink shaded mirror with roses on the border.

"This job is perfect for you, Lisa," Greg persisted, "and don't forget what it might mean to my future. To *our* future," he quickly corrected himself.

"Tell him you'll see that the problem is taken care of," Samantha chuckled. "At least it will mean you won't have to put up with him for a week."

"I'll . . . see that the problem is taken care of, Greg," Lisa said, and Samantha stared at her cousin. Samantha was assigned to J.T., and he was the only person who should be able to hear her. Was there even the slightest possibility Samantha had influenced Lisa with her suggestion? No, of course not. That was a crazy thought. It was just coincidence.

"Thanks, Lisa," Greg said, with a big smile. "I knew you wouldn't let me down." He blew her a quick kiss, then pulled away, his tires squealing against the pavement. "Don't forget to miss me," he yelled back as he disappeared from view.

Lisa only felt alone as she walked into the house. Unseen, Samantha remained at her side.

CHAPTER 6

Greg drove away from the MacGregor home filled with a mixture of emotion. On the one hand, he was pleased with himself for his ability to manipulate Lisa into watching his office while he was away. On the other hand, he was concerned about Rob Jensen. It was evident Lisa hadn't forgotten that loser, even though it had been months since she had seen him. J.T. had told Greg how he had handled the matter, and Greg knew all about the contracted year's separation. Like J.T., he had assumed it would be enough to bring Lisa around to his way of thinking. Now, some three months into the deal, he was beginning to have doubts.

It wasn't that he was so much in love with Lisa. It was just that she was the perfect candidate for his wife. Finding another with all her qualifications would be a difficult task, indeed. A task he wasn't prepared to spend the time pursuing. No, a second choice was not an option. It was obvious he needed help with the problem, and throughout his life, whenever he needed help, he had turned to one person—his father. This was no exception.

Reaching for his car phone, Greg dialed his father's private number for the cellular phone Big Ed kept with him at all times. The phone was programmed to display the name of the caller so that Big Ed could take the call or ignore it, as he chose. Just as he had eagerly taken J.T. MacGregor's call earlier that morning, he took the call from his son now. "Hello, son. What is it?"

"Ed, I have a problem, and I need your help." Greg always called his father Ed. It was a habit he had picked up as a young boy, and one that had stuck.

"What sort of a problem, son?"

Greg drew a deep breath before answering. This wasn't a minor problem he needed his father's help with. But he knew from past experience that he could depend on his father's help if he could convince Ed the request was in his own best interests. "It's Lisa, Ed. She's so hung up on this Rob Jensen, I'm afraid I'm losing her. I told you how J.T. feels about the man, and how he made a deal to get rid of him for a year. But I'm starting to wonder if the year is going to be enough to make Lisa forget Jensen. I need your help on this one, Ed."

Big Ed laughed the scratchy laugh he was famous for. "You want me to get this Rob out of the picture, is that it, son?"

"That's the general idea. A woman like Lisa is a rare find. I can't take the chance on this guy upsetting my plans."

There was silence for several seconds before Ed came back with his reply. "Yes," he said at length. "I think I can oblige your wishes, son. In fact, I might be able to use the idea of getting Rob out of the picture to my advantage as well. Let me do some thinking on it. There's no hurry, is there?"

"No, I suppose there's no real hurry," Greg answered. "But the sooner it's taken care of, the sooner I can go to work mending Miss Lisa's broken heart, if you know what I mean."

"Yes, son, I know what you mean. I'll get on the problem right away. As I said, I believe it fits right in with another plan I'm working on at the moment. I haven't mentioned it to you yet, but I think it's time. And then I think several things will become clear to you. Things I'm sure you've been wondering about. Now if you'll excuse me, I have some other pressing matters to get out of the way."

Greg shut off his phone and smiled to himself. As usual, he had everything under control.

* * *

After Greg drove off, Lisa went straight to her room. Placing the name plaque Greg had given her on the desk, she picked up a five-by-seven picture of her and Rob taken on one of their last dates. It had been a dance, one where Rob's band hadn't been furnishing the music. It had been good to have him close to her, instead of on stage.

I wonder where you are right now, she thought as she looked at Rob's face. *Are you thinking of me? Or have you forgotten me, as my father says you have? Maybe you're dancing with someone else tonight. Maybe you'll even take her out for a ride in a canoe. Oh, Rob. I miss you, and I need you so. Please keep your promise to come back to me.*

Reaching for a tissue from the box on her nightstand, Lisa wiped away her tears. Suddenly the walls of her room were like the bars on a prison cell. Slipping out of her room, she moved to the next door down the hall. Giving a tap on the door, she opened it and peeked inside. "Can I come in, little sister?"

Julie was lying on her bed reading a book, but at the sight of Lisa, she set aside the book and sat up. "What's up?" she asked as Lisa, who hadn't bothered to wait for permission, came in and closed the door behind herself.

"Nothing special," Lisa sighed, crossing the room and sitting down next to Julie. "I just need to talk." Picking up Julie's book, she read the title aloud. "*Angels to the Rescue.* That's a strange title," she said. "What's the book about?"

Julie glanced briefly at the book. "It's about an angel who comes down to help her cantankerous uncle get his priorities straight about the way he's raising his two beautiful daughters."

Lisa looked startled, then laughed. "The two beautiful daughters could almost be us, couldn't they?" she jested.

"Almost," Julie grinned. "Except in our case the author would have to explain how much more beautiful the younger sister is than the older."

"Yeah, right," Lisa groaned, tossing the book back onto the bed. "And the author would also have to tell how *humble* the younger sister is."

Julie smiled. "I'm sure he'd find a way to get that point across," she said.

Lisa leaned back on her sister's bed and stared at the ceiling. "I'll bet the book has a happy ending, doesn't it?"

Julie shook her head. "I haven't gotten that far yet."

"Oh, it'll have a happy ending," Lisa said with a heartfelt sigh. "Look at the cover. It oozes romance. I wish real life could be like that."

Julie looked at her sister sympathetically. "You're thinking about Rob again, aren't you?" she asked.

Lisa nodded.

"You still miss him, don't you?"

"Like I'd miss the sun if it never showed its face again. But enough of this depressing stuff. Rob *will* keep his promise, and I *will* wait for him."

Julie looked at her sister slyly. "You do know that Rob's in town all next week, don't you?"

"What?!" Lisa sat up. "I didn't know. What . . . Where . . . ?" she tried to speak but couldn't.

Julia laughed to see her sister suddenly energized. "I saw a poster at the store where I bought this book. Rob's group is doing a concert at the old theater on 12th Street."

"The band is doing a concert? Here?"

"That's what the poster said."

Lisa jumped off the bed and started pacing around the room. In fact, she nearly walked right through Samantha, who had followed her into Julie's room. "I've got to see him, Julie. I've just got to. I won't exactly be breaking my promise to Dad if I don't talk to him and he doesn't see me. They'll probably use the theater for rehearsals in the afternoons. I could sit at the back, in the balcony. No one would notice me, and I could at least see him."

Julie grinned. "If it were me, I'd be a lot closer than a back-row balcony seat."

"Oh no!" Lisa gasped, remembering her commitment to take care of Greg's office. "I just thought of something, Julie. I have a major problem. Greg asked me to fill in at his office all next week. He's going away on business, and his regular secretary is off on her honeymoon."

Julie rolled her eyes. "Don't you know how to use the word 'no'? It works wonders at times."

"I'd like to say no," Lisa sighed. "But I hate contention. It just seems easier to go with the flow than fight it. Sometimes I wish I could be more like you, Julie. You'd have no problem handling Greg at all."

"You're not suggesting I take him off your hands, are you?" Julie said in mock horror, then laughed. "Not that I couldn't if I wanted to, you realize. But—I don't. Greg is your problem, not mine." Julie smiled complacently.

Lisa put her hands on her hips. "Very funny, Julie MacGregor. C'mon, admit it. Every dance we've gone to has been the same. *I'm* always asked before you."

Julie shrugged and flipped her hair over one shoulder. "That's *only* because the guys think I'm so hot they wouldn't stand a chance with me. Being as gorgeous as I am does have its down side at times."

Lisa chuckled. "Yes, dear sister, you have your problems being too beautiful. And I have my problems with Greg. Seriously, what am I going to do? I can't stand the thought of missing out on the chance to at least see Rob from a distance." She turned to look at Julie with a peculiar gleam in her eye. "Say, Julie—"

"Oh, no," Julie protested, realizing immediately what the look meant. "I'm not filling in for you at Greg's office. If that's what you have going through that head of yours, you can forget it."

"Julie, please. At least do it for a couple of days. You have no idea what it would mean to me to just see Rob. All Greg needs is someone to make phone appointments. And since our voices sound so much alike over the phone anyway, no one will ever know the difference. Greg will think I was there the whole time, and there won't be any trouble. Say yes and . . ." Lisa paused, thinking, "that new green dress you've been begging to borrow is yours to keep. I'll even throw in the green pumps that go with it."

"Listen to your sister," Samantha broke in, forgetting she couldn't be heard. "Julie, *you're* actually the one who needs to be at the office next Tuesday morning. Your whole future may well depend on it."

Julie's expression turned to one of astonishment. "Did you hear something, Lisa?" she asked.

Lisa stared at her sister. "What? Did I hear something? Like what?"

"I don't know—like a voice. Sort of like . . . Cousin Sam's voice."

"You thought you heard Cousin Sam's voice?" Lisa's jaw dropped. "How much sleep have you been getting lately?"

"You heard me?" Samantha gasped, no less startled than Lisa had been. "But—that's not supposed to happen."

"I didn't actually *hear* Sam's voice," Julie tried to explain. "I just sort of felt—kind of—I don't know how to describe the feeling. It was just there."

"Julie MacGregor!" Samantha exclaimed with a shout. "If you can understand what I'm saying, take your sister up on her offer. You're the one who has to be in Greg's office when Eric Roberts shows up."

"There, it happened again," Julie said. "Did you feel it?"

"I—I don't know," Lisa replied. "I do feel something strange. Like someone is here with us. Maybe even Cousin Sam. This is crazy. What do you suppose is going on here?"

Julie shook her head. "I have no idea, but whatever it is I may actually have to help you out. Call me crazy, but I have the feeling there's something bigger going on here than we know. Hmmm . . . throw in that cute little white purse I saw you carrying yesterday, and I'll do it."

"What? My white purse?!" Lisa looked dismayed. "You want that, too?"

Julie stood firm. "You're lucky I'm not asking for more, big sister. Babysitting your boyfriend's office for a week isn't my idea of fun."

Lisa's dismay turned to joy. "You'd fill in the whole week for me?"

"Two days, a week, what's the difference?" Julie shrugged. "Rob will be here all week, and I'd just have to live with your moping if I didn't do this. Throw in the purse, and it's a deal."

"The purse is yours," Lisa promised. "Now what do you say we get out of here? Look at that incredible day outside your window. It's just crying for us to go shopping. That's the best way I can think of to help me forget Rob, Greg, Father—the lot of them. What do you say?"

"That's what I like about you," Julie grinned. "You always have an answer to any problem at hand."

Lisa laughed. "I think shopping is your answer to every problem."

"Of course it is! After all, I learned from the best—you."

Grabbing her purse from the edge of the bed, Julie slid the strap over her shoulder. In three steps she was at the door, motioning for Lisa to follow. "What are you waiting for, slow poke? Let's go!"

"I can't believe this," Samantha said, as she watched them walk away. "They heard me. That's not supposed to happen."

CHAPTER 7

Samantha glanced across the seat at Eric Roberts, and smiled to herself. "I'll bet he thinks this is just another Tuesday morning," she chuckled. "Like any other Tuesday morning. Is he in for a surprise, or what? Just wait until he opens the door to Greg's office . . ."

Samantha was right. Eric didn't see anything out of the ordinary about this Tuesday morning. The traffic was light, it wasn't raining, and his first job for the day promised to be an easy one. For nearly a year, he had worked part time for Ace Brothers' Computer and Electronics Repair. The job suited his needs perfectly. The pay was good, and his hours were flexible, which allowed him plenty of time for school and homework. Not that he particularly enjoyed all the homework. But the coveted degree in electrical engineering was only one semester away, and that made it bearable.

Eric pulled his service truck into the parking lot of the Rockshire Business Complex and parked in front of Greg Reeves's office. He was no stranger here, since the company he worked for held the service contract on all of Greg's office equipment. He had been here only a week earlier, in fact, repairing the fax machine. This time it was Becky's computer that needed his attention. Eric was glad this call was on a computer. Computers were more fun to work on than fax or copy machines. Gathering his tools, Eric made his way to Greg's office.

* * *

Julie sat at Becky's desk, bored stiff. She tossed the magazine she had been reading onto the desk and stared out the window at the lovely day going to waste with her here in this office. "Julie MacGregor," she grumbled aloud, "how could you let your pushy sister talk you into this job? And this is only the second day, for goodness' sake. You'll be climbing the walls by Friday."

Julie had hoped to use this time to catch up on some letter writing, something she was always behind in since she hated letter writing. She had thought that as long as she was babysitting Greg's office, it would be a great time to catch up. September would be here before she knew it, bringing the start of a new semester and a heavy schedule. If she didn't have her letter writing out of the way before then, it would never get done. But the computer on the secretary's desk had completely given up the ghost. Julie had quickly scanned the few magazines in the lobby, and now she had nothing to do but think about her life.

The pursuit of her law degree was anything but easy, but it was a goal she refused to let go of. To Julie, being independent of her father's financial influence was paramount. Not that she didn't love him, because she did. But she couldn't help feeling that somewhere along the way he had allowed a few of his priorities to slip out of order, and she wanted to put herself in a position where he could never use his money to back her in a corner as he had done with Lisa. Julie knew the day would come when she would meet a Rob Jensen of her own, and she wanted to be prepared when that time came. There was still plenty of time for preparation, of course. Meeting her Rob Jensen was something that wouldn't happen for a year or two down the road. Maybe she would meet him in one of her classes, or perhaps even later when the two of them would be thrown together by one of the many dramatic law cases her future was bound to hold in store. Who knew how it might happen? There were thousands of possibilities.

As a matter of fact, Julie was right. There were thousands of possibilities, one much closer than she could possibly realize.

* * *

Eric pushed open the door and stepped into the office expecting to see Becky at her desk as usual. To his surprise, he didn't see Becky at all. His eyes grew as big as sand dollars as he stared at the attractive young woman in Becky's chair and wondered who she could be. The first thing he noticed was her shoulder-length, strawberry blonde hair that reminded him of something out of a Pantene shampoo commercial.

She was absolutely beautiful, he thought. No, she was more than beautiful. She was . . . well, to put it in engineering terms, she was radiant. Sort of like the glow of a hundred brilliantly colored light-emitting diodes.

His heart rushed to his throat, leaving him groping for words. What he managed, and immediately wished he hadn't, was, "I—I was expecting Becky. You're not her."

Eric winced. *What a dumb thing to say,* he berated himself.

Her left hand was in plain sight, and he quickly noticed she wore no ring. Of course that shouldn't matter to him, anyway. He could never bring himself to ask this lady out. She was definitely out of his league, and would just embarrass him with some excuse why she had to say no. Gathering his wits, he closed the door behind him and walked over to the desk.

"I'm here about the computer," he finally said.

* * *

Julie glanced up to see who had entered the office and found herself looking into a pair of the deepest eyes she had ever seen. Who was this guy? With that one little unruly lock of jet black hair hanging down just over eyes that made her insides melt, he looked like someone who might have stepped down off the big silver screen of a sizzling romance movie. From somewhere far away, she heard him say something about her not being Becky.

"Uh—no," she replied. "Becky is off this week. I'm taking her place. Is there something I can do for you?"

Unheard by either of them, an angel named Samantha cried out ecstatically, "YES! It's working! They're already hooked—it's written all over their faces. What can I say, Samantha Hackett? Are you a matchmaker, or what?"

Stepping up to the desk, Eric said, "I'm here about the computer. You know—the one someone called about yesterday afternoon."

"The computer?" Julie said blankly. "Oh, yes, the computer. It's this one here on my desk. Uh—on Becky's desk," she quickly corrected herself. "It's the mouse. It just refuses to work, and I'm not smart enough to use WordPerfect without a mouse." She paused and added with a slight smile, "I offered it cheese and everything, but it didn't help."

Eric laughed. "You probably tried cheddar," he quipped. "That's a common mistake. A computer mouse will usually go for Swiss." A moment later he asked, "So what's the deal with Becky? Is she sick?"

"No, Becky's fine. At least I think she's fine. She's on her honeymoon."

Eric looked surprised. "Becky's married already? Seems like she barely got engaged. So you're covering for her?"

Julie nodded. "The office needed a temporary secretary. Not that I'm much of one. My secretary skills are pretty much limited to answering the phone and reporting computers that won't let me play solitaire. So can you fix the thing?"

Eric smiled. "Sure I can fix it. That's my job." Eric sat down to the task, and in less than two minutes had the cover removed from the computer. Julie was fascinated just watching him. "I'm Eric," he said as he worked. "Eric Roberts. If the name on your desk plaque is right, you must be Lisa."

"No, I'm Ju—" Julie caught herself in midsentence. Lisa had made her promise not to use her own name. She had even insisted that Julie use the name plaque Greg had given her, fearing that if he ever heard about the switch, he would be furious. Much as it bothered her, Julie knew she couldn't give Eric her real name. "Yes, I'm Lisa," she lied.

Eric looked a little confused at her near slip, but said nothing. Glancing over his shoulder, Julie stared in earnest at the inside workings of the computer. "So that's what a computer looks like opened up," she remarked. "What are all those little black things that look like plastic centipedes?"

"Plastic centipedes?" Eric laughed. "Now there's a new one. I've never heard it put like that before. These are PC chips. And this is called the mother board," he said, pointing to one component in particular. "The mother board is the heart of the computer. It contains more intelligence alone than all the computers combined that were used to put man on the moon a few years back. Impressive, huh?"

Julie shook her head. "I'll take your word for it, okay? To me it looks just like a bunch of plastic centipedes."

"Hey, don't feel bad. I'd probably be just as lost looking at some of your shorthand notes."

"Shorthand notes?" she laughed. "Boy, have you got me pegged wrong. I couldn't tell a page of shorthand from a sheet of Mozart's music. I told you before, I'm just filling in on this job as a favor to my—uh . . . to a friend."

Eric grinned. "You're sort of a pseudo-secretary, then."

"Pseudo-secretary?" Julie laughed. "That's one way of putting it, I suppose. I'm actually a law student, or will be when the semester starts next fall."

Eric glanced up. "Law student, huh? I'll bet that could keep you in the books. Ah, here's the problem." He pointed to a connector plug with a damaged pin.

"This is really strange," he said, examining the damaged part more closely. "It's almost like someone did this on purpose."

"Well it certainly wasn't me," Julie assured him. "All I did was turn the darn thing on and *poof!* That was it."

Folding her arms, Samantha looked on with pleasure as nature continued to take its course between the two young people. "Gus," she said, with a certain satisfaction in her voice. "This is one of your contracts that's well on its way to the completion file. My idea of having Maggie program the bent pin on this computer was a stroke of genius, if I do say so myself. All I have to do now is keep Uncle Mac from muddying the water."

As Eric straightened the bent pin, he said, "This should work well enough to get you by until I can get back with a new part, maybe sometime later this week."

Sliding the cover back in place, he secured it with six small screws. Then, taking a deep breath, he made his move, which came as no surprise to Samantha. After all, she had planned this whole thing out in advance.

"Do you like pizza?" Eric asked.

"Of course," Julie said with a laugh. "Everyone likes pizza, don't they? Why?"

"I know a place where the pizza is out of this world," he replied.

"I thought you came here to fix this computer," she teased. "Not to hit on the pseudo-secretary."

"Hey!" Samantha exclaimed. "Cut that out. I didn't go to all the trouble of getting you two together to have you play hard to get. Tell the guy you love pizza, cousin."

Julie found herself torn between an overwhelming desire to say yes to Eric, and dread that her dad would find out. "It's nice of you to ask," she said. "But . . ."

Samantha quickly figured out Julie's hesitation. "Forget about your dad!" she cried out. "Say yes, quick!"

"I don't see a ring on your finger," Eric went on to say. "I'm not out of line here, am I?"

"No," Julie said, looking down at her finger. "I'm not married or anything." She sighed, and allowed her eyes to meet his. "Do you know how many guys have offered to take me out for pizza that's out of this world?" she finally asked.

The disappointment in Eric's voice was obvious as he answered, "I don't know. Dozens, I suppose."

"No," she said, after what seemed an unbearable pause. "Actually, you're the first. I get off at three."

As Samantha looked at both their faces, she giggled. It was a toss-up who looked more excited, Eric or Samantha. "You get off at three?" Eric burst out. "Does that mean I can pick you up then?"

Julie hesitated again before saying slowly, "You can pick me up, but if that pizza's not as good as you say . . ."

At her words, Eric grinned. "You won't be disappointed, I promise. Shall I pick you up here at the office?"

This time there was no hesitation. "That would be great," Julie answered.

"All right!" Eric exclaimed, gathering up his tools and backing toward the door. "I'll see you at three."

Both Samantha and Julie looked on with amusement as Eric managed to back into a chair on his way out. He succeeded in knocking it over.

"Oh . . . I . . . uh . . ." Eric righted the chair and continued backing out of the door, grinning with embarrassment.

Samantha gave a sigh of relief. "Don't you ever scare me like that again, cousin," she said, then added, laughingly, "I could die of a heart attack, or something."

* * *

At the same time that Eric and Julie were managing their first meeting, a scene of a very different nature was taking place on the far side of town.

Conscious of Big Ed's gaze upon him, J.T. nervously thumbed through the stack of papers he was holding. It was difficult keeping his mind on the transaction at hand after the humiliating experience he had just undergone. This was the first time he had been in Ed Reeves' office, and he certainly hadn't been prepared for what he encountered here. It had been intimidating enough having two body guards scrutinizing his every move, but he'd even had to suffer the indignation of a pat-down search when he entered the office. And then one of Big Ed's goons had confiscated his cell phone. What was J.T. going to do, poke someone in the eye with the antenna? It had been unnerving, to say the least. But—he had to admit—it was worth it just for the chance to work with a man like Edward Reeves.

"Well?" Big Ed asked, from the other side of his massive mahogany desk. "Does everything seem in order to you, J.T.?"

J.T. looked up from the papers he held in his hand. "Everything looks perfect. I can't tell you what a pleasure it is doing business on a scale like this with you."

Big Ed stood up and stepped around the desk where J.T. could get a better look at him. The name "Big Ed" couldn't have been more out of place, if it were used to refer to his physical size. He was no taller than five-six, or five-seven, and he obviously weighed no more than a hundred and fifty or so pounds. The skin on his face and hands was wrinkled far beyond his years. His ears seemed much too large for his head, and his nose had a definite hook to the left. The most prominent of his features, however, were his eyes. They were filled with a bitterness that seemed to emanate from the man's soul. It was impossible to be in his presence without feeling this bitterness. Even to a man as hardened to the world as J.T., this was a little nerve-racking. Swallowing nervously, J.T. agreed that the name Big Ed fit the man perfectly—not for the man's size, but for the power he held in one of those scrawny little hands.

"This deal stands to make us both a lot of money," Edward said as he approached J.T. "And after all, isn't making money what this life is all about?"

Even though J.T. had often expressed the same idea, it somehow sounded more impressive coming from this man. "Yes, it is," he readily answered. "And if you ever decide to take on another project like this one, you can feel free to count me in."

Edward put an arm around J.T.'s shoulder and escorted him to the door. "Give the man back his phone," he instructed one of the bodyguards, who had just opened the door in anticipation of J.T. leaving. "I hate to hurry you off like this," Edward said. "But you do understand I have a heavy schedule. You look over those papers. We'll get together soon for the final signing. Very soon, as a matter of fact."

"I understand," J.T. said, as the two men shook hands. J.T. then took the cell phone the guard held out to him, slipping it into his pocket as he walked out the door.

Big Ed was silent until he was sure J.T. was well out of the range of his voice, then he turned to the one of the guards. "Well, Hank?" he pressed. "Did you take care of the switch like I asked you to?"

"No problem, sir," Hank answered, handing Edward the cellular phone he had tucked away in his own pocket. "As you can see, J.T.'s phone is just a standard Nokia model. I had no problem finding an exact match while you had him occupied here in your office. He now has the replacement phone, and you have the one registered in his name."

An evil smile curled the edges of Edward's mouth. "Good," he sneered. "We'll put this little item to good use, you can depend on it. Now I want you to get a hold of George Weathersby for me. I want him here in my office as soon as possible."

"Yes, sir," Hank dutifully replied. "I'll get right on it."

CHAPTER 8

As badly as she had wanted the computer the day before, and even earlier that morning, Julie no longer even cared. The thought of writing letters was the furthest thing from her mind. Eric Roberts had walked onto center stage and taken over. There was something about Eric, something she couldn't put a finger on, that left her with the haunting feeling she had known him before. Or maybe it would be better to say she had waited all her life to know him. However she said it, that persistent little voice in her heart and head only added to the feeling. A little voice that reminded her vaguely of Cousin Sam, although of course that was impossible. Still. . . .

Julie had thought Monday was the slowest day of her life, but now, as she waited for Eric's return, it seemed to take forever for the hands on the clock to reach three o'clock. And even when they did reach that point, Eric still hadn't arrived. Another five grueling minutes passed before the door opened, and Julie saw Eric walk into the room wearing that same warm smile. She forced the frown to remain on her own face, although it wasn't easy.

"You're late," she said. "I was beginning to wonder if you'd changed your mind."

Eric glanced at his watch. "What can I say? I didn't realize that Little Blue was low on gas. I had to take time to stop by the gas station. Since you're a law student, I knew you'd never fall for that old 'out of gas' routine."

"Little Blue?" Julie asked, while shutting down the computer and picking up her purse from under the desk. "If you don't mind my asking, just what is a Little Blue?"

"Little Blue is my car," he explained.

Julie's eyes widened. "You named your car?"

"Why shouldn't I give my car a name? We're talking about a darn good car here."

Julie stepped into the elevator and watched as Eric pressed the ground floor button. "Little Blue," she said again. "Let me guess. It's a shiny blue sports car, right? Probably a Ford Mustang."

"Not hardly," Eric chuckled. "You did get one thing right, Lisa. It *is* blue—except for the rust, which is sort of an orange-red. Little Blue may not be much to look at, but underneath that humble appearance beats the heart of a great car."

As they crossed the lot, Julie got her first look at Little Blue. It was a Ford, all right. But not a Mustang. It was an Escort station wagon. She watched with amusement as Eric opened the door and smoothed the wrinkles out of the terry-cloth towel he used to cover the seat.

"I'll give you this much," she teased. "You certainly weren't lying about how it looked. I hope what you've told me about the pizza is as truthful."

"Don't put Little Blue down like that," Eric pleaded. "You'll hurt his feelings."

Julie laughed. "Cars don't have feelings. They're just machines."

"Don't you ever let Little Blue hear you say that," he scolded mildly. "Machines have feelings. Take your computer, for instance. I treated it with great respect when I checked it out this morning. As a result, it responded to my effort and started doing its thing with no problem. If I had yelled because one of the screws stuck, or something like that, you can bet it would have fought me all the way. That's how it works with a machine every time."

Julie just grinned at him. "You're serious, aren't you?"

"You're darn right I'm serious. I treat Little Blue like a true friend, and you know what? He's never let me down yet. Not once."

As Julie slid in and fastened her seat belt, she reached out and patted the dashboard. "I'm sorry, Little Blue," she apologized. "I'll never say bad things about you again, I promise."

Eric smiled at her as he started the engine. "I told the truth about the pizza, too," he said. "Benny's place isn't far from here, and the pizza should be ready when we get there. I've already called in the order."

"Why did you do that?"

"This is no ordinary pizza we're talking about. It takes forty-five minutes to construct a *Benny Special*. The guy uses twelve kinds of cheese on it."

"Twelve kinds of cheese? I had no idea there *were* that many different kinds of cheese."

"I didn't either. But that's what Benny says, and I know he wouldn't lie." Eric glanced at Julie. "Do you have a last name?" he asked.

Julie bit her lip. She had known the question would come up sooner or later, but she hoped it would be later. She had started this friendship with one lie, using her sister's name, and more lying didn't sit well with her. But giving out her real name was not something she wanted to do, either. Not with J.T. to think about. "I have a last name," she sighed. "But I'd rather not tell it to you just now."

"Why not?" Eric asked.

Julie forced a smile. "You know what they say—a little mystery makes a woman more exciting."

Eric was obviously puzzled, but he shrugged. "Okay, Miss Lisa No-Name, I can always use a little excitement in my life." *Especially when it comes in such a lovely package*, he added under his breath.

"Have you been repairing computers long?" Julie asked, hoping to change the subject as well as satisfy her curiosity.

"I've had this job almost a year now. It fits in great with my class schedule since these guys pretty much let me pick my own hours to work."

"You're going to school?"

"Yeah. I'm working on an electrical engineering degree."

"That sounds interesting. Maybe I'll have you wire up my first law office, or something."

Eric's response was something between a laugh and a grunt.

"What's so funny?" she asked.

"I was just thinking what a pair the two of us could make someday. Sort of like Ben Matlock teaming up with Thomas Edison."

Julie laughed. "Not hardly."

Looking over his shoulder as he drove, Eric gave Julie a smile that made her feel tingly in a pleasant sort of way. "True. You're much better looking than Ben Matlock."

"Oh, brother," she groaned. "I hope the pizza's better than your jokes."

"Hey! That was no joke. I've never even wanted to ask Ben Matlock out for pizza."

"That's because he only eats hot dogs. Anyway, how close are you to getting your degree?"

"About halfway," he answered, a hint of disgust showing in his voice. "I would have graduated a year ago, but I ran into a little problem that set me back. Hey look, here we are."

He pulled Little Blue into a small shopping center and parked in front of Benny's Pizza Parlor.

Julie wanted to pursue the discussion of Eric's problem at school a little further, but she decided to let it go—for the time being, at least. "I must have passed this corner a hundred times," she said. "I never realized there was a pizza place here."

"It's a small place," Eric explained. "But once you taste the food, you'll never forget it."

As Eric pushed open the door to the restaurant, a cowbell sounded their arrival. Julie stepped inside and saw five small round tables crowded into a room barely large enough to hold them. Each table was covered with a bright red cloth and held a single candle in an old soda bottle. Runners of spent wax gave each bottle its own rustic pattern. At the far end of the room, behind the service counter, the kitchen could be seen. There she noticed one cook busily going about his work.

Eric pulled out a chair from one table and motioned for Julie to sit down. "Is that pizza ready yet, Benny?" he called to the big man in the back.

"I'm working on it, guy," Benny called from the kitchen. "What—you think I got a dozen hands? If you're in such a rush, you can come back here and slice the thing yourself."

"Take your time, Benny," Eric replied. "I might as well tell you that . . . you're going to, anyway."

Benny left the kitchen and approached their table. "Say now, would you look at this," he said, smiling at Julie. "Eric Roberts has himself a date. I hope my insurance is paid up. My walls may not be able to stand this shocker."

Eric groaned. "Just concentrate on the pizza, Benny. We can do without your comments. If we wanted entertainment, we'd have gone to a movie."

Benny wiped his hands on his apron and cocked back the chef's hat on his head. "Are you going to tell me this charming lady's name or do I have to drag it out of you?"

"I'll introduce you, as long as you remember she's *my* date. Try horning in, and you'll wear that pizza home for a hat. Lisa, this is Benny. Benny, Lisa."

"Hiya, Lisa," he said, extending a big right hand in her direction.

Shaking his hand, Julie said, "Nice to meet you, Benny."

"It's nice to meet you, too. And I'm darned glad to see you in here with this guy. I'm tired of seeing him ears and elbows in his work and studying twenty hours out of every day. He can use a little time off with a nice-looking lady like yourself."

Eric waved Benny away. "Benny, go finish that pizza and stop embarrassing her."

"Embarrassing her? You're the one blushing like a slice of pepperoni. You hung up on this guy, Lisa? Have the two of you discussed a date, or anything?"

Julie laughed. "We just met, Benny. But if I decide to get married in the next few minutes, I promise to give Eric my strongest consideration."

"Lisa, you have to understand Benny," Eric explained. "This guy thinks he's my mother."

Benny started back toward the kitchen, muttering, "I know when I'm not wanted."

"I'm sorry," Eric said, still blushing. "I should have warned you about Benny's tactfulness."

Julie smiled. "It's okay. I think he's sort of cute."

"Benny cute? How do you see to study your law books, if your eyes are that bad?"

Julie shook a finger at him over the table. "Not nice, Eric."

"So what do you want to wash this down with?" Benny asked as he brought the pizza and placed it on the table between them. "I recommend the carrot juice, sprinkled with a bit of ground liver."

"Yuck!" Julie pulled a face. "Don't you have something a little more traditional, like lemonade maybe?"

"I got lemonade," he grinned. "That would have been my second suggestion."

As Benny went off for the drinks, Julie's eyes took in the pizza. "Oh my," she said, lifting her first wedge of pizza. "This is hot!" It seemed to take forever to stretch the cheese far enough for it to break. "Umm—it is good, though," she added after the first taste.

"Told you so." Eric smiled at her as he helped himself to a slice of pizza.

Julie studied Eric closely as she nibbled a second bite. His eyes were a penetrating bluish-green, but it was more than just their color that fascinated her. It was something that went much deeper than color alone. She couldn't pin down exactly what it was, but it only strengthened the feeling she had of knowing him from somewhere before.

"I take it from what Benny says, you don't date much," she said.

"I guess not," he agreed. "Like Benny said, I spend most of my time working and studying."

"You didn't seem too shy about asking me out."

"Some things are just too good to pass up," he replied. Julie noticed a faint blush under his skin, and she grinned her approval of his remark.

"Liquid lemons on the rocks," Benny said, as he placed the drinks on the table. "If you need anything else, give us a shout." With this, he whisked off to the kitchen once more.

Eric reached for a straw and stripped back the paper. "I know this sounds corny," he said, "but when I opened the door and saw you this morning, this little voice in my head began shouting, 'Ask this lady out!' It refused to go away until I gave in."

Julie looked at him skeptically. "You hear little voices in your head?" she asked, not bothering to mention her own similar experience.

"Not often," he shrugged. "But in your case I did. It was sorta like the time I first spotted Little Blue on the used car lot. I heard one of these little voices then, too, telling me to buy the car. What if I hadn't listened that time? I'd have missed owning a great car."

"Oh, I see. You're comparing me to your car now."

"That's not what I meant," Eric defended himself. "I only meant that—"

"It's okay," Julie said. "I know you meant it as a compliment.

But let's talk about you for a while. Tell me about the problem you mentioned about your graduating."

"Why would you want to talk about that?" Eric asked. Something in his tone of voice caught Julie's attention.

"Uh-oh," she smiled, a little apologetically. "I hit a nerve, didn't I?"

"You could say that, I guess," he admitted.

Never one to back away from a subject she was interested in, Julie decided to press her luck. "Do you feel like talking about it?" she asked cautiously.

"Sure," he shrugged. "It doesn't bother me much anymore." He sipped his lemonade, then said, "I could have had my degree more than a year ago. You see, I earned a full scholarship after graduating number one in my high school class. Everything was paid for. My tuition, my books, even my room and board. Then during my sophomore year, one of my assignments was to design and build a circuit using op-amps."

"Op-amps?"

"Operational amplifiers."

"Some of those little black things in the computer at Greg's office, no doubt."

Eric nodded. "You got it. I went all out on the project. To describe it in terms you would understand, I built a model speedboat that worked on voice control."

"Voice control?"

"Yeah. I could control its speed and direction—I could even cause its flag to raise and lower simply by telling it to do so. And it worked only with my voice; no one else could interfere."

"Just your voice? That's incredible."

"Working with my voice alone is what made the project so special, Lisa. It would be simple to build a voice-controlled boat that would work with any voice."

"You have a strange idea of simple," Julie said, chuckling. "I'd be lucky to build a boat that would float. So what happened? Did something go wrong?"

"Something went wrong, all right. I wanted to take the project one step further, so I secretly recorded my professor's voice. Then I programmed the circuit to function at his command. I figured that little added feature would impress him for sure."

Julie's face showed her skepticism. "Would voice control work with just a tape recording of a person's voice?"

Eric nodded. "That's exactly what it was. I can't remember how many nights I went to bed after midnight only to get up at three a.m. to start in again. But in the end it was worth it. At least I thought so at the time. The darn thing functioned perfectly. I just knew I had an 'A' coming for the project."

By this time, Julie was completely caught up in Eric's story. "So what went wrong?" she asked anxiously. "Did it fail the test at the last minute?"

"Oh no," Eric assured her. "The project worked to perfection. The problem is, someone else got credit for it. The night before the project was due, my roommate, George Weathersby, set me up with a blind date."

"A blind date?" Julie broke in. "Was she cute?"

Eric pursed his lips in thought. "Yeah, she was kind of cute, but not as cute as a certain law student I've met since."

"Oh, that's okay then," she grinned.

"Well, it didn't turn out okay. While I was out on the date, George stole my project."

"He what?!"

"He stole my project and turned it in as his work. He not only got an 'A' in the class, but he also won the thousand-dollar prize money the school had set up for the best project. Now he has the idea patented, and is working with some rich guy trying to market it. Old George will probably end up making a fortune off my idea. As for me," Eric sighed. "I had nothing to turn in for my assignment. I failed the class and lost my scholarship."

Julie smacked the table with her hand. It made her blood boil to think anyone would do such a thing under the guise of being a friend. "And you let him get away with it?" Her eyes blazed with anger.

Julie couldn't believe Eric could laugh about the matter, but that's exactly what he did. "You are really cute when you're angry," he said, smiling deeply into her eyes, "and I like the way your nose wrinkles up."

Julie tried to ignore his words. "Eric Roberts, we're talking about a terrible injustice here, and all you can say is I'm cute? There must be something you can do to prove the model is yours. Didn't you keep notes? What about witnesses? Surely someone saw you working on the project."

"You're even cuter when your lawyerly instincts start showing through. You'd better learn to hide that from a jury, or you'll never send the bad guy away. But as for your question—yes, I kept notes. I kept them with my project. When George stole the model, he took the notes with it. As for witnesses, there were none. Like I said, I did most of my work at three o'clock in the morning. Who in their right mind would be up at that time when they didn't have to be?"

"I don't understand you, Eric." Julie stared at him, bewildered. "How can you be so calm about this thing? If George Weathersby, or anyone else, did something like that to me I'd . . ."

Eric became more serious. "You'd what, Lisa? Buy a gun and shoot the man? Believe me, there were times I wanted to do just that, but what would it have gotten me in the end? You understand the law. Who would have come out on the short end of the stick if I had hurt George?"

"I didn't say you had to shoot him. There are other ways."

"Other ways," he nodded soberly. "Other ways, as you put it, are only possible if someone believes you. No one believed me. George was a politician from the get-go. He had the whole faculty in the palm of his hand. I darn near got expelled for accusing him of doing any such thing."

Julie could see she was suggesting nothing that Eric hadn't thought of before. She felt helpless, and she hated it. Being helpless was something she wasn't used to.

"Do you hate the man?" she asked. "I mean, if that happened to me, I'd hate him."

"Yeah," Eric admitted. "I hated him at first. I hated him with a passion you can't believe. Sometimes I'd lie awake nights thinking up ghastly things I could do to him. I wanted to make him as miserable as he made me. I became so obsessed with hating George I couldn't think of anything else. I couldn't concentrate on my school work, so I quit trying. I dropped out of the program for more than a year.

"But in time I came to realize my anger was like a poison that was hurting me—Eric Roberts—not George Weathersby. I mean, he went on with life like nothing had ever happened. He didn't quit school. He didn't lose any sleep at night. He didn't lose his appetite and drop more than twenty pounds. I was the one who did all those things. After realizing this, I came to the conclusion that I had to get the poison of hate out of my system, or it could mess me up for the rest of my life."

Julie took another bite of pizza and stared at Eric. "So?" she asked. "How did it work out? Did you actually start feeling better about George?"

"It took a long time and a lot of effort," Eric confessed. "But I can actually say I've forgiven the man now. He may have even done me a favor by stealing my idea."

"You can't mean that," Julie protested.

"Actually, it helped me get my head straight again," Eric said. "I'm back in school now, and I intend to graduate this time. And the best part is I'm doing it on my own. Before I was depending on the scholarship. Now I know I can do it myself. And what the heck, I can invent better things than voice-controlled boats. I know I can now. If it hadn't been for George's little stunt, I might never have gained this confidence."

Julie was silent, awed at Eric's strength of character in forgiving someone who had done him such a terrible injustice. Eric misunderstood her silence.

"I hope I'm not boring you with all this," he said. "Here I am going on about myself like this on a first date. I know how unimportant this all must sound to someone like you. I mean, you must go out on interesting dates all the time."

"Well, you're wrong," Julie said. "I very seldom date. I almost turned you down."

"Yeah, I got that feeling. What made you change your mind?"

She grinned. "Some things are just too good to pass up," she said mischievously. "I mean, this pizza is fabulous."

"Gee, thanks a lot," Eric groaned. "I really needed that boost to my ego."

"I'm joking," she assured him. "I am glad I didn't turn you down. And I do mean for more than the pizza, although it is great pizza."

"I'm glad, too," Eric quickly agreed. "This sure beats eating alone, like I usually do."

Julie tried to imagine what it must be like having to eat alone. It was something she hadn't thought of before. She always had Lisa, and Dad, of course. Even with his ornery streak, he was still good company—most of the time, at least. "Why do you have to eat alone, Eric," she asked, in concern. "Don't you have family?"

"Yeah, I have a family. But I don't get to see them often. Dad's in the service, and he goes where the job takes him. Right now they're living in the East. I flew back and spent Christmas with them, but I haven't seen them since. How about you, Lisa? Is your family close by?"

Julie bit her lip, and wished she hadn't mentioned the word family. "I'm sorry, Eric. I really don't want to talk about my family just now. Would you think me too awful if I asked you to let them be part of my mystery? I'd really appreciate it."

As Eric opened his wallet to pay for the pizza, Benny shook his head. "Keep the money in your pocket, pal. This one's on the house."

Eric couldn't believe his ears. "What do you mean 'on the house,' Benny? You usually charge me for an extra olive that gets on my plate by accident."

Benny put one arm around Eric and the other around Julie. "Look, guy, if I want to give you a pizza, I'll give you a pizza. And if I only do it when you bring a date in here I won't lose very much in the deal, will I? Now get out of here, both of you, before I change my mind and ring you up double."

If the wait in Greg's office seemed too long for Julie, the date and drive back to her car made up for it by rushing by much too quickly. She wanted to linger a while before saying goodbye, but couldn't think how to do it without appearing too obvious.

"Which one is your car?" Eric asked as he pulled into the parking lot. When Julie pointed to the red BMW she had driven that day, Eric's mouth dropped open. "That's your car," he choked. "The BMW 325I?"

Julie nodded.

"No wonder you had a hard time saying yes to a date with me," Eric grumbled.

"And just what's that supposed to mean?" she asked pointedly.

"Isn't it obvious?" he said. "Anyone who can afford to drive that car is definitely out of my league."

Julie slugged Eric in the shoulder. "Come off it, Eric Roberts! It's not fair for you to judge me by the car I drive. And anyway—it's not exactly mine."

"Your parents'?"

"Yes, sort of."

"Are they wealthy?"

Julie's anger eased a bit as she realized his question was perfectly natural. Glancing down at her purse, she fumbled with the strap. "Look Eric . . ." She paused, searching for the right words. "Some things aren't easy to explain, and I don't want to hurt your feelings. It's just that my life is rather—let's say, 'complicated' at the moment."

Eric pulled his car to a stop in the space next to the BMW and turned off the engine. "If there's someone special in your life, Lisa—"

"Oh, no!" she assured him quickly. "That's not it at all. It's just . . . something I'm not comfortable explaining. Please, can't we just let it go at that?"

For a long time, Eric sat watching Julie, who didn't look up at him. "I'd really like to see you again," he said at last.

Julie was torn. "I—don't know," she stammered.

"I'll make you a deal," Eric bargained. "If I can see you again, I promise not to pry. We'll let it go with what I know already. You're a law student playing pseudo-secretary for Greg Reeves, you have no last name, and you're very beautiful. How's that?"

Julie lifted her eyes until they met Eric's. She couldn't keep from smiling. "You think I'm beautiful?" she asked softly.

"Yeah," he chuckled. "I think you're a knockout. And I'd like to see you again."

Julie wanted to say yes. She knew she wanted to see Eric again. But she needed time to work this through, to plan her defense so that her father wouldn't interfere as he had with her sister and Rob. "Let me think on it," she said. "I'll talk to you when you come back with the part for the computer, all right?"

"All right," he sighed. "If that's the best I can get, I'll take it as a definite maybe."

"I'd better be going now, Eric," she said, then watched as he circled the car to open her door. Julie had never been one to let a guy open doors for her, but with Eric she didn't resist. Somehow, with Eric, it seemed acceptable, even nice.

Once inside her car, she started the engine. "Thanks for taking me out for pizza," she said. "I enjoyed it." Returning his smile and giving a shy wave, Julie backed out and pulled away. She watched him in her rear view mirror for as long as possible.

What are you doing, Julie MacGregor? she asked herself. *First you get talked into the masquerade at Greg Reeves' office, then you actually go out with a guy just because he has the most gorgeous eyes you've ever seen. And you even let him think he was dating your sister. This is crazy, and you know it.* By the time she reached home, she had made a decision. She would never go out with Eric again. There was too much chance of her dad finding out, and then meddling in her affairs as he had done with Lisa. It was better not to give him an opening. She would just concentrate on her law degree and let it go at that for the time being. Pulling the BMW into its parking place, she shut off the engine and walked slowly toward the house.

"Who do you think you're kidding, Julie MacGregor?" she asked aloud. "You can't wait to see him, and you know it."

CHAPTER 9

J.T. ran the brush through his thick, coarse hair one last time. For a long time he stared at the image looking back from his mirror. Where had the years gone? Wasn't it only yesterday when he noticed a couple of white hairs showing through the black? Now the game had reversed, and it took some doing to find a sprinkle of coal showing through the snow.

There were wrinkles, too. Far too many wrinkles for a man who hadn't quite turned fifty. Not that he'd always looked older than his years. When Katherine was alive, he had looked vibrantly young for his age. But life had been much simpler back then. After her death, many things changed. That was when he had come into the first phase of his fortune. He had buried himself in his work, to the point that it became an obsession. He couldn't even remember the last time he had slept more than four hours.

He sighed and reasoned to himself that looking older was a small price to pay for the lifestyle he had provided for Lisa and Julie. The lifestyle he would have given anything to have offered Katherine.

Then he noticed something else in the mirror. Actually it was someone else. She was standing right behind him, wearing that aggravating smile of hers.

"Sam," he said, spinning to face her. "I've got to know. Is it really you, or am I losing hold on reality?"

"It's really me, Uncle Mac," she assured him. "That's not to say you haven't lost hold on reality, though. That's the reason I'm here, as a matter of fact."

"But—this makes no sense at all. You were killed in that awful elevator accident. I was one of your pallbearers. How can I be seeing you now, Sam?"

"I told you, Uncle Mac. I'm an angel now."

"Are you—you know—all right?"

Samantha had to laugh. "Yes, Uncle Mac, I'm fine. I've never been happier. And I know what you're going to ask next, so I'll just tell you. Aunt Katie is fine, too. She misses you, but other than that she's perfectly happy. I talked to her again this morning. She tried to get a one-time pass to see you, but she was turned down. One-time passes are hard to come by under the best of circumstances, and with your own niece already working this close with you, it was too much to ask."

J.T. stared at her in bewilderment. Gathering his wits, he put his thoughts into words. "You've seen Katie? Is she like you are now?"

"She is," Samantha assured him. "She looks a little younger and more beautiful than you remember her, but other than that she's the same Aunt Katie you lived with for more than fifteen years. She sends her love and told me to tell you she still thinks one of her kisses will someday turn you into her Prince Charming."

"She said that?" J.T. asked, a hint of moisture in the corner of his eyes. "Katie always teased me that I was still being a frog waiting for one of her kisses to make me into her prince."

"I know," Samantha said with a smile. "She told me all about it. I love it. It's hard for me to imagine that you have one romantic bone in your body, but Aunt Katie tells me I'm wrong about you."

J.T. continued to stare. "Uh . . . I don't suppose . . . I could hug you, or anything, could I, Sam?"

"Sorry, Uncle Mac," Samantha said, a tear glistening in the corner of her own eye. "I'd love one of your hugs, but angels can't hug mortals. It doesn't work that way. I've been given approval for you to see and hear me, but that's as far as it goes."

"What about your cousins? Will they be able to see you?"

"No. But they're the reason I'm assigned to you. You need to do a little adjusting of priorities where they're concerned. I'm here to help you make that adjustment. And while we're at it, that's another thing Aunt Katie wanted me to pass along to you. Her exact words were 'Tell him I said to get off Lisa's back and let her marry Rob.' She said it's none of your concern who either of the girls marry, and your interference is throwing destiny off course. So there, I've told you."

"Blast it, Sam. Don't tell me Katie said that. I know what's best for my girls, and believe me, a second-class, dead-broke singer is not what's best. And don't try telling me you think marrying someone with a lot of money is such a bad idea. You were going to Bruce Vincent when you were killed in that elevator, and Bruce is a wealthy man in his own right. Deny that if you can."

Samantha glared at J.T. "You have no idea what you're talking about, Uncle. I *chose* not to marry Bruce. Bruce is a wonderful man, but I'm not in love with him. I'm not now and I wasn't back then. How I went about choosing to marry Jason is a long and involved story, but I did it because I love him. I gave up fifty or so years that could have been mine right here on this side. And yes, I gave up the chance to live those years with Bruce."

J.T. narrowed his eyes as he stared at Samantha. "I have no idea what you're talking about, Sam. But this much I do know. When you were killed you were cheated out of the chance for a wonderful life. Bruce could have given you the world."

Samantha laughed. "Jason's given me a lot more than the world," she said. "Believe me, Uncle Mac, I wasn't cheated out of a thing."

J.T. scratched the back of his head as he contemplated all of this. "So whatever happened to Bruce?" he asked after a bit. "He was pretty torn up at your—you know . . ."

"My funeral, Uncle Mac. It's okay to use the word, it's not poison. And Bruce made out just fine. I had a lot to do with that, in fact. You know who Arline Wilson is, don't you?"

"Of course I know who Arline Wilson is. She's your friend who was in the radio business for a while. She has her own TV show now."

Samantha gave a little smile of satisfaction. "I got Arline and Bruce together. They plan to be married soon, thanks to me. I worked with them—sort of like I'm working with you now. And while we're on that subject, we have a lot of ground to cover if I'm going to get your relationship with my cousins back where it belongs. You've been treating them pretty rotten lately, you know."

J.T. shook an angry finger at Samantha. "You may be my favorite niece," he grumbled. "But that doesn't give you the right to interfere in the way I'm raising my girls. Back off, Sam."

Samantha couldn't keep from laughing. "I can't believe you, Uncle Mac. You'd think you're still raising my cousins. They're grown women, not the little girls who used to sit on your lap and listen to you sing those old Elvis songs to them. Let them go."

"Enough of this, Sam!" J.T. sputtered. "I demand that you stay out of my daughters' affairs. If you insist on haunting me, it's one thing. But leave the girls out of it!"

"You demand?" Samantha asked, lifting an eyebrow. "I'm sorry, Uncle Mac. Maybe you'd better take stock of who's in charge here. I'm an angel, you're a mortal, remember? If demands are in order, I'll make them. Now if you don't mind, I'd like to get on with why I'm here this time. Do you think you can control yourself long enough to make our second little visit to your past?"

"Humph!" J.T. scoffed. "Like you're offering me a choice? I thought you were pushy when you were alive. I swear, you're worse than ever. Where are you planning on taking me this time?"

"I could tell you, but why not show you instead? Hang on, Uncle. Here we go."

"HO BOY . . ." J.T. gasped, sounding like an echo from the old television series *Quantum Leap*. With no control of his own element, he felt himself being hurled through the dimensions of time and space just as before. Knowing what to expect helped some, but still, his heart was in his throat when he realized where Samantha had taken him this time. "Why did you bring me here?" he groaned. "Of all the places you could have taken me, I would have chosen this one for last. Please, Sam. Have a heart. Don't make me look at this."

"Forget it, Uncle," Samantha insisted. "You're going to watch every second of this little show. And if you'll just lighten up, you might even enjoy it. Now tell me what you see."

J.T. shook his head in disgust, but did as she asked and described the scene. "It's Charley Briggs' horse-drawn carriage. Charley was a friend of mine in those days. He moonlighted in the evenings driving lovers around the city in his carriage. He often picked up his customers in front of the hotel where I worked. Charley learned what I had in mind for this particular evening and offered his services to me at no charge. It was there in Charley's carriage, under a full moon, that I asked Katie to marry me."

"And did she accept?" Samantha pressed.

"You're not kidding me, Sam. You already know the answer to that, or you wouldn't have brought me here."

"I'm proud of you, Uncle Mac. You're catching on to how this works. Now just keep watching; the big moment is about to happen. You've just popped the question."

J.T. held his breath and watched as a crying Katherine leapt from the carriage and darted off into the night. A younger J.T. jumped from the carriage with the intention of going after her, but at the last second changed his mind.

"You could have gone after her," Samantha said. "What stopped you?"

J.T. had trouble getting the words past the lump in his throat. "What good would it have done to go after her?" he asked. "She ran away that time. Who's to say she wouldn't have run away the next time?"

"She did look a little upset," Samantha agreed. "I've heard of wild proposals in my time, but yours must have been a real humdinger. What did you say to her, anyway?"

"Cut it out, Sam. You know it wasn't how I asked her to marry me that upset her. Just seeing me against her parents' wishes was enough to worry her half to death, so when I popped the question it just tipped the scales. She found herself facing a situation she wasn't ready to deal with. So, she ran away. I tried calling several times over the next few days, but she refused to take my calls. I was sure I had lost her. I know now she would have been better off if I'd let it go at that."

"In your own favorite word, Uncle Mac—hogwash! If you could ever get past that mile-wide guilt trip of yours, you'd realize just how dumb that sort of thinking really is."

J.T. stood looking into the darkness where, for the second time in his life, he had watched Katherine run from his proposal of marriage. "It was her parents," he answered glumly. "They forbade her to have anything to do with me. They wanted her to marry into the security the other fellow had to offer."

Samantha clucked her tongue. "My, my, does that sound familiar or what? It seems to me a couple of my favorite cousins are having a similar problem at the moment. Let's see, I think their names are Lisa and Julie."

"Cut that out, Sam," J.T. grumbled. "Katie's parents were right about who she should have married, just as I'm right about who my daughters should marry. And don't you ever forget it."

Samantha looked at him slyly. "What do you say we move forward a month or so, and take a look at Aunt Katie's wedding day? Or what was *supposed* to be her wedding day."

J.T. looked startled, then angry. "No, I absolutely refuse! Enough is enough. Take me home this instant!"

"If I do take you home now, will you promise to bug out and let my cousins live their own lives?"

"Of course not!"

Samantha shrugged. "It's your choice. Get ready, the scene is about to change."

Suddenly, the night of the carriage was gone. It was now a crisp autumn afternoon with J.T. and Samantha standing just outside the open doors of a little white chapel.

"Go ahead," Samantha encouraged. "Step inside. Everything's just as it was that day."

J.T. let out a loud sigh. Then walking to the open door, he peered inside. "It was to be a magnificent wedding, with hundreds of guests," he said ruefully. Searching the room, he spotted his younger self seated on a back row. "I tried to stay away, Sam. You'll never know how hard I tried. I just loved her too much. I slipped quietly inside, trying to remain unnoticed. That's me over there."

"I see you," Samantha acknowledged.

J.T. strained to see the intended groom at the front of the room. "Everything is so blurry, Sam," he remarked. "I can't make out what he looks like."

"That's because you never looked his way the day this all happened," Samantha explained. "You were too busy watching for Aunt Katie to even notice him. Like I said, you can only see now what you actually saw then."

The organ struck up the wedding march and, just as he had all those years before, J.T. turned to see Katie enter the chapel on her father's arm. She looked even more radiant in her wedding dress than he remembered. "Please, Sam," he begged. "Spare me having to watch this."

"My offer is still open, Uncle Mac," Samantha replied. "Give me your promise, and you can go home now."

J.T. didn't bother to answer. Great drops of perspiration formed on his forehead as he watched the events unfold.

Not more than a few steps into the building, Katherine heard her name called. A hush came over the whole congregation when she stopped and turned toward the young man who had spoken her name.

"I don't know what came over me, Sam," he whispered. "I should never have called out her name. But she looked so beautiful . . .'"

The two of them watched as Katherine froze in her tracks. There she stood, her eyes fixed on young J.T., for what seemed an eternity. Then, to the chagrin of everyone watching, her bouquet flew high into the rafters of the church. In an instant, she was in his arms smothering him with a kiss that most felt should have belonged to her waiting groom.

J.T. sighed at the reality of the visual memory. "I've never been kissed like that, Sam. Not before that moment, and certainly not since."

What happened next threw everyone in the building into shock. Grabbing J.T. by the hand, Katherine quickly led him outside and down the steps. From there, it was into J.T.'s battered and time-worn 1960 Plymouth coupe, and they made their escape.

"It all happened so fast," J.T. said as he and Samantha watched the car speed away. "We went to the hotel where I worked, and they gave her a room at no charge, until we could be married two weeks later." J.T. wiped his eyes, which were beginning to tear up. "Please, Sam, take me home. I can't bear to look at more of this."

Samantha was unyielding. "I'll take you home on one condition," she said.

"Blast it, Sam," J.T. swore. "I'm not about to make a promise I can't keep."

Samantha smiled. "Relax," she said. "I have something else in mind for now. I'll get back to the problem of your meddling in Lisa's and Julie's lives when the time is right."

J.T. glared at her. "How many times do I have to tell you? I am not *meddling* in their lives. I'm *protecting* them from their mother's fate. I had to watch as Katie's radiant smile began to fade as the years passed. I tell you, Sam, Katie married the wrong man, and I'm going to see to it that Lisa and Julie marry the right men. No matter what it takes, I'll see to it. So you might as well go back to your cloud and practice your harp lessons for all the good you'll do here, Sam. My mind's made up."

Samantha glared right back. "When the time comes for you to crawl, I'm going to enjoy watching it, Uncle Mac."

Uncle and niece stood nose to nose in a heated moment, until Samantha decided to try another approach.

"I think you ought to take a trip to the cemetery so you can put flowers on Aunt Katie's grave."

J.T. was taken aback. "I was planning to go tomorrow or the next day. I visit her grave several times a week. A nosy angel like you should know that."

"I do know that, Uncle Mac. But I think you ought to visit her grave tomorrow morning, first thing."

"Why?" he asked suspiciously.

"I have my reasons, Uncle Mac. Now do we have a deal, or do you want to see some more?"

J.T. sighed helplessly. "Take me back," he said. "I'll go to the cemetery tomorrow morning."

CHAPTER 10

Julie had met lots of guys over her lifetime, some even cuter than Eric. Well—maybe if not cuter—then at least as cute. Okay, maybe it would be safe to say some were almost as cute, but that didn't justify the fact she couldn't get the image of his face out of her mind for one waking second. And the worst part was, she couldn't tell anyone. It was like the joke her father used to tell about the golfer who called off work on the pretext of being sick so he could sneak in a few holes. He made a hole-in-one on the most difficult green but couldn't tell anyone about it.

Julie certainly couldn't tell her father. That was a given. And she couldn't tell the person she would most like to tell, her sister, Lisa. How would Lisa react if Julie told her she'd let Eric believe he was dating Lisa, instead of Julie?

Julie remembered another old saying: when you find yourself in a hole—stop digging. That's what she should do in this case, she decided. Stop digging. She would come clean with Eric the next time he showed up. She would tell him her name was really Julie MacGregor, and she would tell her father all about Eric. Sure she would. So she could end up just like Lisa and Rob. Forget it. This is one time she'd have to keep digging no matter how deep the hole became. Who knows, maybe she'd even manage to dig up some buried treasure along the way.

Wednesday and Thursday passed with no sign of Eric returning with the computer part, and Julie was beginning to wonder if he'd ever show up at all. It would probably be for the best, she sighed, then thought, *Like heck it would.* She couldn't keep her eyes off the outer office door, constantly hoping it would open and he would walk through.

Friday afternoon about two o'clock she got her wish. The door opened, and Eric came through it, and Julie's heart took flight like an eagle soaring in the clouds.

"Well, what do you know?" she said casually, doing an unbelievably good job of hiding her excitement. "You did come back. I'd about given you up. The goofy computer you supposedly fixed lasted less than a day."

Eric lifted his eyebrows. "The computer? Is that all you can think about? I was sort of hoping you'd like to see me again for other reasons."

Julie leaned forward, elbows on the desk, and rested her chin on one hand. "Who says I'm not glad to see you?" she teased, as her face finally won the battle and broke into a smile. "I lied about the computer. It's been working fine."

"It has?" Eric beamed. "I mean, yeah, I thought it would." He paused, getting up his courage, then asked, "Would you consider going out with me again?"

"That all depends," she answered flirtatiously. "What do you have in mind?"

Eric laid his tools on the counter and leaned over it. "I was thinking we might go to the county fair. It opened yesterday and I've been told it's pretty good this year."

"Well, I don't know," Julie said slowly, pretending to consider it. "Do you promise not to get pushy about my last name?"

"Word of honor."

"Will you buy me some dinner?"

"How does a hot dog at the carnival sound?"

"Do I get a soft drink with it, and maybe an order of fries?"

Impatient with her stalling, Eric grumbled, "Two orders of fries. Now will you go with me, or not?"

Julie was having too much fun to resist a mischievous, "Do you think Little Blue will make it that far?"

Eric glared at her. "You're enjoying this, aren't you?"

"Every second of it," she laughed. "I'd love to go to the fair with you."

"All right!" he exclaimed. "I'll get the computer fixed now, then I'll come back and pick you up in an hour when you get off work."

"I have a better idea," Julie said, picking up her purse and rounding the desk. "You can forget the computer, and we'll go right now."

Eric was startled. "But—what about your job? What about the computer?"

"I get off at three, remember? Besides, I haven't had a single call all day, and it's my last day here. As for the computer—it's working fine. You can come back another time to fix it."

Eric didn't argue. Within minutes they were traveling across town to the fairgrounds. True, Little Blue wasn't as comfortable as the BMW Julie was used to, but she admitted to herself it was a fun car just the same. Especially with such a cute chauffeur at the wheel.

With the tickets he had just bought in hand, Eric led Julie onto the fair grounds. Since Julie didn't care for crowds, she was glad to see that there weren't many people there. The further from a crowd she could get, the better she liked it.

"What shall we do first?" Eric asked. "Midway, exhibits, food? Take your pick."

Julie grinned. "Food. I want the hot dog you promised."

Eric was quick to agree. "I was hoping you'd say that. I was too rushed for breakfast this morning, and I'm starved."

Julie chose a table with an umbrella that provided a little shade from the warm afternoon sun. From her shady spot, she watched as Eric waited in line at the hot dog stand. *What is it with you, Julie MacGregor?* she asked herself. *You haven't flipped over a guy like this in ages. What if you hadn't agreed to fill in at Greg's office for Lisa? What if the computer hadn't broken down?* Then she had another thought. *Good grief! If I'd refused to fill in for Lisa, she would have been the one to meet Eric. Now that's a frightening thought. I know Greg can't make her forget Rob, but I'm not sure Eric couldn't. Of course,* she added humorously, *I could have taken him away from her, but that would be a rotten thing to do to my sister after what happened to her with Rob.*

"Here you go," Eric said, returning to the table with the order. "One hot dog, one soft drink, and two large orders of fries, as promised. Now aren't you glad you said yes to this date?"

"Could be," she answered with a teasing smile. "But don't go getting too proud of yourself just yet. You forgot the mustard. What's a hot dog without mustard?"

Shaking his head, Eric returned for the mustard. Julie saw that he was trying so hard to please her that she couldn't help but laugh at him when he held out several small packages of mustard. "Here," he said. "Am I forgiven now?"

"You're forgiven," she laughed. "But don't *ever* let it happen again."

As Julie spread the mustard on her hot dog, she noticed Eric staring at her. "What are you looking at?" she chuckled. "You're hoping to see me get mustard all over my shirt, aren't you?"

Eric quickly looked away. "I'm sorry," he said. "I was just wondering . . ."

"You were wondering about why I'm so guarded with my last name?"

"Well, yeah, that's part of it."

"Believe me, Eric. The less you know about my personal life right now the better it is for both of us. Not that I'm a criminal, or anything," she hurriedly added. "I just have a few complications, that's all."

"Enough said," he yielded. "Is your hot dog okay?"

"My hot dog is perfect," Julie said with a smile. "But I was only kidding about a second order of fries. I'll be lucky to finish one order, let alone eat the second."

"What?" Rob feigned irritation. "After the hassle you gave me when I picked you up? There's no way I'm letting you off without downing every last one of those fries. I know my rights. No judge in the world would convict me on this one."

"Oh, I don't know," Julie teased. "I think she might see it my way."

"She?" Eric asked.

"That's right. I'll have you in front of Rhoda Milestone, the toughest woman judge you'll ever hope to meet. And she's especially hard on men who force women to eat two orders of fries."

"Okay, you can forget the second order of fires. I know when I'm licked."

When they had finished eating, Rob tossed their leftover wrappers away. "Come on," Eric said as he stood up. "Let's go over to the midway and see what's there."

Julie agreed that might be fun, and so they started out for the midway. As usual, they found it alive with the noise of rides and hawkers begging the passers-by to stop and test their luck and skill. As they made their way through the light crowd, Julie noticed a young boy, about ten, standing in front of one of the booths counting some change in his hand and looking very dejected. Something in his expression tugged at her heart strings.

Julie drew Eric's attention to the small boy. "I just saw a special on television telling how a lot of these games are rigged," she said. "And this game is one of the worst. I hate seeing that little boy cheated out of his money."

Eric looked at her. "Does it really bother you that much?" he asked.

"Yes, it does." Her answer was emphatic. "Once, when I was just a little girl, I tried to win a small stuffed animal at a place like this one. I ended up wasting all the money I had. Back in those days, my family had little to spare so I paid for my mistake. I had to watch as my older and wiser sister used her money for cotton candy and peanuts. It's one of those crazy little memories that never seem to go away."

Eric looked at her compassionately for a moment or two, then stepped up to the boy who by this time had tears rolling down his face. "What is it, big guy?" Eric asked, as he knelt to the young fellow's level. "Did you lose your money at this booth?"

"Yes," the boy whimpered. "I wanted one of those little white bears for my sister. She's home sick. The man kept saying, 'Just one more try and you'll have it.' I lost my whole ten dollars and this is all I have left, but he won't give me another ball because I'm a dime short."

Eric looked up at the hawker. "Do you really need customers so badly? You ought to give the kid back his money, or at least give him the bear he was after."

The hawker laughed. "Forget it, son. I'm a businessman. This kid took his chance just like anyone else. Ya win some, ya lose some. This just happened to be his time to lose. If I gave away a prize for every kid that pulled a crying act, I couldn't stay in business very long, now could I?"

Eric nudged the young boy toward Julie, who put a protective arm around him. Stepping up to the counter, Eric said, "You say you're a businessman? How about if we make a deal, here?"

"What sort of a deal?" the hawker asked suspiciously.

Eric opened his wallet and removed a ten-dollar bill, which he laid on the counter. "I get three balls," he said, looking the hawker straight in the eye. "If I knock the bottles down three times, I win. If I don't, you win. If I do win, I keep my ten—the boy gets his money back—and you cough up two of those little stuffed bears like the boy wanted—one for him and one for me. If I lose, you keep it all and we walk away empty-handed. You seem to like taking money from boys. How do you feel about chancing it with a man?"

The hawker eyed the ten-dollar bill. "In the first place, son," he sarcastically responded. "You're not a man. You're still just a runt of a kid yourself. In the second place, I have to be tough to survive in my world. This is the big city. Taking money from kids don't mean a thing to me. But you've got yourself a deal. Just remember, the bottles have to be *all* the way down. Leaning against each other don't count."

Julie stepped forward to protest. "Eric, you won't be proving a thing by losing your own money. I'm telling you, these games are rigged and this one is one of the worst. The bottles are weighted down so they wouldn't fall over if a tornado strikes."

Eric shrugged. "Hey, let me at least try. If this guy cheats me, I'll hire you to take him to court, okay?"

"That's a laugh! What makes you think you could afford my fees?"

"Well then, you leave me no choice. I'll just have to knock those bottles down. May I have my first ball, sir?"

Julie looked on with keen interest as the hawker stepped aside. Eric took a full windup and released the ball with astounding speed. The impact sent the bottles tumbling in three different directions. Julie couldn't believe her eyes and, from the look on his face, neither could the hawker.

"I'm ready for my next ball," Eric chided him with a huge grin.

The hawker obliged by handing Eric another ball, but there was no smile on his face. In righting the bottles, he was careful to place them exactly where they would be most difficult to dislodge.

Again, Eric took a full windup and let the ball fly. Once again the bottles scattered.

Julie squealed with delight. "I don't believe this," she cried. "You're actually doing it!"

The hawker took his time in setting the game up again. This time he held onto the ball. "You some kind of professional pitcher, son?" he asked sternly.

"Nah, I'm no professional. I lettered all four years in high school. I was good enough the California Angels wanted a look at me, but I never followed up on the idea. I enjoy the game, but not enough to make a career out of it."

"So you came over here with the idea of getting even with me for taking money from the kid?"

Eric shrugged. "Something like that, I suppose. But then, that's just the way life is in the big city. Ya win some, ya lose some. Now, if you'll let me have my last ball, we'll see which it will be with me."

"Forget it, kid," the hawker said, laying ten dollars on the counter in front of the small boy and retrieving two stuffed bears from the trophy counter. "Do me a favor, lady," he said to Julie. "Get this guy as far away from my booth as you can, okay?"

"It will be my pleasure," Julie responded, taking the stuffed animals from him. Then after a hug for the lad, she gave him one of the little white bears.

"Thank you," he sniffed.

"Give your sister a kiss for me, too," Julie said, as she watched him walk away smiling. Turning to Eric, she exclaimed, "I can't believe it! I've never seen anyone win a prize at this booth."

Eric shrugged. "Like the man says, ya win some and ya lose some. I just got lucky this time."

"You're not kidding me for one minute," Julie said, snuggling close to her little white bear. "You knew perfectly well you could beat that game from the start."

"I knew I had a good chance," Eric admitted. "Pitching baseballs is something I'm pretty good at."

Stealing this girl's heart is something you're pretty good at, too, Eric Roberts, Julie added to herself. "Let's go find the rides," she suggested. "That's my idea of what to do at the fair."

"You like the rides?" Eric asked.

"You bet. The faster the better, too. I never got to ride them much when I was a girl. My sister hates the rides, and my—" A hand shot to her mouth as Julie caught herself saying more than she had intended.

"You have a sister?" Eric smiled at his small triumph of learning this much, but pushed the subject no further. "I love the rides, too," he said. "Let's go."

"Thanks, Eric," she said softly, knowing he understood what she meant.

As they walked, she felt his hand slip into hers. Holding hands with a guy always seemed awkward to Julie. But somehow with Eric it felt pretty darn good.

"Are you game for the roller coaster?" he asked, stopping in front of the first ride they came to.

"Just try and keep me off it," she responded with bubbling enthusiasm. "And after that, I want to go on the loop. I haven't been on one of those since I was ten."

The roller coaster was great, and so was the loop. Then came the hammer and the rocket. At last they chose a more gentle ride, and sat arm in arm at what seemed the top of the world on the large double Ferris wheel.

They spent the rest of the evening enjoying the displays, listening to the bands, and eating cotton candy. All too soon it was time to leave. Then, just before they reached the exit gate, something caught Julie's eye. "Look," she squealed. "It's a dress-up photo booth. Can we?"

Eric swallowed hard when he noticed the prices. Trying to keep Julie from noticing, he checked his wallet. There was barely enough left, especially if they wanted to stop for snacks on the way home.

"I've always wanted to have my picture taken at one of these places," Julie went on. "And look at this old-fashioned white dress, with a hat and a parasol. This dress reminds me of something my mother once wore. And you could wear this outfit!" she said, holding up a silky vest of an old suit that looked like something Clark Gable wore in *Gone With the Wind.*

Eric gulped, but there was no question in his mind what he would do. He followed her to the back of the booth to where the attendant stood.

They both managed their best smiles as the shutter clicked and the light flashed. Eric took a wallet size for himself, and bought a five-by-seven for Julie. Though he didn't know it at the moment, the time would come when he would be very thankful Julie had talked him into having the picture taken. Even if it did mean that driving through McDonald's for soft drinks was the best he could manage on the way home.

"I had a great time," Eric said, as he opened the door on Julie's BMW. "I'd really like to see you again."

Julie lay the little white bear and her picture on the seat next to her. "I'd like that, too, Eric," she admitted. "But there's a problem. I won't be working at Greg's office anymore."

Eric's eyes widened. "That's right. I forgot. How can I contact you? I have no idea where you live. I don't even know your last name."

Julie smiled. "Would you think me bold," she asked, "if I invited you out on a date?"

"No, I wouldn't," came his quick response. "In fact, I'd really love that. What do you have in mind?"

"Well," she replied. "Since I can't tell you where I live, I guess you'll just have to tell me where to pick you up. How does a week from tomorrow sound? Say around ten in the morning?"

"Yes, yes, my address," Eric chattered nervously while digging through his pockets for something to write on.

"Here," Julie said, handing him a note pad and pen she took from her purse. "You can use this." He quickly scribbled his address and phone number on the pad, and handed them back to her.

"I had a great time, too," she smiled. Then, catching him completely off guard, she leaned over and kissed him on the cheek. "That's for being such a good sport about my closed-book life," she said as she slid into the BMW.

It was a toss-up which was bigger—Eric's smile or his blush. "Hey," he said after a heavy sigh. "What are good sports for, anyway?"

"Do you always blush so easily?" she teased.

"Gorgeous law students do this to me. It's just something I've never been able to get a handle on."

"Until a week from tomorrow," she said.

"Until a week from tomorrow," he happily replied.

It was sometime in the early morning hours when the thrill of the day finally faded enough to allow Julie's mind to drift off into a beautiful dreamland of sleep. From his perch on the night stand next to the bed, a little white teddy bear lay smiling at her.

CHAPTER 11

The grave was completely shaded now by the willow tree that had been little more than a twig on the day of the funeral. Memories flooded Lisa's mind as she stared at her mother's name on the faded gray marker stone. Among her memories was one so vivid, it played through her mind like a familiar old movie on the silver screen. It was the morning she and Julie had gone with their mother to the portrait studio to have their picture taken. *It's funny how some memories fade over the years,* Lisa thought, *while others cling so tightly even the tiniest details remain.* The way her mother had looked that morning was one of those clinging memories. She wore a beautiful white dress and matching hat with a funny little turned down brim on one side. Lisa had thought that while her mother was always beautiful, that morning she was even more beautiful than usual. She was radiant.

On the way home from the portrait studio, Julie had asked if they could go to a movie and Katherine had happily agreed. They had enjoyed the movie tremendously and laughed a lot, then stopped off for pizza and root beer floats. They had planned to take a walk around the lake in Dove Park, but just as they reached the park an afternoon thunderstorm had struck. So instead, they stood in the protection of the covered pavilion and enjoyed the sound of rain pounding on the aluminum roof, and the noisy birds chattering their pleasure at the unexpected shower. Lisa couldn't remember ever seeing it rain so hard before or since that afternoon. And from that day on, she had loved the rain. It always brought memories of that special day, a day that proved to be one of the last spent with her mother, who died less than a month later.

Lisa knelt and placed the flowers she had brought with her at the edge of the headstone. "I miss you, Mother," she said aloud, moving her hand tenderly over the time-worn letters of Katherine's name.

"I miss her, too, Lisa," came her father's familiar voice from behind. "I miss her so much, I think at times I can't go on without her."

"Father?" Lisa said, rising to face him. "What are you doing here?"

"I uh—promised someone I'd come here. Unless I miss my guess, that someone knew I'd find you here." J.T. knelt down and placed his flowers next to Lisa's, then stood up beside her. "What brings you here today, Lisa—if you don't mind my asking?"

Lisa had had the same question. Why indeed had she come here, when she had planned a different afternoon altogether? It was that little voice again. The same little voice that had been in her head prompting her to do this or that for the last couple of weeks or so. Try as she would, she couldn't shake the prompting until she gave in. "I'm not sure, Father," she replied. "I just sort of felt like coming here." She gave a little chuckle. "Maybe an angel talked me into it."

"Humphhh," J.T. responded. "I wouldn't be surprised. Probably a downright stubborn angel, at that. Those are lovely flowers you brought." He was silent for a moment before he said, "I wonder if you'll ever come here to put flowers on my grave."

Lisa was so surprised she couldn't believe she had heard him right. "What?" she gasped, stepping back and looking up at him to see if he was serious.

J.T. gazed at his daughter. "I'm just wondering if you'll put flowers on my grave after I'm laid to rest here. That's not such an unusual thing for parents to think about, is it?"

"Father, that has to be the craziest thing I've ever heard you say. Is something wrong?"

"It's just his guilty conscience talking," Samantha explained, though she didn't expect Lisa to hear her. She had come up beside them, unnoticed even by J.T. "He's thinking about what he did to Rob Jensen. Deep down he knows he was wrong, and he knows how he hurt you in the bargain."

J.T. gave Samantha an irritated glance, but he didn't say anything. He didn't want to make a fool of himself in front of his daughter. "Why shouldn't I wonder if you'll ever visit my grave?" he asked. "Everyone has to die sometime. I'm no exception. I'd like to think I'll be remembered fondly."

Lisa stared at her father. She had a good idea what he was getting at, and she had to search deep within her own heart for an honest answer to his question. While she had always loved her father, it was true that he had hurt her, and it was obvious from the way he was talking that he was fully aware of it. Gathering her courage, she decided to address a subject she normally would have avoided at all costs. "Are you asking if I can ever forgive you for stealing a year out of my life, and depriving me of the right to be with the man I love for that time?" she asked.

J.T. swallowed hard at the forthrightness of his normally easy-going daughter, before answering her with a question of his own. "Is that what you think? That I'm stealing a year out of your life?"

"What am I supposed to think? That is what you're doing, isn't it?" Reaching for the gold chain around her neck, Lisa let it roll smoothly through her fingers. Then, summoning up more courage than she had ever thought she possessed, Lisa added, "You haven't kept me from loving him, Father. And you haven't kept me from seeing him. I've honored my word not to speak to him, but I have seen him. He's here in town for a concert, and I couldn't make myself stay away from him. I love him too much, Father. You and all your money can never change that. Not in one year, not in a lifetime."

J.T. blanched. "What? You've seen Rob Jensen?" he asked in alarm.

Lisa looked at her father calmly. She had already decided to speak openly to her father about certain things she normally would have kept hidden in the chambers of her heart. She found that the words came more easily than rain water falling from a drenched roof. "Only from a distance, Father. Every day this week I've crept into the back row of the balcony and watched him. My heart ached to call out his name and call him to me, but I somehow held my tongue. I've been true to my promise, though it's been the hardest thing I've ever done in my life."

J.T. was horrified. This was something he might have expected from Julie, but not from Lisa, who had always been so sweet and submissive. As he opened his mouth to speak, Samantha stepped directly in front of him. "Ah—ah," she said sternly. "Think about what you just saw yourself do when someone tried to interfere with your right to see Aunt Katie. You don't have to like Rob Jensen, but you'd darn well better wake up to the fact that your daughter is in love with him."

Burning with frustration, J.T. pressed his lips together as he tried to decide what to do. Taking advantage of his silence, Samantha pushed the point further. "You want those flowers on your grave when the time comes? What you do right now will have a big influence on whether or not you ever get them."

J.T. wanted to ignore her and he tried to, but Samantha's words had struck home. Not that they changed his mind entirely on what he thought was best for Lisa, but they did loosen his heart a notch or two. "Blast it, Lisa!" he grumbled. "It does hurt me to keep you from the man you think you're in love with. But try and see it from my point of view. I can't be around forever to look out for you, and I want you married to a man I can trust to take care of you the way you deserve."

J.T.'s voice trembled a little and Lisa thought she saw a tear sparkle in his eye. Softening, she reached her arms around her father and put her head on his shoulder.

"I know, Father," she said softly.

J.T. cleared his throat, then continued. "Lisa, I'm sorry, but I just don't believe Rob is that man. I believe Greg is the one, and I believe in time you will come to love him and appreciate what he has to offer you."

Lisa closed her eyes as she leaned against her father's strong, wide shoulders. She had always felt warm and protected in the circle of her father's arms, and although her father's words pained her, she knew he loved her and wanted what was best for her.

"Not too bad, Uncle Mac," Samantha said, pleased with the progress that her uncle had made that afternoon. "At least you listened when Lisa was trying to tell you how she felt. Now listen to what I'm telling you. I brought you and Lisa here, to Aunt Katie's gravesite, to give you the chance to get to know each other a little better. Forget about Greg Reeves for the moment and tell her about the things you've just been allowed to relive from your past. These are things you've never mentioned to your daughters. It's time you opened up, and let them see a side of their father that's been hidden from them all their lives. And remember this, Uncle Mac. You're not holding a little girl in your arms, you're holding a woman. She's all grown up. What she needs from her father is a friend, not a marriage counselor."

J.T. closed his eyes and let the meaning of Samantha's words sink into his heart. Then, with a loud sigh, he took her advice to heart. Backing away a step, he spoke to Lisa. "How well do you remember her?" he asked. "Your mother, I mean."

"How well do I remember her?" Lisa asked. "I remember her like I might remember the warmth of a summer day long into the cold nights of December. I remember her smile, and her tender touch. I remember how she could kiss away the pain of a scrape or bruise, and how one word from her lips could ease the pain of much deeper hurt that came from facing the realities of a little girl's everyday world. I remember the love she always brought to our dinner table, and how she would tuck me in bed at night. I remember the pain of losing her and the empty place her leaving left in my heart." Lisa choked up and was silent for a moment. J.T. didn't speak, but waited for her. After a few minutes, she continued.

"But most of all, I remember the good times. One of my favorite memories is the day we listened to the rain on the roof of the pavilion in Dove Park. In fact, I was thinking about that very day when you came up a few minutes ago."

J.T. smiled tenderly at her. "I should have known. I've over-heard you and Julie talking about that day dozens of times. It was the morning the three of you had the picture taken, the one I keep in my study." His eyes were distant. "It was her last picture, you know. She died less than a month after it was taken."

Lisa stepped forward and slid her arm around her father's waist. "I know that, Father," she said. "And even though you never say it, I know how much you miss her. Sometimes I wish you missed her less. Then maybe you wouldn't have to try so hard to be both father and mother to Julie and me. And don't pretend you don't know what I'm talking about, either."

J.T. pressed a brief kiss to the top of Lisa's head. "You're right, Lisa. I do miss her. Losing your mother was the toughest pill I've ever had to swallow." Then after a moment's contemplation, he added, "Especially since I'm the one who killed her."

"What?!" Lisa stepped back from her father so she could look up into his face. "You know perfectly well Mother died of cancer. There was nothing you, or anyone else, could have done to save her."

J.T. pulled out his handkerchief and wiped his brow. He glanced at Samantha, almost as if he hoped she would tell him to hold his tongue on the matter, but she didn't.

"Don't stop now, Uncle Mac," she replied instead. "You're doing fine. Go on with your story. Getting it off your chest will do miracles for easing your self-appointed guilt trip."

After years of silence brought on by the heavy load of guilt kept deep in his lonely heart, the words didn't come easy for J.T. But—for the first time ever—he managed to get them out. "You're wrong, Lisa," he said slowly. "It wasn't cancer that killed your mother. The surgeons were able to remove all the infected tissue. She later developed a staph infection, and that's what killed her."

"Staph infection? You never mentioned this before."

Stooping down beside the grave, J.T. brushed back a few blades of grass that had grown over the corner of the headstone. "When Katie took ill," he explained, not looking at Lisa, "every dime I had to my name was tied up in a land deal. I had no money to pay for the operation she needed, so she ended up in a county hospital. The rotten irony of the whole thing is, the land deal came through less than a month after she died. That's when I came into my money, Lisa. One lousy month after she died. If I hadn't invested in that crazy land deal, I might have been able to scrape up enough cash to pay for the proper care she needed."

Lisa's voice was quiet but firm. "You can't do this, Father. You can't play God. You have no cause, and you have no right, to blame yourself for Mother's death."

"What she's saying is true," Samantha added. "And another thing, Aunt Katie is not here in this cold hole in the ground. As I've already told you, I talked to her just this morning."

"Why don't you sit down here for a minute." J.T. said. "There are several things about me you and Julie don't know, and I think . . . uh . . . someone wanted me to explain some things I've never told you or your sister."

"Now you're cooking, Uncle Mac," Samantha encouraged. "It's not as hard as you thought it would be, is it?"

J.T. grimaced at her, but he had already made up his mind. When Lisa had settled herself on the grass, J. T. began, "Lisa, before your mother married me . . . she was engaged to another man."

"She was?" Lisa asked in surprise. "Who was he?"

"I don't know. I never met him. And your mother never told me his name. I do know he was wealthy. The night I met Katie the two of them had just had a bitter fight. They were attending a social event that evening at the hotel where I worked as a valet. I never knew what their fight was about, but whatever it was, it was bad enough that Katie left him there and rushed angrily out of the hotel. She ran right into me. Believe me, Lisa, she knocked me off my feet in more ways than one that night." J.T. paused as he let the bittersweet memory play out in his mind once again.

Samantha couldn't resist. "And you know what else," she broke in. "It was no accident that she had that argument and ran into you on the way out of the hotel. It was all part of the plan to get the two of you together, because you had a contract like Jason and I have. I've read the unedited version of the incident in Gus' report. I know you don't understand right now what that contract means, Uncle Mac. But trust me when I say it's the most important document you'll ever have your name tied to. It dwarfs the deal you think you have going on the super mall. It makes the deal you have with Edward Reeves look like of couple of little boys trying to sell mud pies."

"Don't stop now, Father," Lisa pleaded. "I'm dying to know what happened next."

J.T. smiled at her eagerness. "What happened next is—we fell in love," he said softly.

Lisa reached out and took hold of her father's hand. "Oh, that gives me goose bumps!" she said. "Tell me how you proposed to her. I've always wanted to know."

J.T. told her the whole story—the moonlight proposal, Katherine's running away, her wedding day, he covered it all.

Lisa listened intently, and as he concluded she laughed. "You old fox, I had no idea you could be so romantic. And I'm proud of you for standing up to her parents like you did." After a moment, she added thoughtfully, "Probably just like I should do to you about Greg."

J.T. tensed at her words. "Katie's parents were a lot wiser than I gave them credit for back then," he said. "And I'm wiser than you give me credit for now. Greg is a fine man, and he would be a good husband to you."

Lisa's eyes had glowed as J.T. had talked about his courtship and marriage, but now her eyes darkened. "Father, I gave you my word to give Greg a chance. Well I've done that, and I don't feel I owe either him or you any more chances. I don't love him, and for that matter I don't even respect him. And you know what? The next time I see him, I'm going to tell him just that. I'm in love with Rob, just like you were in love with my mother. And I'm going to wait for him if it takes ten times the year you've imposed on me."

The apprehension in J.T.'s eyes was never more evident. "No, Lisa. You don't mean that. Just give Greg a little more time."

Lisa shook her head. "He's had all the time he's going to get." Lisa couldn't believe she was saying these things to her father, but it felt good. It felt darn good. For once in her life, she was acting more like Julie than herself. And the funny thing is, it wasn't so hard to do after all. Once she set her mind to it, it just seemed to flow naturally.

However, J.T. was speechless at this change in his usually docile daughter, and he just stared at her.

"I think she means it, Uncle Mac," Samantha grinned. "And if you think you'll have any more luck picking some rich jerk for Julie, you're not as smart as I give you credit for."

J.T. pointed a finger at Samantha, but lowered his hand when he caught Lisa staring at him strangely. *I'll deal with you later,* he thought to himself. "As for you," he looked at his daughter sternly, "you'll see that Greg is the right man for you, Lisa. And I'd like to add that I don't approve of you going to Rob's concerts either."

The tenderness of the meeting with her father had vanished as suddenly as it had occurred. Lisa stood up and put her hands on her hips. Looking down at him, she said coldly, "I've had it with you, Father—you with your two faces of what's right and what's wrong. I've had it with you, and I've had it with Greg Reeves. I'm in love with Rob Jensen, just as surely as you were in love with my mother. And just as you faced every obstacle that threatened to keep you away from her, I'll face my own obstacles. I'm serving you notice right now—the next time I see Greg Reeves, I'm sending him down the road."

Not giving her father a chance to answer, Lisa practically ran toward her car, which was parked a short distance away. When she reached the car, she looked back just long enough to say one last thing. "Of course I'll put flowers on your grave when the time comes. You're my father and I love you. That will never change. But right now, I don't like you very well. I pray that will change, but that depends completely on you."

* * *

It was late when the young man was ushered into Edward Reeves' personal office.

"You wanted to see me, sir?" he asked eagerly.

Edward was working at his desk. He didn't bother to get up but only lowered his glasses to stare at the nervous young man. "It's about that idea you've been trying to interest me in," he said without preamble. "The toy boat."

At the mention of the boat, the young man took courage and jumped in with his pitch. "Yes, sir, the boat. But it's much more than a toy, you see—"

"I know what the toy does," Edward said sharply. "I'm not interested in the idea just to satisfy some kid who wants to sail it in his father's swimming pool. I have other uses for the device. I'm willing to pay you well, provided you can rework it to do what I want."

"What do you have in mind, sir?"

Edward leaned back in his chair and placed the tips of his fingers together in front of his face. "I need an explosive device," he said candidly. "And I want the device detonated by the ringing of a telephone."

"It would be no trouble at all to redesign the mechanism as a detonator. And using the sound of a phone in place of a voice is simple."

Edward leaned forward. "Perhaps I'm not making myself clear. I'm not interested in a detonator that will be set off by just any telephone. I want it to work only at the sound of a specific telephone, which I have in my possession. Can you do that?"

"I—think so," came the hesitant answer.

Fire flared in Edward's eyes. "You think so? Now what sort of answer is that, young man? Either you can do it, or you can't. I know your device can be limited to one unique voice; my question is can it be limited to the sound of one unique telephone? Don't play games with me, boy. A simple yes or no will do. Can what I'm asking for be done, or not?"

George Weathersby had never found himself in a situation quite like this one before. Nevertheless, he wasn't one to let go of an idea he felt would bring in a bundle of money. "Yes, sir," he answered forcefully. "I can redesign the circuit to do what you want. I'll need the phone, though. The one you want used to set off the detonator. Uh—if I'm not being too bold, how much did you have in mind paying me?"

At this, Edward laughed. While he didn't understand electronic circuitry, this young man's greed was something he understood perfectly. "I see you have no trouble getting right to the point," he said. "I like that in a man. If you can deliver a working device to me by ten o'clock tomorrow morning it would be worth, say—twenty-five grand."

"Twenty-five grand?" George choked. "Yes—yes, sir. I can have it to you by then."

Edward smiled. "And if it works as well as you say it will, we'll think about making it an even thirty grand."

Edward opened his center desk drawer and removed the cellular phone his henchmen had taken from J.T. Handing the phone to George, he motioned for his bodyguards to usher the young man out of his office.

"Until tomorrow morning," he said as George stepped through the door. George nodded, and moved away while the bodyguard closed the door behind him.

Once Edward was sure the coast was clear, he lifted his phone and dialed a number he had used on many occasions before. "Joe," he said into the phone when the party on the other end answered. "I have a little job for you and your boys. Can you meet me here in my office tomorrow morning, say around noon?"

CHAPTER 12

As Julie turned the BMW into the parking lot of Eric's apartments, she thought about how simple life had been before Eric had walked into Greg's office that morning. Maybe life would be simple again if she could just get Eric Roberts out of her mind. But getting him out of her mind wasn't that easy. So, with a trumped-up excuse about spending the day with some girl friends, she set out to see Eric Roberts once more.

A glance at the clock on the dash told her she was right on time. She spotted Eric at the opposite end of the lot, waving his arms madly.

"What are you doing?" she asked, pulling up next to him. "Let me guess, you're trying out for cheerleader, right? If I'd known you were into this sort of thing, I'd have brought along my old high school pom-poms for you."

Eric moved toward the car and leaned in the window. "So I got a little carried away," he defended himself. "I wanted to make sure you saw me, that's all."

Julie wouldn't have admitted it, but his interest in her was more than a little flattering. "Would it bother you," she asked innocently, "if I hadn't seen you and had driven away?"

Eric's smile was just as innocent. "No question about it. I sure don't want to lose the friendship of anyone who can get a free pizza out of old Benny."

Reaching through the window, Julie placed her hand against his chest and gave Eric a push backwards. "You can get your own door, fella. Taking a guy on a date is one thing, but I draw the line at opening doors for him."

Eric wasted no time in getting in the car. "I'm at your mercy," he said. "What's the plan? I think you should know my mother taught me to be in before midnight. You will have me home by then, won't you?"

Julie's glance toward Eric showed her skepticism. "Your mother wants you home by midnight? Ha! I might believe it of Benny, but not your mother."

But Eric's tone was serious. "Hey, you should see some of the letters I get from my mom. She's always warning me about leaving myself at the mercy of women in racy cars. Especially beautiful women," he added softly, leaning toward her to whisper in her ear.

Julie shook her head and laughed at him. "Trust me," she said. "I have an afternoon planned that even a worried mother would approve of."

Eric's face was doubtful. "Yeah, well, I hope so. For all I know you could be up to no good here. How do I know you're not kidnapping me?"

Julie smiled calmly. "You don't."

Eric's face grew more worried as he pretended to consider the danger of his date with Julie. "You might even hold me for ransom for the keys and title to Little Blue," he speculated.

"That I doubt," she laughed. "I couldn't handle owning a car I'd have to talk to. And while we're at it, what's wrong? Why are you staring at me like that? Do I have something on my face?"

"Was I staring?" he asked, looking a little embarrassed. "Sorry. But I can't help thinking how great you look in red."

"Yeah, sure," Julie giggled. "I'll bet you use that line on all the law students you date."

Eric nodded. "You're right, every last one of them. At last count there have been—oh, let me see—one."

Slipping the car into gear, she pulled out of the lot. After a few blocks, she turned left onto Hillview Road.

"Oh!" Eric exclaimed. "We're going to the mountains. I've got it, you're taking me fishing."

Julie cringed. "Fishing? I don't think so."

"Okay then, you're taking me water skiing."

"Strike two. I'm in no mood for getting my hair wet. I didn't bring along a hair dryer."

"Well, that brings us back to kidnapping. That must be why you refuse to tell me your last name. You want to keep your identity hidden in case I happen to escape."

Julie laughed, and let the subject drop. For the next few miles, they rode without speaking. Soon they were surrounded by trees, and Julie rolled down the windows using the automatic switch. "I love the smell of pines," she said. "Don't you?"

"Yeah," he responded with a deep breath. "I really do. So when can I ask my mother to make a trip home to meet you?" His pointed question caught Julie completely off guard.

"I beg your pardon?" she gasped, turning to Eric and nearly driving off the road. "You want your mother to meet me?"

"Yeah, I do. What's wrong with that? Since my dad is in the Air Force, she gets free travel. She can fly here whenever she likes."

Driving more carefully, Julie studied Eric's face out of the corner of her eye as her thoughts raced. Although she was flattered, she felt a little concerned that this relationship was moving so quickly. She forced herself to speak lightly. "Gee, I've always heard if a guy wants you to meet his mother, it means he's getting serious. I wonder if there's any truth in that saying."

Eric's voice was noncommittal. "Could be," was all he said.

"Eric," she cautioned. "You hardly know me. And I'm talking about more than just not knowing my last name. What do you say we put meeting your mother on hold for now? Let's take this one step at a time, all right?"

"Okay," Eric reluctantly agreed. "I guess I was getting a little carried away."

And so am I, Julie admitted to herself. *This is crazy, but I've never felt for a guy what I feel for you. It makes me wonder—could there be anything to the old idea that some people are destined for each other?*

"Besides," she added, poking him in the shoulder, "after what I have planned, you may never want to see me again, anyway. Have you ever heard of the North Wind Ranch?"

"I've seen the name around here," Eric responded.

"It's just around that curve up ahead," Julie said mysteriously.

"So . . . is that where we're headed now?"

"It is."

Eric stared at her a moment before his next question. "What is it about this ranch that I might not like?" he asked.

"You'll see in a minute," she grinned. "We're almost there."

Sure enough, as they rounded the curve, there was the sign advertising the ranch. Julie turned onto the road leading toward the ranch, but didn't stop at the house. Instead, she continued on toward a group of stables that lay some distance behind the house.

Eric's earlier mock concern became real. "A horse?" he asked. "You expect me to get on a horse?"

Julie gave Eric a disappointed look. "You don't like horses? I was afraid of that. Okay then, you can spend the rest of the afternoon waiting here in the car while I ride up the mountain to one the most beautiful places in this whole world."

"Give me a break, Lisa," he pleaded. "I've never been on a horse in my life."

"That's what I figured," Julie said nonchalantly. "But if you were serious about wanting me to meet your mother when the time comes, you had better learn to appreciate horses. Riding is my first love, and I don't plan on giving it up."

"Never?"

"Ever."

Eric sighed. "Okay, Lisa, but I know horseback riding doesn't come cheap. How much is this afternoon setting you back?"

Julie stepped out of the car, and closed the door. "You can put your mind at ease. I know how guys can be about a woman paying for a date, but these horses aren't costing me a dime."

"Let me guess. Like the BMW, this all belongs to your wealthy father, right?"

She shook her head. "No, this place doesn't belong to my dad." She looked at him mischievously. "Who it belongs to is for me to know and you to wonder about."

The ranch actually belonged to one of her father's business associates, but Julie thought it best not to give Eric any more details of her life. The less Eric knew about her, the better.

"So the mystery woman has friends in high places?" Eric asked.

"Now, now," Julie said, wagging her finger at him, "you know I'm not going to tell you anything more about my family just yet. Just wait here for me while I get our horses, okay?"

Eric shrugged. "Okay, I'll wait. It's a long walk back to town anyway."

A few minutes later, Julie emerged from the stables leading two horses that even Eric had to admit were beautiful. One was coal black, the other was brown with splashes of white.

"They sure look big," he said cautiously. "Do they bite?"

Julie broke out laughing. "No, Eric, they aren't going to bite you. These horses are as tame as they come. The brown one is Buster. I picked him especially for you because he's the most gentle horse at the ranch. The black one is Midnight. He's my favorite."

After a brief ten-minute training and demonstration session, Julie managed to get Eric on the horse.

"At least you're facing the right end," she laughed at him.

"How do you steer this thing?" he asked helplessly.

"With the reins," Julie explained patiently. "When you want the horse to move to the right, you pull gently on the right rein. If you want the horse to move to the left, pull the left rein. Okay? I'll be leading the way on Midnight, and Buster will just naturally follow. You won't have to do anything but stay in the saddle. Surely a brilliant engineer like you can manage that much," she teased.

"Wouldn't it be just as much fun to hike up the trail, and let these horses have the day off?" Eric suggested.

"Forget it, Eric," Julie said sternly. "I'm going to teach you how to put some fun into your boring workaholic life, even if it kills you. All you have to do is hold onto the saddle horn, and let Buster do the rest."

Clutching the saddle horn with one hand, Eric gingerly patted Buster's neck with the other. "You hear that, Buster? I think she means it. How about a deal? I promise to be good to you, if you'll do the same for me."

They started up the trail with Julie leading the way and Eric holding on tightly to the saddle horn. He soon learned that Buster would follow Midnight naturally, which left him free to figure out some of the other, more troublesome, aspects of riding. "How do you do that?" he asked after half mile or so.

"How do I do what?" Julie asked, glancing over her shoulder to check on his progress.

"How do you move in the same direction as the horse? Every time I go up, Buster goes down. That part's not bad. But every time I come down Buster goes up. That part I hate."

"The whole secret is to relax. Just allow yourself to become one with the animal."

"I have been becoming one with the animal, every time we meet in the middle."

Julie giggled. "You're not relaxing."

"How much further are we going?"

"It's about an hour's ride to the most beautiful place I've ever seen," Julie said enticingly. "Really, and I want to share it with you, Eric."

"An hour's ride you say? How wonderful."

* * *

It took Eric a while, but at last he was able to get his ups and downs in the right order. That alone was a huge improvement. *What have you gotten yourself into here?* he asked himself as he followed Julie up the trail. *I mean, sure, Lisa is a great lady and all—but she was right when she said you know nothing about her. You don't even know her last name, let alone where she lives and what her family's like. All you do know is what you've felt ever since meeting her two weeks ago. How can you feel this strongly about someone you hardly know? It doesn't make any sense.*

Eric stared at Julie's back ahead of him. She had to be the most beautiful woman he had ever laid eyes on. He loved the way her pony tail bounced back and forth with the motion of the horse. He was still a little embarrassed that he'd mentioned wanting his mother to meet Julie. How could he have been so stupid as to bring that up the way he did? *It's a good thing I didn't scare her off, coming on so strong like that.* But his heart had shifted into high gear, and there seemed to be no way to convince it to slow down.

There must be some way to melt her doubts and get her to open up, to tell me what she's been afraid to tell me, he reasoned to himself. *But how?*

* * *

At last they came to a point where the trail widened, and Julie dropped back to ride next to Eric. "How are you doing?" she asked.

"I've gained a lot more respect for Clint Eastwood," he moaned plaintively. "Anyone who can ride one of these things in as many movies as he did has my admiration."

"Look at the bright side, at least you're doing better than when you started."

Eric smiled at her tiredly. "That's because I'm relaxed now, Lisa. I'm one with the horse. How close are we, anyway?"

"About halfway," she grinned.

"Halfway? By the time this trip is over, I may wish you were studying medicine instead of law. I think I'm going to be seasick, not to mention saddlesore."

However, it wasn't long before they crested a hill, and Lisa brought Midnight to a stop. "This is it," she said, as she pointed to a scene that unfolded like an artist's canvas before them. Eric caught his breath as he gazed across a meadow-like clearing surrounded by a thick forest. Tall green grass swayed to the movement of a gentle breeze. The sound of running water drew his attention to a little stream at the far end of the meadow.

"Wow," was all he said, as he breathed in deeply and admired the beauty of the view. Meanwhile Julie had dismounted and offered Eric a hand down, but he refused her offer and somehow managed on his own.

"Was I lying to you?" she asked. "Or is this the most beautiful sight you've ever seen?"

"You're right," he admitted, rubbing his backside. "But getting here didn't come easy for some of us."

"Sometimes it takes a little pain in order to expand your horizons," Julie informed him kindly. "There are places in this world you just can't get to in Little Blue."

Taking Eric's hand, Julie led him over to the bank of the nearby stream. "What about the horses?" he asked. "Shouldn't we tie them up, or something?"

"I never tie my horse when I'm up here. Animals deserve the right to a good time, too. Let them alone; they'll be fine."

"What if they run away?"

"Then you'll be stuck up here with me. Is that such a terrible thought?" Julie picked out a large flat rock near the water's edge, there she sat down. "Here," she beckoned. "Come sit beside me."

Eric hesitated momentarily. "To tell the truth, I'm not too sure I want to sit after an hour of bouncing in that saddle, but I'll give it a try." Moving slowly and carefully, he took a seat beside her.

Julie leaned back and drew in a deep breath. "Isn't this great?" she sighed. "The best part is what you can see with your ears. Close your eyes, Eric. Just listen for a while. Nature has a music all its own."

Eric closed his eyes, and to his amazement he discovered she was right. He actually did hear nature's music. There was the sound of the little stream rushing along its rocky course. In the tops of the trees, a soft wind rustled through the branches. There was a blue bird, and some crickets. Somewhere off in the distance a pine cone fell. Nature had even added its own drummer in the form of a woodpecker.

"Go ahead, Eric," Julie challenged. "Tell me this wasn't worth the ride to get here."

"I give up," he conceded. "Especially since I'm in the company of my favorite law student. Of course, this is going to cost me tomorrow, when I have to spend all day on my feet."

Julie slid over next to Eric, and put her arm around his shoulders. "This is my most favorite place in the whole world," she whispered in his ear. "I wanted to share it with you. And if it means anything, you're the first guy I've ever shared it with."

"No kidding?" he brightened. "I'm the first?"

Julie's smile deepened, and suddenly she felt an overwhelming urge to kiss him, almost as if some unknown force was pushing her toward Eric. But she couldn't do that. A first kiss had to come as the guy's idea, not the girl's.

Unknown to her, there was indeed an outside force nearby. Two of them, in fact. "Give it a rest, Sam," Jason chuckled. "You can tell her to kiss him until whaling turns to a sport in Death Valley, but she can't hear you. Believe me, I should know. I spent enough years trying to communicate with the most beautiful mortal I ever saw—you—with no luck. It didn't work then, and it won't work now. If this is how you've been trying to operate, it sounds like you needed my help a lot sooner. "

Samantha poked an elbow into her husband's ribs. "Jason Hackett, I've been doing just fine without your help," she defended herself. "I know she can't actually hear me, but I'm sure she's getting my message just the same. I made this work once before, when I got Julie to take Lisa's place at Greg's office. Besides, look in her eyes, Jason. She's dying to kiss him."

"I'm telling you, Sam, you have a lot to learn about this angel thing," Jason said. "Rules are rules, and the rules state you can't talk to mortals unless you've been cleared. If you insist on keeping this assignment, then stick with your Uncle Mac. He's the one you're assigned to."

Samantha leaned over and kissed Jason's cheek. "I know you could never get through to me in all those years," she agreed. "But something is different here. Maybe it has to do with me being so close to my cousins while they were growing up. I don't know what it is, but I know it's working. She understands what I'm trying to get across to her." Samantha tried again. "Go ahead, Julie, kiss him. You know you want to kiss him, just do it."

Jason rolled his eyes. "You're wasting your time, Sam."

"Wasting my time, am I?" Samantha burst out with smile. "Take another look, my doubting ghost."

Jason was speechless as he watched Julie put a hand gently on Eric's face and turn his head to meet hers. Eric was obviously caught off guard by her actions, but he quickly understood her intentions and leaned forward to press his lips against hers.

"Well?" Samantha taunted, folding her arms and grinning at Jason. "What have you to say for yourself now, Mr. Hackett?"

"Coincidence," Jason grumbled. "Nothing but coincidence. There's no way she actually heard you."

Samantha didn't give up easily. "What about the time you were trying to keep Bruce from going home because there was a robbery taking place at his house."

"Sorry, Sam. Maybe I *almost* got through to him, but not quite. In the end, it was your call on his mobile car phone that saved his life. We angels can't communicate with mortals unless someone like Gus clears the way first."

"I'll make you a deal," Samantha smiled, slipping both arms around Jason's neck and rubbing the tip of her own nose against his. "If I can convince Julie to do one more thing, like I did with the kiss,

I want you to do two things. First, acknowledge that I can communicate with her. And second, stop hassling me about taking this assignment. If I fail, I'll give up and admit you're right about the whole matter. Is it a deal?"

Jason looked thoughtful. "That all depends on what it is you have in mind for her, Sam. What do you propose trying to convince her to do?"

"I'll get her to take a drink of water from the stream, okay?"

"No way. That's something she might do on her own. Pick something harder."

"All right, smarty. The hardest thing I can think of is a rock. I'll have her sit on any rock you point out. No fair making it a sharp one, though."

Jason shook his head no. "That's still not hard enough. How 'bout if you get her to take down her pony tail?"

"Take down her pony tail?" Samantha looked at her husband in surprise. "Why would you want her to do a thing like that? You're infatuated with her long hair, aren't you? That's why you want her to take it down, isn't it?"

"I do think she has beautiful hair," Jason admitted. "But that has nothing to do with my suggestion. Letting her hair down is something she wouldn't normally do up here in the mountains. You wanted to prove you can convince her to do something hard, well, that's it."

Samantha shook her head in disgust. "You men are all alike. If a girl has long hair, that's all you can think about. Well, I like my hair short whether you do or not. I look hideous with long hair so you're out of luck if you expect me to ever grow it long. You'll just have to put up with me the way I am."

Jason put his arms around Samantha. "You're putting words in my mouth, Sam. I wouldn't change your hair, or anything else about the way you look. You're the most beautiful woman I've ever seen, and I love you just the way you are. Julie's hair is great on her, and your hair is great on you. Now can we get back to the subject at hand? Let's go with the rock idea. Only instead of Julie sitting on a rock, I want her to get Eric to throw a rock. If you can get her to do that, you win. But when you fail—"

Samantha wiggled out of his arms. "When I fail? Pretty sure of yourself, aren't you?"

"You're darn right I'm sure. I know a heck of a lot more about this sort of thing than you do, Sam. I've been at it a lot longer."

"Hmmm. . ." Samantha stared hard at Jason. "You're sure you like my hair the way I wear it?" she asked again.

"Sam," Jason said patiently. "I love your hair. Now let it drop, will you?"

"All right," she agreed, "we'll go with Eric throwing a rock." They sealed their bargain with a kiss, and Samantha wasted no time getting started.

"Come on," Julie said, taking Eric by the hand and leading him along the little stream toward the thick forest at the end of the clearing. "There's something else I want to show you while we're up here."

"Is that a waterfall I hear?" Eric asked.

"It is," Julie responded, "and just wait until you see it, Eric."

He didn't have to wait long. As they came around a bend in the stream, Eric suddenly found himself overlooking a majestic canyon that seemed to run for miles into the distant mountains. "Wow," he exclaimed. "This is breathtaking."

Julie slid her arm through his and pulled him close. "This may not be the top of the real world," she said. "But I've often thought of it as the top of my own personal little world. When something is bothering me, I come here. Big problems have a way of shrinking when I look out over this canyon. They're called Butterfly Canyon Falls. Are you impressed, or what?"

"I'm impressed," Eric agreed. "It must be more than two hundred feet to the canyon floor."

"It's closer to three hundred feet. How'd you like to throw a baseball that far?"

"That would be a real kick. But unfortunately, I don't happen to have a baseball with me."

Julie leaned down and picked up a small round rock. "Here, this is close enough. See what you can do."

"Well, I can't guarantee winning you a little white bear this time," Eric joked.

That was the wrong thing for Eric to say. Standing on top of a mountain, next to Julie MacGregor, it was not wise to mention bears. She was quick to take advantage of Eric's small blunder. "I don't think you'd enjoy winning any of the bears that roam these parts," she teased convincingly. "They're not as cuddly as the one you won for me at the fair."

"There are bears up here?" Eric asked, nervously.

"Sure, hundreds of them. And mountain lions, too."

Eric glanced quickly around. "Are you sure it's safe for us to be here?"

"I usually manage to outrun them," Julie assured him.

When Eric stared at her, she broke out laughing. "Gotcha, Eric. There hasn't been a bear or lion in these parts for forever. They say some guy named Jim Bridger had the last one for breakfast over a hundred years ago. Now let's see how far you can throw that rock."

Eric grimaced. "You just cost me ten years off my life with that little stunt. Forget the rock. I have half a notion to throw a certain strawberry blonde over the canyon."

"Now, now, Eric. I have a feeling you'd regret that, and I know I wouldn't care for it. I'd rather see you throw a rock over the edge."

Eric reached out and pulled her close. "I'm not in the mood to throw a rock right now," he said softly. "I'm in the mood to kiss the most beautiful law student to come along since Jim Bridger finished his bear and egg breakfast."

Julie felt her heart quicken. It wasn't as if Eric was the first guy she had ever kissed. So why did her knees go weak when he pulled her to him? Why did she melt like a rag doll in his arms? Why did the top of this mountain suddenly become even more beautiful than before? Even the sound of the falls was different—sort of like in the movies when music comes out of nowhere for the big, climactic scenes. There could be only one answer to all of this—Julie MacGregor was definitely falling in love.

As the kiss ended, Julie's mind was spinning so rapidly she hardly noticed when Eric turned and threw the rock out over the canyon. Then, throwing tradition after Eric's rock, she pulled him to her and kissed him again. And unseen by either of them, Samantha was enjoying a victory kiss of her own.

Eric found the ride back down the mountain even worse than the trip up, especially since he had to spend most of the time standing in the stirrups. "I have to admit, you showed me the most beautiful place I've ever seen," he told Julie as they drew near to the ranch. "But I'd have liked it much more if I could have driven there in a comfortable car."

Julie laughed. "I suppose I can tell you now," she confessed. "There *is* a road that goes nearly to the falls, and it's not a long walk after that."

"What?" Eric bellowed. "There's a road? You mean we could have driven up there instead of riding these horses?"

"The Echo Mountain Mine is a half mile or so from where we were," she chuckled. "The mine is abandoned now, but the road up to it is still usable. But if I'd told you about it earlier, you would never have ridden the horse up the mountain and enjoyed the real beauty of the day. Like I said, riding is one of my favorite things. Do you forgive me?"

"I forgive you," he sighed. "The company was worth the pain, there's no doubt about that. But if we ever go up there again . . ."

"There is one thing, though," Julie said very seriously. "Just because you tricked me into letting you kiss me, doesn't mean I liked it."

"What!? I tricked you into kissing me? I don't think so, lady. You kissed me first, and besides—you enjoyed my kisses as much as I enjoyed yours."

Julie just smiled. "If you say so," was all she said. Still, she was glad he had admitted that he'd enjoyed them, too.

With the horses stabled, they were soon on their way back down the mountain. "I'm really glad your BMW seats are softer than Little Blue's," Eric joked. "I love that old car, but right now this one feels pretty good."

"The BMW is nice," Julie agreed. "But you don't have to worry about hurting its feelings. You don't even have to talk to it. It's only a piece of machinery. "

Eric looked troubled. "I hate to say this, Lisa. But you're making a big mistake saying things like that in front of the car. I'm not kidding. That sort of talk will stir up the car gremlins every time."

Julie laughed. "Car gremlins?"

Eric glanced around nervously. "I'm telling you, lady, this

BMW is a great car, and it will take good care of you if you stay on its good side. But you're pressing your luck with talk like this."

"You sound just like my sister," Julie said, shaking her head, "only with her it's her plants. She even plays music to them."

"You've mentioned this sister of yours a couple of times. Is she half as beautiful as you?"

"My sister," Julie said, "is the reason I keep you in the dark. If you ever got one look at her, I'd never see you again."

Eric rubbed his hands together appreciatively. "Wow, she does sound exciting. Come on, be a sport. At least tell me—"

Suddenly, a loud bang sounded from under the back of the BMW. "What was that?" Julie cringed, as she fought to bring the swerving car under control. They finally came to a rest at the edge of the road.

"That," Eric answered smugly, "was the sound of a perturbed car gremlin. You just blew a tire, Lisa. Offhand, I'd say it was the right rear."

"There was nothing wrong with that tire," she huffed, as the two of them stood looking at the flat. "My dad had four new tires put on less than a week ago. He always takes good care of my car. You have to understand, he's very overprotective of my sister and me. And I see that look in your eye, so don't even think of asking me more about my dad. Just get the tire fixed, okay?"

"I wasn't thinking about your dad," Eric said as he opened the trunk and took out the spare. "I was thinking about the car gremlins. Those little guys couldn't care less how new something is. If you get them riled—they go for it."

* * *

"Jason, that wasn't one bit funny," Samantha scolded. "I thought when you disappeared back there on the mountain you were up to no good. How did you ever convince Gus to blow out a tire, anyway?"

"It was easy," Jason bragged. "When I told him I had agreed to help out with this project, he was happy to do a little favor for me. At least he understands that my expertise is needed if this job is to be done right."

"Yeah, right," Samantha laughed. "Like I couldn't handle it alone if I wanted to. And what does blowing out a tire have to do with getting this job done right?"

"I had Gus blow out the tire because Julie deserved it. She's been downright mean to Eric. If the two of them have a contract, then he has the right to confront J.T. and win the woman."

Samantha looked at Jason appraisingly. "Oh, now you think Cousin Julie's mean, do you? A short time ago you were telling me how wonderful she is because of her long, beautiful hair. But now you think she's mean? Exactly what is it you do think about her, Jason?"

"How did we get back on this hair thing again?" Jason asked, bewildered. "And even if I do like her long hair, what does that have to do with thinking she's mean to Eric? The two things have absolutely nothing to do with each other."

"Maybe not, but you just remember whose assignment this is. You're only here to help out when I need you. Don't go getting any ideas about taking over the operation. And don't pull any more stunts like this blown tire."

"You're forgetting something, Sam," Jason reminded her. "I have a lot more experience in these matters than you do. I suggest it's time you let me take over."

"Let you take over?" Samantha asked, disbelieving. "After the way you almost blew it with Arline and Bruce? Nothing doing. I'll handle this assignment my way. And from now on, you're no longer a ghost in my eyes. From here on out, you've been demoted to car gremlin."

* * *

With the tire changed, Julie and Eric got back in the car. "All right, all right" she said, patting the dashboard of the BMW. "I apologize to you, car. Now will you get me home with no more surprises, please?" When Eric laughed, Julie rolled her eyes. "And what exactly is so funny?" she asked.

Eric leaned over and kissed her quickly. "Jim Bridger may have taken care of the bears and lions," he teased her, "but there seems to be evidence of a few car gremlins."

Thirty minutes later Julie pulled into the parking lot of Eric's complex. "When can I see you again, Lisa?" Eric asked.

"I don't know," she quipped. "Maybe we should clear it with your car gremlins before we discuss it."

"I've already cleared it with them. They said if you didn't make it soon, they'd be even more perturbed."

Catching him completely off guard, she moved forward and gave him a quick kiss. "Thanks for being such a great guy, Eric."

"You think I'm a great guy?"

"Well, of course. From now on I'll let you change all my flat tires."

Eric cupped her face gently in his hands. "Thank you for a great date, Lisa. I may have to stand up all day tomorrow, but I can't remember when I've enjoyed a day more than this one. You will call me, won't you?"

"I will," she smiled. *Even your car gremlins couldn't stop me from calling you again, Eric Roberts,* she added to herself.

That evening Julie added a pine cone to her collection of a five-by-seven photo and cuddly white bear placed on the nightstand next to her bed. Other than remembering to answer to the name Lisa, it had been a great day. But it was a day that left her with a dilemma to face.

Once, when Julie was very young, her mother had given her a big red balloon. Filled with helium, it floated almost magically at the top of a thin ribbon tied to Julie's wrist. She must have been around five at the time, and what a wonderful thing the balloon had seemed to her young mind. She wanted to keep it forever, so she could enjoy its beauty and magic. When her daddy had come home from work that afternoon, she had run out the door to meet him—magic balloon and all. As he always did, he scooped her into his arms and kissed her cheek. Even now, with the memory nearly twenty years old, she could almost feel his stubby whiskers against her soft skin.

Greeting her father as he came home from work was a ritual that had lasted well beyond the day he accidentally tore the ribbon loose, releasing the cherished balloon to drift upward into the afternoon sky.

Eric Roberts was much like that balloon. He brought a wonderful new magic to her life that she wanted to hold onto forever. But like the balloon, Eric seemed to be at the end of a very thin string just waiting for her father to tear it from her hand. Just as Rob had been torn from her sister Lisa's.

CHAPTER 13

"You're sure you want to go through with this, Uncle Mac?" Samantha asked as J.T. approached the door to Greg Reeves' office. "Just remember, I have a job to do and I'm going to do it one way or another. You can agree to my wishes right now and get off light, or you can do it the hard way and go through with this meeting. Just remember, I gave you the choice."

As J.T. pushed the door open, he paused long enough to answer Samantha's proposal with one of his own. "I'm the one with a job to do here, my pushy niece. This deal I have cooking with Big Ed stands to make me more money than King Tutankhamen spent building his famous pyramid. Now, as you say, we can do this the easy way or we can do it the hard way. The easy way is for you to leave me alone. Go find yourself another uncle to haunt."

Having said this, J.T. pushed the door the rest of the way and entered the office. "Hi, Becky," he called out as she looked up to see who had come in. "Are you feeling like an old married person yet?"

Becky beamed. "No way, Mr. MacGregor. Roger is the best thing that's ever happened to me. Our honeymoon has only begun, you can be sure of that."

"Now there's a happy woman," Samantha exclaimed. "Like your daughters could be if you'd bug out of their lives and leave them alone."

J.T. glared at Samantha. Why did she have to be so stubborn? Life had been so much more pleasant before she showed up as a fix-it-all angel. "Is this the lucky guy?" he asked, picking up a picture from Becky's desk.

Becky nodded. "That's Roger. Isn't he handsome?"

"He's very handsome," J.T. answered, doing his best to ignore the irritating smile on Samantha's face. "Is Greg in his office? He should be expecting me. His father asked me to stop by this morning."

"He knows you're here. I buzzed him when I first saw you at the door. You can go on inside if you'd like."

"Thanks, Becky," J.T. said, returning the picture to her desk and stepping to the door to the inner office. "Give Roger my best, will you? And tell him I think he's a very lucky guy."

"Ah, J.T.," Greg said as J.T. entered the room. "Pull up a chair and sit down. My father has all the papers ready for you to look over."

J.T. was a little surprised. "Your father sent the papers here to your office for me to look over? Why didn't he have me come to his office?"

"Why does my father do anything?" Greg asked. "I gave up trying to second-guess Ed years ago."

Samantha wrinkled her nose as she looked at Greg. "Take a close look at this guy you think you want for a son-in-law, Uncle Mac," she said. "You can tell from his shifty eyes that the only person he's ever been in love with is himself. He might be able to provide material things for Lisa, but he'll never give her the love and affection she deserves. And if you have any idea this guy would ever be faithful to her, you can forget it."

J.T. squinted angrily at Samantha. He had to admit, there were a few things he didn't like about Greg. But he wasn't going to tell Samantha that. All in all, he still saw Greg as the best prospect for a future son-in-law.

Greg lifted a box of cigars from the top of his desk and offered one to J.T., who declined. "Do you mind if I have one?" he said.

"Of course not. It's your office." The cigar smoking was one of the things J.T. most disliked about Greg. But he figured that if the man could afford the habit, he had every right to enjoy it, regardless of how J.T. felt about it.

Holding a match to the end of the cigar, Greg drew a deep breath. Swells of smoke formed in front of his face, then drifted upward until they dissipated their stagnant odor into the air. Dropping the spent match in the ash tray, he pulled a stack of papers from an upper desk drawer and handed them to J.T.

As J.T. took the papers, he looked them over briefly. "You can tell your father I'll look these over more carefully tonight. If I find them in order—as I'm sure I will—we can get together to finalize the deal later this week. That is, if your father is ready to finalize the deal."

"Oh yes, he's ready for that, all right," Greg assured him. "He's talked of little else for the last several weeks. He's coming here to my office later today for a meeting. He says he wants to fill me in on all the necessary details before finalizing the deal. I'll have Becky give you a call when I learn where and when he wants all of us to meet."

"You know, Greg," J.T. said, looking up from the stack of papers he was holding, "this mall deal your father came up with is a stroke of genius. We all stand to make a bundle on this one. I've already laid all the groundwork on my end. I think the five million I'll be putting up for the land will be the best money I've ever spent. Of course, it helps knowing that your father's put in two hundred million to back up the rest of the deal."

"The best money you've ever spent?" Samantha laughed. "You know it's going to take every dime you can scrape up, plus securing some heavy loans. Where will you be if Edward Reeves decides to leave you hanging out to dry on the deal, huh? You'll be dead broke, that's where you'll be."

J.T. only leaned back in his chair and grinned. When it came to money deals, he knew what he was doing. *Sam may be an angel, but she knows nothing about making money,* he thought smugly.

"I'm aware of the money to be made on this deal," Greg replied, staring at the cigar he held between a thumb and one finger. "Not only that, but it will get my name in front of a lot of people. To me, that's even more important than the money. As you know, I have my sights set on the state senate this next election."

"Oh yes," J.T. responded. "I'd forgotten about your political aspirations. I suppose the publicity associated with this deal could be a big boost for you. And for Lisa, of course."

"Yuck," Samantha said. "The only thing I can think of worse than this guy being in the state senate is having him in the family as Lisa's husband. Take my word for it, Uncle Mac, it isn't going to happen. I'll see to it with Lisa, and the people will see to it with the senate. Most of the voters out there have better vision than you seem to have, Uncle."

By the time J.T. got back to his car, he was annoyed to see Samantha already waiting for him in the front passenger seat. "Why do you insist on hanging around like you do?" he fumed. "You're my niece, not my mother. I swear, you and Julie are just alike in that department."

"Ha!" Samantha chortled. "It's lucky for you I'm not your mother. I'd have pinched your head off years ago."

"Let me ask you a question, Sam. Do angels ever take a lunch break?"

"Of course we take lunch breaks, Uncle Mac. Why?"

"I was sort of hoping you'd take one right about now. A long one. Say about twenty years."

"Very funny. But for your information, I did take a breakfast break this morning before coming to supervise your meeting with Greg. I had a great meal at the Paradise Palace with my little sweetheart Jason."

"Supervise my meeting? Hogwash!"

"Would you mind reaching over here and pulling down my sun visor so I can use the mirror, Uncle Mac? I didn't have time to reapply my lipstick after breakfast."

"Good grief, Sam! I don't believe you! Why not pull the darn thing down yourself, if you want to use the mirror?"

"I can't," she said, giving him a quick demonstration of her hand sliding through the visor. "Angels can't do things like that."

"I just don't believe this is happening to me," he grumbled, while reaching across to pull down her visor. "You may be my favorite niece, but you do aggravate me at times. Why can't you just bid me a fond farewell and go back to your angel world, wherever that is, and let me get on with my life?"

Samantha opened her purse and rummaged through it until she found her tube of lipstick. Opening it, she applied a fresh coat. Only after she had finished and returned the tube to her purse did she answer. "If I went away now, you have no idea the mess you'd be left with. Things are coming down fast. I give you my word, before you go to bed tonight you'll be seeing things in a different light."

J.T. shook his head and reached for the keys to start the car, but he paused to ask a sincere question. "You really do believe you're here to help me, don't you, Sam?"

Samantha looked back to the mirror and smoothed her lipstick with the end of her little finger. "Of course I believe I'm helping you. I *am* helping you. And, my sweet husband, Jason, should be doing his part on the project right about now, too."

"Oh come on, Sam! Give me a break. No more angels haunting me, please. Even if he is your husband, I don't want him bothering me."

"Don't worry about it, Uncle," she laughed. "Jason won't be working with you. That's my job. He'll be working with your future son-in-law."

J.T. was curious in spite of himself. "He's going to show himself to Greg?"

"Not hardly," Samantha scoffed. "The guy I'm referring to you haven't even met yet. You will meet him, though, a lot sooner than you realize right now." Just then, Samantha noticed something in the mirror. "Gus?" she asked. "What are you doing here?"

"Gus?" J.T. echoed. "Don't tell me there's another angel after me now. Who's Gus?"

"I'm Gus, pal," came a voice from the back seat. "And you can put yer mind at ease. I've been out of the hauntin' business for centuries now. I'm just here ta check up on Sam. This bein' her first official assignment and all, I thought she might need my assistance with somethin'."

J.T. shot a quick glance to the back seat. "Good grief!" he bellowed. "Will they never stop coming? So who are you, Sam's father-in-law?"

"What do you mean you're checking up on me?" Samantha turned around to ask over the back of her seat. "What you're really saying is you don't trust me with this assignment."

"Ya got it all wrong, Sam," Gus said placatingly. "I just thought ya might need some help."

"I know where to reach you if I get in trouble, Gus," Samantha reminded him. "Didn't my performance with Bruce and Arline count for anything?"

"Good grief!" J.T. shouted. "Not only am I being haunted by two creatures, they're even having an argument in my car. Would it be asking too much for you to take your dispute elsewhere and let me get on about my business?"

"Be quiet, Uncle Mac," Samantha scolded. "I'll get back to you when I finish with this other stubborn male that's annoying me. As for you, Gus, say what you have to say and get back to your office. I can handle this assignment without your interference."

"It's not that I don't have confidence in ya, Sam. I just wanted ta see how things are goin', is all. But one thing I'd like ta mention is when ya need help with somethin', come ta me and not to Maggie. I'm the one who's supposed ta handle the field jobs. Maggie takes care of the office."

"You're just jealous because I asked Maggie's help in breaking down Greg's computer."

"Will somebody please tell me what's going on here?" J.T. begged, seeing that his request for them to leave had fallen on deaf ears.

Gus pursed his lips. "Of course I'm not jealous of Maggie. It's just that things should be kept in their proper order, Sam. And the proper order is I take care of the field. Blast it, Sam. I do deserve some respect, ya know."

Samantha shook her finger at Gus. "If you want my respect, then start acting like a person of your position in the eternities ought to act. A Special Conditions Coordinator shouldn't go around getting his feelings hurt over trivial matters like his secretary doing something a little beyond her duties once in a while. And if a Special Conditions Coordinator had been paying attention to his business, he wouldn't have messed up a certain contract in the first place."

J.T. was growing more anxious by the minute. "Listen, you two," he shouted. "If you insist on using my car for your argument, could I at least know what the argument is all about?"

Gus turned his attention to J.T. "I don't envy ya, pal. Dealin' with Sam here is like tryin' ta hold a Tarzan by the tail."

"That's a tiger, you nut basket!" J.T. exclaimed. "The expression is holding a tiger by the tail."

Gus shrugged. "Tiger, Tarzan, what's the difference? I can see that Sam has everythin' under control here, so I'll just be runnin' along."

"Now hold on a minute!" J.T. exclaimed. "You can't just show up suddenly in the back seat of my car, carry on an argument with this pushy niece of mine, and then walk away without at least explaining who you are and what you're doing here."

Gus paused before stepping out of the car. "Sure, pal," he said. "What would ya like me ta explain? Sam's already told ya she's here ta help get destiny back on track, hasn't she?"

"The only thing she's told me is she wants to straighten out my thinking. I don't need my thinking straightened out. I had everything under control before she showed up."

"That's not true, Gus," Samantha countered in her own defense. "I've told my hardheaded uncle exactly why I'm here. I can't help it if he refuses to listen to me."

"Well, say something that makes sense," J.T. fumed. Turning to Gus, he said, "Look Gus, as long as you're here, explain it to me in man's language. What is it she's trying to do to me?"

Gus tried to explain. "Sam is here workin' with you because you're her assignment. It's not like I couldn't have sent a more experienced angel, but Sam is a special friend of mine. Ya see, she asked fer the job, Lisa and Julie bein' her family, and all."

"What assignment?! What job?! Why is she working with me when I'm perfectly happy just the way I am? I don't need anyone telling me how to run my life."

"Yeah, well," Gus said, "ya better start changin' yer mind on that point, pal. Whether yer willin' ta admit it or not, yer on a course that's taken destiny askew. That's somethin' we just can't tolerate in our business. And whether ya like it or not, ya better listen to Sam. Now if ya'll excuse me, I gotta be goin'."

As J.T. looked on in astonishment, Gus got out of the car, shut the door, then simply vanished.

CHAPTER 14

For Eric Roberts, life had never been sweeter. He could think of nothing else but a wonderful woman named Lisa. Even his dreams at night were filled with the wonder of her charm. Other than wishing to know her last name, he could think of only one thing that would make life better. That would be a phone number he could call so he could hear her voice on the other end. As it was, he would just have to wait for her promised call.

By the middle of the week following their date to the mountains, Eric was hard pressed for ways to keep his mind off the anticipated call. He was glad for a busy week at work, but the evenings were a problem. He tried doing some research on a project he had in mind for a miniature video camera, but concentration was impossible. Going for walks helped, but he couldn't walk all night every night. In desperation for something to do, he set out to give Little Blue its third bath in that many days. With a bucket of soapy water and a few rags, he stepped from the kitchen of his apartment into the living room, but he never made it to the front door. For there, directly in his path, and right in the middle of his living room, stood a man. Eric stared dumbfounded at the man.

"Who are you?" he asked, as soon as he managed to get his wits together. "And what are you doing in my apartment?"

"Name's Jason Hackett," the man replied matter-of-factly. "And I'm here to help you, if you'll give me the chance."

Somehow, Eric had a strong sensation he had nothing to fear from this fellow. Still—what good reason could there be for him being here? He must be up to no good.

"Are you sure you don't mean *rob* me?" Eric dropped the rags and took the bucket in both hands. "So help me," he threatened. "Either you back out that door, or you wear this bucket of hot soapy water. I'm not kidding, bud."

Jason rolled his eyes and let out a rueful sigh. "Here we go again," he sighed. "I hate first-time encounters. Do you have any idea how many times I've had to go through this before? I know how hard this is for you to grasp, Eric, but—"

Eric was caught completely off guard by the use of his name. "What is this?" he demanded. "What do you want, and how do you know my name?"

"I'm trying to explain if you'll just let me," Jason said patiently. "Why not think of me as sort of like one of your car gremlins." Jason smiled, proud of himself for having thought of this idea. "That's it, think of me as a car gremlin."

"What are you talking about?" Eric asked, bewildered. He thought car gremlins were his own little joke.

"Wait a minute, Eric, don't turn this car gremlin thing off too lightly," Jason protested. "It really is a great way to explain myself. After all, I was the one who caused the blowout on Ju—uh—that is, on Lisa's car. You know, up on Hillview Road, after you rode the horses up to the falls."

Eric was stunned. *How does this guy know about me? Has he been following me? Why?* Did it have something to be with his old roommate George Weathersby? Did he send this guy to take something else from him? Eric held up the water bucket threateningly. "What do you want?"

Jason wasn't fazed in the least. "I just thought you might be interested in learning a little more about your new girlfriend," he said. "You know, like what her last name is and where she lives and why she's so secretive about her life. And I have to warn you, throwing that bucket of water at me won't do anything but leave you with a mess to clean up. We car gremlins are waterproof."

Eric saw the opportunity to learn more about the new woman in his life, and he intuitively trusted the stranger, who seemed too honest to have any dealings with George Weathersby. "You know where I can find Lisa?" he asked cautiously.

"I do," Jason assured him. "That's one of the main reasons I'm here, to take you to her."

Eric lowered the bucket. "You're not lying to me? You want to take me to Lisa?"

"I'm not lying," Jason assured him. "But I think we should get a few of the preliminaries out of the way upfront. This is always the hardest part, getting someone to keep their cool when they realize I really am an angel."

"You're an angel? You mean like Monica on the television show?"

Jason laughed. "I've never been compared to Monica before," he admitted. "There are some similarities, I suppose, though not many. For instance, Monica can open doors. I can't."

Eric wasn't buying it. "Why not try telling me the truth? Who are you really?"

Jason shrugged. "I guess we need a little demonstration. Toss me one of those rags at your feet."

Eric looked startled. "Why?"

"Just toss me the rag, Eric. You'll know why when I try to catch it."

Eric set the bucket of water on the floor and picking up the rags, tossed one of them to Jason. To his surprise, the rag simply passed through Jason's body like it wasn't even there and fell on the floor behind him.

"What do you think of that, Eric?" Jason grinned. "That should convince you I'm either an angel, or one of your concocted car gremlins, shouldn't it?"

Eric threw a second rag with the same result. He couldn't believe what he had seen. "How did you do that?" he gasped.

"I told you, Eric. I'm an angel. You want to see me walk through a wall, or something?"

Eric shook his head, dazed. "No, that's all right. I've seen enough. But—I still don't understand. If you really are an angel, where are your wings?"

Jason slapped a hand to his forehead. "Please, Eric," he moaned. "Just take my word for it. Angels don't have wings. We don't play the harp, either. I'm here to help you get together with the woman you love, but first, we need to solve the mystery she's left you struggling with. Now are you ready to let me do my thing, or do we have to stand here arguing the rest of the day?"

Eric was more astounded than ever. "You know about Lisa's mystery?" he asked eagerly.

Jason nodded. "Yes, I know everything there is to know about her mystery. I'm here to take you to her, but you have to agree to do things my way. There's a lot more involved than simply providing you with your girlfriend's address."

Eric's head spun in confusion. How could this be happening? He had seen proof of Jason's claim to being an angel. How else could the rags have passed through him like they did? Eric desperately wanted to believe, especially if it meant learning Lisa's last name and where he could find her. "Then you really are an—angel?" he asked.

"Dyed in the wool, one hundred percent true blue. And please, don't call me Casper. I've been there, done that, got the t-shirt. My name's Jason Hackett."

"Jason Hackett, eh? Well, tell me, Jason, did you really cause Lisa's tire to blow out?"

Jason smiled. "Nice touch, wasn't it?"

"And you're here now to help me find Lisa?"

"You got it. But like I said, we do it my way or we don't do it at all. I'm going to have to ask you to do some pretty strange things before you get to see her. How do you feel about that?"

"You're not going to ask me to break any laws, are you?" Eric asked.

Jason scratched the back of his head. "That all depends on whose law it is we're talking about. I give you my word, I have the approval of the higher authorities on this plan. That overrides any other law. And I know what you're thinking, but don't ask. I hate trying to explain who the higher authorities are. Just take my word for it. When they approve something, no one had better argue about it."

It took more than a little effort to trust Jason, but the stakes were high enough for Eric to chance it. "I'll take your word for it, Jason," he said. "Just lead me to Lisa."

"That's the old spirit, Eric. I have the plan all worked out. Well, actually my cute little angel wife has the plan worked out, but that's another story. We're going to use your talent with electronics to open the eyes of a stubborn old man who just may turn out to be your father-in-law one day."

The word "father-in-law" jarred Eric to the quick. He stood quietly listening as Jason took the next several minutes to explain his plan. Jason had put it mildly when he said he was going to ask Eric to do some strange things. Eric struggled with his decision, but in the end it was his hope of finding Lisa that turned the tide. After hearing Jason's plan, he quickly gathered up the things he would need. This done, he and Jason set out to put the plan into action.

"How ya doing, Becky?" Eric greeted her cheerfully. "I happened to be in the building and saw your light still on. You're working a little late tonight, aren't you?"

Becky looked up from her desk, surprised. "Oh, hi, Eric. Yeah, Greg asked me to stay late tonight. He has a big meeting planned with his father, and he wanted me here to be sure they're not disturbed. What's up with you?"

Eric glanced at Jason, who gave him a thumbs-up sign to move ahead with their plan. "Greg called me earlier about his computer, said something about it locking up on him." Eric handed Becky the fake work order Jason had instructed him to make up. "Is it okay if I disturb him long enough to check it out?"

"Oh, you won't be disturbing him," Becky answered. "He's out just now. I'm expecting him any minute, though. His meeting is only a few minutes away. How much time will you need to get his computer working?"

"You know me, Becky. I'll have it going in no time at all. Is it all right if I go on in and get started?"

Becky smiled. "Be my guest," she replied. "But if Greg shows up . . ."

"If he shows up, I'll leave," Eric promised. "But I'm sure I can have the computer fixed in a matter of minutes."

Eric stepped into Greg's office and went right to work. Unzipping his tool pouch, he removed a small box and secured it to the bottom side of the desk.

"How am I supposed to get my transmitter back, Jason?" he asked. "This little baby cost me too many days' pay just to play finders keepers with these guys."

"You'll have no problem getting it back," Jason assured him.

"After tonight, Greg Reeves will have too many things on his mind to worry about his office. Just make sure you have the volume on that thing turned up high enough. We don't want to miss one word of their conversation."

Eric laughed. "No problem. This little baby can pick up an ant crawling on the carpet on the other side of the room. I should know, I designed it myself." Crawling out from under the desk, he pushed the chair back in place. "All finished," he said. "I've never done anything like this in my life. Are you sure I'm not going to end up in big trouble? I mean this Big Ed character has bodyguards and everything."

Jason started for the door. "Not to worry, Eric. I have a guy named Gus on my side. All the bodyguards Big Ed might hire could never outmaneuver Gus. Like the fellow in the Allstate commercial says, 'You're in good hands.' Now let's get out of here."

"All done, Becky," Eric said as he walked by Becky's desk. "I'd rather you didn't mention to Greg that I was here. He thought I was going to take care of this little job sooner than this, but I couldn't get to it. You know how it is."

"Don't worry," she winked. "Your secret's safe with me. So long as he's happy with his computer, why should he care when you fixed it?"

Eric left the building quickly and slipped behind the wheel of Little Blue. There he waited for the next part of the plan to develop. It didn't take long.

"This will be Greg now," Jason explained, as a green Porsche convertible pulled into the lot and parked next to the building's entrance. A few seconds later, a second vehicle rolled to a stop in the space next to the Porsche. This one really caught Eric's eye. It was a solid white Cadillac stretch limousine.

"Wow," Eric said. "I'd say that vehicle is a little out of place in this neighborhood. Can I assume it belongs to Big Ed Reeves?"

"One and the same," Jason agreed.

As they looked on, two hefty bodyguards got out of the limo, and one of them opened Ed's door. By this time Greg was out of his car, and the four men made their way toward the building.

"So that's Big Ed?" Eric asked. "Is he really as rich as they say?"

Jason smiled. "He's rich, all right. But he didn't get that way by selling Girl Scout cookies. He's had his finger in just about every illegal enterprise there is. Among other things, he's ruthlessly planning the downfall of two people, Eric—your future father-in-law and your future brother-in-law."

"My future what?"

"Never mind. You'll understand it better before this night is over. First things first—is that recorder ready to go?"

"Everything's ready," Eric assured Jason. "But I'm still not too sure about all this. Big Ed isn't the sort of guy I'd ordinarily risk running into."

Jason gave Eric an encouraging smile. "Put your mind at ease, Eric. The higher authorities have had their eye on Ed Reeves. Alongside one of them, he's about as powerful as a butterfly in a hurricane. With them on your side, you have nothing to worry about."

Eric was still not a hundred percent convinced. "This whole thing hinges on you really being an angel," he said. "Granted, I've believed in car gremlins all my life, but angels take a little more work. I didn't actually think of them as looking like—well you know . . ."

"Like an ordinary man?"

"Yeah. That about sums it up."

"Sort of takes some of the fun away, doesn't it?" Jason smiled.

"Sorta, I guess," Eric admitted.

"Well, that's just the way it is. I'm nothing more than a man who lived his life here in mortality much like you're doing right now, Eric. You have your problems, I had mine. In fact, our problems were alike in a way. Only mine took longer to solve. I spent a lifetime looking for the woman I loved. And by the time I found her, I was already an angel. I'll tell you this much, though, she was worth the wait. Would you like to hear my story?"

Eric listened intently as Jason set out to tell him of his plight. He told of his own life and death, leaving out the part about choking on a chicken bone, of course. He told of watching Samantha grow up, and about courting her as an angel. As his story unfolded, Eric's doubts began to vanish. By the time Jason reached the part where he and Samantha passed through the light into the next dimension, Eric was a believer. "You must really love her, Jason," he commented at the close of the tale.

"Absolutely. And the best part is, I have a contract making her my forever angel. I know you don't understand that part just yet, but you and Ju— uh, I mean, Lisa are covered by a similar contract. Which is a big part of the reason I'm here, to be sure that contract is secured. Uh-oh, another minute or so and we better turn on that recorder. It's almost show time. But first, take a look at Greg's Porsche, at the license plate specifically. There's a clue there I want you to see."

Eric strained to see the plate. "Well, I'll be—it's Lisa's name. Are you telling me Greg somehow fits into Lisa's life? Is that why she was working for him when we first met?"

"I'm telling you to hang loose. Very soon now you'll learn for yourself how Greg fits into the picture. Are you ready?"

Sliding on the earphones, Eric punched the record button just as the meeting in Greg's office was beginning.

* * *

After instructing his two bodyguards to wait in the outer office and securing the door, Big Ed moved to the chair behind Greg's desk and took it for himself. When Greg had seated himself in one of the client chairs, Ed got right to the point. "I know you're wondering what this meeting's all about, son," he began. "And I suppose you're wondering why we're meeting in your office instead of mine."

Greg nodded. "Both questions have come to mind," he admitted.

"I'm a powerful man, Greg. I didn't get that way by taking needless chances. Believe me when I say there are those out there who would like to bring me down. I have the best security money can buy, but I've learned that means nothing when someone wants to learn my secrets. There's too great a chance that my office may have ears. On the other hand, who would have any reason to bug your office? Now, understand me when I say that what I have to tell you must never get out. Is that clear?"

"I understand."

"Good, because what I intend to tell you today is going to come as a shock. This is something I've never told any living person. As I said, I expect you to keep these things to yourself. No one is ever to know any of it." Big Ed glared at his son for emphasis.

"Yes, Father," Greg said obediently.

"Now, let me begin by asking you a question. Why do you suppose I've navigated the project on the super mall and brought in J.T. MacGregor?"

Greg shook his head. "I never understood why, because I've never seen you dabble in real estate before. I just figured you had your reasons. To tell you the truth, it didn't bother me that you were helping J.T. make a few bucks. I sort of like the old boy. He's on my side with Lisa, you know."

Ed slammed his fist hard against the top of the desk. "Don't ever let me hear you say you like that old fool. If you're a son of mine, you'll learn to hate him the way I hate him."

Greg's eyes widened in shock. "But—I thought you . . . that is, you sought him out to do business with you. I thought you must like him."

"That's exactly what I wanted you to think. And that's what I wanted MacGregor to think. I learned a long time ago, son, it's always best to profess cooperation. That way you can usually catch the other guy with his guard down, and slit his throat clean through—just as I plan on slitting MacGregor's throat." Big Ed's eyes glowed with pleasure as his raspy voice nearly caressed the words.

"Now wait a minute, Ed," Greg protested. "I have big plans for MacGregor's daughter. If you ruin him, where will that leave me with Lisa?"

Ed smiled and leaned back in the chair. "You have plans for his daughter, do you? I like that, son. You have no idea how satisfying I find the thought of being a father-in-law to his daughter. And I intend to do everything in my power to see to it that you get what you want so you can put your mind at ease. I always cover my tracks. MacGregor will never know what hit him. He'll think we both got caught in the same swindle."

The primary emotion Greg had for his father was admiration. Not the kind of admiration that made him want to be like his father, but the kind that demanded his respect nevertheless. However, when it came right down to it, Greg was nothing like his father. They didn't look alike, nor did they think alike. Greg held no interest in pursuing the same lifestyle that had made his father wealthy. Ed may have found satisfaction in the underworld of big crime, but Greg wanted to follow a different path. Not that he didn't plan to maintain the family fortune his father would someday leave him; he had no intention of ever giving that up. It's just that he wanted to take his career a step further, by adding personal power to the wealth he could already claim. He had it all figured out. First step, state senate. Next, governor. Then federal congressman, and finally the White House.

To Greg, appearance was a huge factor in his career path. That's where Lisa MacGregor fit into the picture. She would make the perfect lifetime running mate. She looked good in front of the cameras, handled herself wonderfully with people, and sparkled with a warm, sweet charm. There was just one obstacle—Rob Jensen. And so, although Greg didn't care all that much about his father's super mall deal with J.T. MacGregor, he understood that his father had the connections necessary to get Rob out of the picture permanently. Leaning forward, he gave his father his undivided attention.

"When you first started seeing Lisa MacGregor," Ed began, "the name MacGregor stirred something long buried in the tunnels of my memory. I couldn't put my finger on where I had heard his name, so I hired a detective to check him out. What I learned astounded me. You had somehow become involved with the daughter of a man who had crossed paths with me years ago. A man I've hated passionately ever since. You see, son, I was once engaged to marry the woman who later became Lisa's mother."

Greg wasn't sure he had heard his father right. "You were what?"

"You heard me right. I was in love with Katherine Allen, and she had agreed to be my wife. Then J.T. MacGregor came along. He completely swept her off her feet. Her parents were on my side and she agreed to have nothing more to do with him, but the fool actually came to the wedding and stole her away before I knew what was happening. There I was, standing alone at the altar in front all those people while J.T. MacGregor stole my bride. Can you even begin to imagine my humiliation, son? For a thousand nights I lay awake devising ways of making the man pay. I've never forgotten him. Then, when you brought him back into my life, it was like he'd been handed to me on a golden platter. I swore that I would get even with J.T. MacGregor and I would enjoy it more than I've enjoyed anything in my entire life."

Greg was still in shock. "I can't believe this, Ed. You almost married Lisa's mother? And MacGregor ran off with her in the middle of your wedding? That certainly explains your sudden interest in this real estate deal. You're setting MacGregor up for a big fall."

Ed laughed his whiny, evil laugh. "I've set him up, all right. The old fool didn't just nibble at the bait, he lunged headlong into my trap. He knows I'm wealthy enough to buy and sell him a thousand times over. And he's just naive enough to think I'm about to help him double, even triple what he has now. But I have other plans, you can be sure. Tomorrow morning I plan to get his signature on the bottom line, and once I do—he'll be in for the surprise of his life.

"You see, son, I bought an old abandoned warehouse down on Waterfront Drive, and I've filled it with tons of inferior materials that will never pass code. I have papers in my office safe, forged, naturally, showing that MacGregor bought and stocked the whole warehouse. I also have witnesses ready to come forward to swear he offered them bribes to cover up his use of those materials in the mall."

Greg rubbed the back of his neck as he contemplated what his father was saying. "Using substandard materials in a project like the mall is serious, Ed. You can have him put away for years on a charge like that."

"That was the general idea, son. Until you helped me come up with a better one."

Greg looked at his father in surprise. "I helped you? Just how did I manage that?"

"This fellow you talked about—you know—the one you want out of the picture . . ." Even though Big Ed had chosen not to mention Rob by name, Greg knew exactly who he was talking about. "I've devised a second part to the plan," Big Ed continued. "There's going to be an explosion at the old warehouse where the materials are stored. A couple of my boys are setting it up at this very minute, although the explosion itself won't occur until sometime next week. I'll wait for a couple of days after MacGregor has signed the papers. Then I can more easily pin the explosion on him."

Greg wrinkled his brow in confusion. "How do you plan to pin the explosion on J.T.? And what would his motive be for blowing up the warehouse, if he's supposedly keeping the materials there for the new mall?

Ed laughed again. "That's the difference between you and me, son," he said. "You need to be able to see the bigger picture in matters like this. It'll cost me a few dollars, but I can make it look like someone is blowing the whistle on MacGregor's intention to use the inferior materials. It will then appear that he blew up the warehouse deliberately in an attempt to destroy the evidence. That's where your friend comes in . . ."

"Go on," Greg said eagerly.

Big Ed smiled. "We'll lure him to the warehouse on the pretext of signing a contract with a friend of mine in the entertainment business. Once he's inside, all that's necessary is to close the door behind him. There's only one door to the warehouse that's not chained and locked, and I'm having that door rigged to lock on its own once it's closed. So there will be no escaping once he's locked inside. All I have to do is make one phone call, and the whole building goes up in a cloud of smoke."

"A phone call?" Greg asked. "I don't understand."

"That's the most ingenious part of my whole plan, son. That's how I can pin the explosion on MacGregor with enough weight to hold up in any court in this country. You see, I managed to get my hands on his personal cell phone, and I have a contact who has devised a detonator that will trigger at the sound of his phone. I've instructed my boys to leave MacGregor's cell phone in the warehouse, but in a location where it will be somewhat protected from the blast. That will allow it to remain intact enough to become evidence. We lure your friend to the warehouse, and once he's inside, all I have to do is make a phone call to MacGregor's phone. It'll appear that MacGregor enticed this young man to the warehouse, and set off the explosion in his desire to get rid of him. Unfortunately, it will appear as if he dropped his phone in the process."

Greg fidgeted in his chair. "That doesn't make sense, Ed," he argued. "Why would J.T. rig his own phone to set off the blast? And won't the fact that the only door to the place was jimmied raise some questions?"

Big Ed grew impatient. He didn't like being questioned. "Come on, son, use your head," he said sharply. "Do you think the police will be intelligent or resourceful enough to figure those things out? You have to understand, son, cops are stupid. Just as soon as they learn about the bad feelings between MacGregor and your friend, they'll consider the case closed. They'll never even notice the door, and they'll figure he used a simple remote device to set off the explosion. I'll sit back and enjoy my revenge on MacGregor, and your friend will be out of the way so you can . . . pursue your interests. And I'll tell you one thing for sure. Once MacGregor is locked away in a dreary little cell, I'll sleep better than I ever have in the last twenty-five years."

* * *

Eric's stomach was churning. "What have I gotten myself into, Jason?" he asked. "Is my Lisa the one these guys are referring to?"

Jason just smiled calmly. "Could be. But you'll have to wait a little longer to know that for sure. You can shut off the tape recorder now. You have enough there to do the trick. And their meeting will be coming to a close in the next few minutes."

"This Big Ed is a fruitcake," Eric said as he shut off the recorder. "You can see how he's let thoughts of revenge poison his mind but good."

"You should understand how that works, Eric," Jason was quick to point out. "You've had some experience with that sort of thing yourself."

Eric was taken aback by Jason's statement. "George Weathersby?" he asked. "You know about George?"

"Oh yes," Jason said. "I know about George. He was part of my briefing for your case. But pay attention here. Greg is going to come out the door in a few minutes and get in his green Porsche. He's going to pick up a young woman for a date tonight. We're going to have to follow them without being seen."

Eric glanced toward the door. Although Jason hadn't mentioned Lisa by name, he was putting things together in his own mind by this time. He also knew enough about Big Ed to be more than a little worried.

"What if I end up in that warehouse with the other guy?" he asked as he waited for Greg to appear.

"You still don't get it, do you?" Jason sighed. "You have an angel on your side. Ed Reeves is going to have a lot more to worry about than you, my friend. But, hey, if you don't want to know the answer to your Lisa's mystery, we can shut this project down and go home right now."

"Of course not," Eric quickly responded. "I'll follow this guy anywhere, if he leads me to Lisa."

CHAPTER 15

"You're going to do what?" Julie stared at her sister in shock.

"I said I'm breaking it off with Greg," Lisa answered. "That's what you've been wanting me to do, isn't it?"

"Yeah, but why not do it over the phone? Why go out with him one last time just to tell him to get lost? Why spend any more time with him than you have to?"

Lisa's explanation was simple. "You and I are two different people, my dear sister. You might be one to break off with Greg over the phone, but I'm not. I have to look him in the eye when I tell him. That's the only way I can be sure he understands that I mean what I'm saying. And that's the only way I can trust myself to make my decision stick."

Surprised and impressed by her sister's sudden show of forcefulness, Julie willingly conceded her sister's point. "Okay, okay, I get the picture. Whatever it takes for you to get rid of that dud once and for all. Do you want me there when you tell Dad what you're up to?"

Lisa rolled her eyes. "I've already told him, thank you. Not that he believed me, but he will after tonight. I mean it this time, Julie. I've had enough."

Julie stared at her sister. "You told Dad you're breaking it off with Greg? I'm impressed. There may be hope for you yet, Lisa. But watch out for Greg's reaction when you drop the bomb on him. He's not going to take the news lightly, and you know how persuasive he can be when he puts his mind to something."

Lisa nodded soberly. "That's what I'm trying to tell you, Julie. That's why I don't want to do this over the phone where he'll try to smooth-talk me into changing my mind. If he's right there in front of me, I won't forget what a self-centered jerk he is. Believe me, I know what I'm doing and you can bet I'm not about to back down."

A familiar car horn sounded at the front of the house. "I think the object of our conversation is here for you, big sister," Julie said with a grin. "Be careful, and call me if you need me to pick you up somewhere."

"Thanks," Lisa responded calmly. "But I really don't think that will be necessary."

Julie watched as her sister stepped outside and closed the door. *I hope not,* she sighed. *But knowing you the way I do, I worry you'll give in again. Good luck, big sister. You'll need it.*

* * *

Eric whistled when he saw the elegant home where the Porsche had pulled to a stop. "Whew! That is some house. If this is where Lisa lives, no wonder she wants to keep me at arms' length. I'd be a real embarrassment for her to bring home to meet her folks if they have this kind of money. I'm out of my league here, Jason."

Jason was quick to reassure him. "You're not out of your league, Greg. Just have a little patience, and everything will work out fine. You'll see."

Eric wanted to believe Jason, but seeing this house suddenly made it a lot harder. He should have known Lisa would live in a place like this after seeing the BMW she drove. What chance did he have against Greg Reeves, if Greg truly was his rival? Greg had both the financial and social advantages to fit perfectly into this picture, while Eric felt out of place just parking across the street.

As Eric watched, he saw the figure of a young woman leave the house and walk to the Porsche. Although Eric strained to see her face, the sun had already begun to sink and what daylight was left was too dim to make her out clearly. He thought she might be Lisa—she was the right size, and her hair was the right length—but he wasn't sure. He bit his lip in concentration, watching the car lights come on as the Porsche pulled away from the house.

"I know exactly what you're thinking," Jason comforted him.

"But listen to what I'm saying. The answers to all your questions are in that Porsche. Don't lose sight of it."

* * *

Once clear of the driveway, Greg made a left turn onto Hillview Road. "What's this?" Lisa asked, breaking the silence for the first time since getting in the car. "Are we going to the mountains? I'm not really dressed for skiing. You said to dress up."

Greg answered her without taking his eyes off the road. "We're going to the North Wind Ranch," he said. "And don't worry, the dress and heels you're wearing are perfect for the evening I have planned."

"We're going to the ranch?" Lisa's surprise was evident on her face. "I've gone to the ranch with Julie before to go riding, but if that's what you had in mind, I'm not really dressed for it."

"Don't be ridiculous, Lisa," Greg scoffed. "We have more important matters to attend to tonight than riding horses. Some very important people will be there tonight, and I want you to meet them."

Lisa's voice revealed her irritation. "Oh yes, of course. Thanks to your insinuations, all your friends think of us as the happily engaged couple. We have to keep up our appearances."

"Why don't you just accept the fact that we're perfect for each other?" Greg said reasonably. "Relax and be your charming self. I want these people to see you at your very best. A politician's wife can be a very valuable asset, you know."

Unfortunately for Greg, it was the wrong thing to say. If Lisa needed something to bolster her courage to tell him like it was, this was it.

"I think you need to be looking for your 'politician's wife' elsewhere, Greg," she said firmly. "After tonight, I don't want to see you again." There, she had said it.

"What?" Greg nearly drove off the road in his surprise. "That's absurd. You know perfectly well your father isn't going to stand for you breaking up with me, not for one minute."

"I'm through listening to my father, Greg. I don't love you. I don't believe you love me—or that you even know how to love anyone besides yourself. Furthermore, the two of us have nothing in common whatsoever."

Greg shot a worried look at Lisa. He had never heard her sound so determined. "It's that Rob Jensen, isn't it? You're still pining over him, aren't you?"

Lisa frowned at the patronizing tone of Greg's voice. "Yes, I am in love with Rob, and he is in love with me. And my father can either accept Rob, or he can watch me pack my bags and walk away. My mind is made up."

It took Greg only a moment to regain his composure before he managed the condescending smile that Lisa knew so well. "No, sweetheart, I don't think so," he chided. "You won't stand up to your father. You and I both know that. You may talk a good story, but in the end you understand where your bread and butter really come from."

Lisa could see exactly where this conversation was headed, so she made a quick decision. Although her mind was made up, she decided to go along with the charade this one last time. When Greg took her home she would make her point again, as clearly as necessary. That way, at least, she would be within walking distance of her own front door.

She shrugged indifferently. "I'll give it some thought, but I'm not promising anything." Changing the subject, she asked, "So tell me, Greg, what's the big occasion tonight?"

Greg preened smugly at his companion's apparent renewed interest in their evening's plans. "Justen Phelps reserved the ranch for a fund-raising event tonight, and don't tell me you've never heard of Justen Phelps."

"I've never heard of Justen Phelps," Lisa said evenly.

Greg hit the wheel in exasperation, sending the car into a deep rut that jolted the Porsche severely. "I can't believe you, Lisa. You should make an effort to know more of what's going on in the world. Justen Phelps is a longtime friend and associate of my father. He's being primed to run for the U.S. Senate in the next election. You saw him once, at the fund-raising dinner we attended in April."

Lisa's lack of interest couldn't have been more obvious. "Wonderful. I can't wait to see him again," she said. "Who knows, I might even get his autograph."

* * *

A hundred or so yards behind the Porsche, Little Blue plugged along in relentless pursuit. "They must be headed for the ranch where Lisa and I took out the horses last week," Eric muttered. "Why would they be going there? I hope it doesn't require my getting on another horse."

"You won't have to get on a horse," Jason promised. "That much I can tell you."

Glancing at the recorder on the seat next to him, Eric decided to press his luck. Jason hadn't answered any of his earlier questions about the tape, but maybe he was ready to talk now that they'd been on the road a while. "What about this tape?" he asked. "Can you at least give me a hint what I'm going to do with it?"

"That tape," Jason said, "is very important to your future, as well as the future of a few others. I hope you have a good set of batteries in the recorder. You're going to have to play the tape a couple of times before this night is over."

"No sweat," Eric smiled as he patted his tape recorder. "I have the little pink bunny in there, and you know what the commercial says about the way he keeps on going. Hey, look," he pointed to the Porsche ahead of them. "I was right. They are turning off at the ranch. What do I do now?"

Jason's instructions were simple. "You park the car in the darkest spot you can find, and there you wait."

* * *

"Since I'm riding home with you tonight, Greg," Lisa said quietly, as the two of them entered the ranch house, "I'd appreciate it if you'd keep your distance from the bar."

Greg was still smarting from their earlier conversation. Her words had worried him and he was looking forward to a couple of stiff drinks. "C'mon, Lisa, loosen up," he said sharply. "One or two drinks have no effect on my ability to drive. It wouldn't hurt you to have a drink yourself. It might put you in a better mood."

"Forget it, Greg. By now, you should know better than to even bring up such an idea."

Greg wasn't surprised. It was one of her peculiarities that he had hoped would change as they spent more time together. "Well," he grumbled, "you could at least mingle with the guests. And put on a smile. I want to make a good impression. Everyone here thinks we're engaged, so remember that anything you do reflects on me, too."

Lisa's sigh went unnoticed by Greg, who was looking over the crowd. "I'll try not to embarrass you," she replied sweetly.

Greg was so busy scanning the guests that he missed her sarcasm. "If you'll excuse me, I have some mingling to do." Without another word, he walked away, leaving her alone.

The room was so filled with cigarette smoke, Lisa immediately began to make her way to the large double doors at the far side of the room. Stepping outside onto the patio, she took a deep breath of the fresh mountain air and leaned against the wooden rail to enjoy the beauty of the crystal clear night. Thousands of glittering stars dotted the blackness like tiny diamonds against a backdrop of pure black velvet. She marveled at the difference between this sky and the one at home where the city lights deprived it of such striking beauty.

Then another thought came to mind. In much the same way as the sky differed between two locations, so did her life differ from Greg's. Greg was in his element inside the smoke-filled house with all its crowd, noise, and commotion that came with his desires and aspirations. She was in her element out here, enjoying the clean air and peaceful quiet of the fragrant, star-filled night.

For several minutes, she remained spellbound by the beauty of it all. Then, after another deep breath, she wandered down the large stone steps to the garden just beyond the patio. A brick path leading through the garden was too inviting to pass up. After walking only a short distance, she found that nearly all traces of the loud rock music were left behind. Now the night truly was perfect, as it furnished its own music.

Believing herself alone in the garden, she was surprised when she heard a voice from the darkness near the edge of the brick path. "Hello there," came the voice.

Peering through the darkness to see who had spoken, she discovered a woman sitting alone on a bench. "Won't you join me?" the woman asked, patting her hand on the empty seat next to her. "I'm Evelyn Phelps. I'm sure you've heard of my husband, Justen Phelps."

Lisa paused a moment, then walked over to where the woman was seated. She remained standing. "I'm Lisa MacGregor. It's nice to meet you, Evelyn."

"Well, Lisa MacGregor," Evelyn said, looking up at her, "I hope you'll excuse me for not standing up. You see, I've had just a teensy weensy bit too much to drink. But then I always have a teensy weensy bit too much to drink." She squinted her eyes trying to get a better look at Lisa. "Say, aren't you the one who's engaged to Greg Reeves?" she asked.

"So rumor has it," Lisa replied.

"He's a nice boy. He has lots of pretty money and that's what makes him such a nice boy. Justen has lots of pretty money, too," the woman sighed. "Justen used to be a nice boy. Are you going to sit down?"

"I'd rather stand, if you don't mind."

Evelyn Phelps didn't seem to mind. "Do I look like a happy woman to you?" she continued. "I *am* a happy woman, you know. Are you happy, Lisa MacGregor?"

The question caught Lisa by surprise. "I—I'm not sure," she answered. "I suppose I'm happy."

"You will be happy when you marry that good boy with all the pretty money." The woman was silent for a few minutes. Lisa was getting ready to excuse herself, when Evelyn asked another question that surprised Lisa. "Does your pretty boy ever kiss you?"

"Sometimes."

"Justen used to kiss me. Not any more, though." Evelyn squinted at Lisa again and sighed. "You're a beauty, aren't you? I was beautiful once. They say I used to look like the movie star who plays that pioneer doctor on television."

"You mean Jane Seymour?"

"Yes, that's the one. I suppose I did look like her once. But then, we all have to change sometime, don't we?" Abruptly, Evelyn changed the subject. "I suppose I had better go back inside now," she said, trying to stand up. She made it only a few inches, then fell back to the bench. "On second thought, I think I'll wait a teensy bit longer."

Lisa forced a smile. "Maybe I'd better make an appearance inside. It's been interesting talking to you, Evelyn."

Inside the house, Lisa scanned the room for Greg, but before she could spot him a man approached her.

"Good evening, gorgeous lady. And who might you be?"

Lisa studied the man closely. He was at least the age of her father. He was wearing an expensive, well-tailored dark blue suit and held a glass in his hand. She answered his question with reluctance. "I'm Lisa MacGregor."

The man looked at her appraisingly. "Oh, Greg's fiancée?"

"So to speak."

"I'm Paul Foster. I see you're dry; let me get you a drink."

"No, thanks, I never indulge."

"I hope you indulge in other things," he said suggestively, looking her up and down.

"Excuse me," she responded, pushing past the man and hurrying away.

"Wait!" he cried out, but ignoring him, she moved to the far side of the room as quickly as possible. To her relief, he didn't follow.

Lisa looked around the room filled with people and felt nauseous. *Is this the kind of life my father wants for me?* she thought. *These people are all phonies. They put on their best smiles and pretend to be something they're not. Not one person in this room is as happy as I remember my mother being.*

As Lisa searched the room for Greg, she spotted him near the bar conversing with two women in very revealing cocktail dresses. As she had suspected, he was holding a glass of his own. She wouldn't be surprised if it was his second, or even his third. Slowly, she made her way through the crowd toward him.

"Greg," she said, interrupting their conversation. "I'd like to leave. Will you take me home now?"

He glared at her. "The party has only begun, Lisa. Get yourself a drink and loosen up, for crying out loud."

"Please take me home," she persisted, "or at least call a taxi for me. I can't stay in this place another minute."

Impatiently, Greg set his glass down on the bar so hard that it splashed over the side. Grabbing Lisa roughly by the arm, he pulled her away from his companions. "What's the matter with you, Lisa?" he snapped. "You're acting like a child."

"Never mind!" she said, pushing him aside. "I'll call my own taxi." Turning abruptly, she hurried away.

Greg stared after her as she made her way toward the bedroom, where she expected to find a telephone. "Excuse me, ladies," he said, turning back to his friends. "It seems I have a problem to attend to."

"What does he possibly see in a little snip like her?" one of the women said, making sure her voice was loud enough for Greg to hear as he hurried after Lisa.

Greg caught Lisa by the arm and yanked her to a stop just as she reached the bedroom door. "Go to the car. I'll take you home! I've never seen you like this, Lisa. You've embarrassed me enough for one night."

She pulled free and angrily pushed her way through the crowd to the front door. Attempting to appear in control, Greg followed, his head held high. By the time he reached the Porsche, Lisa was already snapping her shoulder harness in place. He jumped behind the wheel and slammed his door. With tires screeching, he pulled the car out of the lot and turned down Hillview Road in the direction of town.

* * *

Eric sat patiently in his old Escort station wagon, listening to an old Elvis song on the radio. It was one he had never heard before, about some guy searching for a lost lover in the cold Kentucky rain. He didn't care for the song, although it seemed somehow appropriate at the moment. Suddenly, he noticed the headlights of a car leaving the property. As it passed, he recognized the green Porsche convertible. "That's them, Jason!" he cried out. "Shall I follow them?"

"At least we can try," Jason said. "The mood that guy's in, I'm afraid he'll be pushing that car of his to the limit. You may have a challenge keeping up with him."

Eric fired up the Escort and jammed the accelerator to the floor. Jason was right—the Porsche was moving away so quickly that Little Blue was soon left in its dust. Eric's heart raced wildly as he watched the tail lights vanish into the darkness of the night. Pushing his car to the limit, he shot forward in frantic pursuit.

* * *

Greg gripped the wheel with vengeance as the car sped down

the winding mountain road. "What were you trying to pull back there?" he shouted at Lisa.

"I just had my fill of that awful mess," she answered, not hiding an ounce of her contempt. "Those people turn my stomach."

"I think it's time you get something through your head, lady. These people are my friends, and I will not allow you to embarrass me in front of them again. Do you understand me?"

"That, Greg Reeves, is the least of your worries. I'll never embarrass you again, because you and I are finished!" Lisa spoke definitely. The words hadn't been that difficult for her to say, but Greg didn't seem to be getting the message.

"Finished? I think not. I think it's time for a little talk with your father. I'll let him handle you. It's obvious I can't."

Glancing at the speedometer, Lisa saw that Greg was pushing his Porsche to nearly eighty miles per hour. "Greg, the speed limit is only forty-five miles per hour. Please slow down."

Greg merely glared at her. Clenching his jaw, he jammed the accelerator even harder to the floor while Lisa gazed in terror at the narrow road rushing toward them at frightening speed. Then suddenly, the car darted to the left of the road's center. Abruptly, Greg jerked the wheel back, causing the car to overcorrect and nearly bounce off the road to the right. Stubbornly, he refused to slow the vehicle, though it was swerving violently.

Terrified, Lisa grabbed the ignition key and switched it off. She tried to pull it out, but with the car in gear it wouldn't release. Although Greg slammed his fist repeatedly against her hand, she held onto the key with her last ounce of strength and finally the car began to slow down. As the speedometer needle approached twenty miles an hour, Greg managed to get her hand off the key, but before he could restart the engine, she grabbed the shift lever and jammed it into park. Instantly the front wheels locked and the car skidded to an abrupt stop.

Lisa's seat belt held her firmly in place, but Greg, who as usual had not taken the time to fasten his belt, was thrown forward into the windshield. Before he could regain his senses, Lisa had the keys out of the ignition. Jumping from the car, she threw them as far as she could into the darkness, then broke into a run in the direction of town. Her lungs were giving out when she heard heavy footsteps behind her. A moment later, she felt his hand gripping her arm.

* * *

In the excitement of the moment, Eric had completely forgotten that Jason was even there. All he could think of was Lisa in the hands of a maniac like Greg as he pushed the old Ford to its limit. His mouth was dry and his head was throbbing as he strained to see into the darkness ahead. Just when he thought he could stand it no longer, he saw a pair of tail lights barely visible in the distance. As he sped on, he soon realized the vehicle ahead was motionless. And not much later, he saw that it was indeed Greg's Porsche.

Eric could see Greg and the woman he hoped was Lisa at the far edge of the car lights. Greg was shaking her violently. In the midst of screeching rubber and flying dirt, Little Blue skidded to a stop. In two bounds Eric had reached them. Grabbing Greg by the hair of his head, he whirled him away from Lisa and flung him face down to the ground. Lisa broke free and dashed into the darkness.

Shouting and swearing, Greg was up and running after her, but with little effort Eric overtook him, throwing him down once again. Greg struggled to his feet and swung a fist at Eric, who easily managed to duck the punch.

"Hey, pal," Eric cried, grabbing Greg's arm and twisting it painfully behind his back. "You seem to like picking on women. Let's see how well you do against another man." In an instant, Greg's face was shoved against the grimy, black pavement with Eric's knee hard against his back.

Greg continued to struggle for a few more seconds before he finally appeared to realize that he was beaten. When he was still, Eric reached down with his free hand and removed one of Greg's shoes, tossing it to the side of the road. He then did the same with the other shoe, tossing it in the opposite direction.

"This is certainly a side of you I've never seen before, Greg," he snapped.

"Who are you?" Greg demanded. "How do you know my name?"

"I'm Eric Roberts. You know, the guy who keeps your computer working. That is, I *used* to keep it working. You can get someone else next time. I'm particular about whose computer I work on."

"Eric Roberts?" Greg shouted. "Well, you'd better let me up, Roberts, or I'll see to it you never work again."

Eric had long since lost his respect for Greg or his father. "Don't be too sure about that, Greg old boy," he said. "You may not know it, but I have an angel on my side. You're the one who may be on the verge of losing it all."

"You're insane! Let me up this instant!"

"I'll let you up," Eric said, getting up and hurrying back to Little Blue. "But don't expect me to offer you a lift back to town. That's your problem."

Less than a minute later, Eric had pulled alongside the running woman.

"Get in!" he yelled, bringing the car to a stop next to her. As soon as she realized the driver wasn't Greg, Lisa yanked open the door and leapt inside, and the two sped off toward town.

Eric could hardly see her face in the darkness. "Lisa, is it you?" he asked hopefully.

"Yes," she said, puffing, still out of breath, "I'm Lisa. But—who are you?"

Eric reached for the dome light and switched it on. His heart went numb. "I—I'm sorry. I thought you were someone else."

"I don't know who you thought I was, but I'm glad you came along when you did. You may have just saved my life."

After taking a moment to clear his head, Eric concluded it might be good to introduce himself. "I'm Eric Roberts," he told her.

She responded with a smile. "It's a pleasure to know you, Eric. I'm Lisa MacGregor."

Confused and disappointed, Eric voiced his frustration. "I don't understand. I was sure you were her. All the pieces fit perfectly."

Lisa studied Eric closely, still trying to catch her breath. "You called me by my name. Can I assume the woman you mistook me for is also named Lisa?" she asked.

"Yes," he sighed. "Her name is Lisa, too." Then changing the subject, he asked, "Are you hurt? That guy wasn't playing around back there."

"I'm fine," Lisa replied. "A little shaken up, but other than that, I'm fine, thanks to you."

"Well, Lisa MacGregor, as long as you're in my car, where would you like me to take you?"

She thought about it a moment. "I'm not sure, Eric," she said. "You can't believe how badly things are twisted up in my life right now."

Eric drew in his breath and made a decision. "Let me guess, the guy you were just with is Greg Reeves. Your father wants you to marry him, but apparently you don't love him."

Lisa's expression turned to one of surprise. "How do you know all that?" she asked.

"It's time, Eric," Jason broke in. "You have to find a way to get her to listen to the tape. Believe me, if you ever want to find your Lisa, you have to get this Lisa to listen to the tape." Eric gave Jason a slight nod to let him know he understood. He would play the tape just as soon as the right opportunity presented itself. "Before I go into how I know about you, Lisa, let me tell you a few more things that I know. Your father doesn't go by his name; rather, he goes by his initials, which are J.T. Your mother's name is Katherine, and she almost married another man several years ago. Am I right?"

"Yes, you are exactly right. But how . . . ?"

"I'll bet you didn't know the man she almost married was Greg's father, did you?"

Lisa's eyes opened wide. "No, I didn't know that. My father doesn't even know that. How do you know all this, Eric? Are you a detective?"

"No," Eric answered, chuckling. "I'm not a detective. At least I wasn't one until tonight. I'm just an electrical engineer who got caught up in all this while trying to find a very wonderful woman named Lisa."

Lisa was a little bewildered, but for some reason she couldn't explain she accepted Eric for who he said he was. "I'd sure like to know more about what's going on here," she said. "Could we go somewhere and talk?"

Eric knew that would give him an opportunity to play the tape for her. "Sure," he said. "Are you hungry?"

"No, but a cold drink sounds inviting."

"I know just the place, if you like lemonade."

"You have no idea how good that sounds."

In the back seat of Little Blue, Jason leaned back and smiled. He knew Sam would be pleased at the way he was handling his part of this assignment. But then, what could she expect? After all, he was the one with all the experience in these matters.

CHAPTER 16

Benny set two lemonades on the table, one for Lisa and the other for Eric. "You know, pal," came his offhand observation. "For a guy who never dates much, you really take the cake. Not only do you suddenly start showing up at my place with these gorgeous women, but they all have the same name."

"Don't you have something to do?" Eric asked gruffly. "Or am I the only customer who ever comes into your place?"

"I have plenty to do," Benny shot back. "In fact, I happen to have a huge catering job on tap for tomorrow night. So as much as I'd like to stay here and talk with you, I've got work to do, so you'll just have to excuse me."

"It breaks my heart, Benny, but I'll live with it."

With a wink of his eye and a tip of his hat, Benny was off to the kitchen leaving Eric and the real Lisa MacGregor to their own discussion. Stirring her icy lemonade slowly, Lisa said, "I take it you brought your Lisa here, too?"

"It was our first date," Eric replied. "I can see why Benny is confused. You not only have her name, but it's uncanny how much you resemble her. You could almost be her sister."

"Well, Eric, I do have a sister, but I can assure you that my parents didn't name us both Lisa. There's something I don't understand, though. Why did you mistake me for this other Lisa up there on the mountain?"

"It's a long story," Eric sighed. "You see, Lisa—that is, the other Lisa—has some problems that she refused to share with me. She never told me where she lives, or gave me a phone number where I could call her, or anything. I don't even know her last name."

"I hate to be the one to break up this delightful little conversation," Jason interrupted. "But if you don't play that tape we're never going to get this show to center stage."

Eric paused for a moment, then motioned to the recorder on the table. "I suppose you're wondering why I brought this along?" he asked Lisa.

"The thought had occurred to me, yes," she said brightly.

"This tape," he explained apologetically, "concerns you, and your family. I'm a little embarrassed for you to hear it. I hope it doesn't give you the idea I make a habit out of sticking my nose into other people's business. I've never done anything like this before in my life. It's just that I was desperate to . . ."

"To find your Lisa?" she asked.

"Exactly."

Lisa studied Eric's eyes closely. There was a softness there that she was certain could mean only one thing. "You're in love with her, aren't you, Eric?"

Eric swallowed hard and fumbled with the strap on the recorder. "I've only known her a short time," he shyly confessed. "I've never been in love before, and I'm not sure what it's supposed to be like. But if what I feel for her isn't love, it feels pretty darn close."

Thoughts of Rob and feelings of her own came to mind. "You're in love, all right," she said. "I do know what love feels like, and I can tell from what you're saying you've got a heavy dose of it."

"The tape recording," Jason prompted.

"I made the recording earlier this evening," Eric explained. "A friend of mine talked me into it. He said it would help me find my Lisa. The recording contains a conversation between Greg and his father. Your name came up, and I just assumed—well, you know. Then after I'd made the tape, I saw your name on Greg's rear license plate. I followed him to your place, where he picked you up."

Lisa was beginning to get the picture. "You followed us to the ranch," she said. "That's how you happened to be there to save me from Greg."

"You have to understand—"

"That you thought I was this other Lisa. Yes, Eric. I do understand."

Eric shook his head in disbelief. "All the pieces fit together so perfectly. In the darkness you even looked like her. How was I to know I was following the wrong Lisa? My gosh, I figured since I had met her in Greg's office in the first place—"

"Wait a minute!" Lisa broke in, a gleam appearing in her eyes. "You say you met your Lisa in Greg's office? She didn't happen to be a substitute secretary at the time, did she?"

Eric looked hopeful. "Yes, she was. Are you saying you might know who she is?"

Lisa started laughing. "Yes, I think I might know who your mystery woman is. Unless I miss my guess, I know her as well as I know my own sister. You don't by chance have a picture of her, do you?"

Eric yanked out his wallet. "Here!" he said, hurriedly handing her the picture taken at the county fair. "This is Lisa. Do you recognize her?"

Lisa looked at the picture and broke out laughing again.

"Hey," Eric said, a little embarrassed by her laughter. "It wasn't my idea to wear that suit, and besides, I don't think I look that funny."

"Eric," she said, reaching across the table to give his hand a pat. "You can put your mind at ease. I know who your Lisa is, and I know why she's kept you in the dark about a few things. In fact, she's kept me in the dark, too. I had no idea she was seeing someone. Boy, am I going to make her pay for this one."

"You know her?" Eric nearly shouted. "Will you take me to her?"

"Well now, I don't know if I can do that," Lisa said. "But I can probably convince her to call you. Will that do for the moment?"

Disappointment filled Eric's eyes. "You won't tell me where to find her?"

"I'm sorry, Eric. I really am, but I promise to have her call you right away. She does know your number, I assume."

"Play the tape, Eric," Jason insisted, a little louder this time. "I guarantee it will change her mind on the matter. After she hears the tape, she'll take you to your Lisa in a heartbeat."

This was all the prompting Eric needed. "I think you should listen to this tape, Lisa," he said. "There are things on it you should be aware of. And so should your father."

Lisa eyed the recorder curiously. "Okay," she said. "If you think it's that important, let's give it a listen."

Eric drew a deep breath, and pressed the "Play" button.

* * *

"You can't go," Samantha said sternly.

J.T. shot an angry glance in Samantha's direction. "What do you mean I can't go?" he huffed. "I like walking in the park. That's where I do my best thinking. And that's where I feel closest to my Katie."

"I know, Uncle Mac," Samantha responded soothingly. "And Aunt Katie likes to walk with you there, too. She told me so. But we have other more pressing business to take care of tonight."

"Blast you, Sam!" J.T. grumbled. "You keep talking about Katie like she was just in the next room. If what you say is true, bring her here and let me see her."

"I'd love to bring her here to see you and I know she'd love that, too. But rules are rules, and as I've already explained to you, she couldn't qualify for a temporary pass."

Slipping into his jacket, J.T. nevertheless headed for the door. "I'm going for a walk in the park, and there's nothing you can do about it, Sam."

He was halfway to the door when her words brought him to an abrupt stop. "You say you want me to go away and stop haunting you? Well if you stay here and finish the business I have planned for tonight, I give you my word to do just that. But if you walk out of this house, I give you my word just as strongly that I'll stay with you and haunt you the rest of your life."

Narrowing his eyes, J.T. gave Samantha a sharp look. "You're not lying to me, Sam? If I stay at home tonight, you'll stop pressuring me about my daughters? You'll go back to your cloud and leave me alone?"

Samantha smiled and folded her arms. "You have my word, Uncle. But one way or the other, you're not about to miss the show I have planned for tonight. Even if I have go get Gus to handcuff you, or something. Now why don't you sit down and watch some TV for a change. It won't kill you."

"I don't like watching television," he snapped. "Too many ridiculous angel shows."

"Then go count your money, or something. Just don't leave the house."

J.T. considered joining Julie in the family room, but he dismissed the idea. He could hear the music she was listening to, and he wanted no part of it; it reminded him too much of Rob Jensen. In disgust, he went to his study, where he ended up watching a rerun of an old Michael Landon angel show. At least he could get rid of this angel by pressing the "Off" button on the remote any time he chose.

* * *

Too stunned for words, Lisa sat staring at the tape recorder long after it had been turned off. At last, she gathered her thoughts enough to speak. "I always knew Greg's father was no good," she mused aloud. "But I never supposed anything like this. The man's carried his grudge for more than twenty-five years, and now he wants to destroy my father. The whole thing is sick, Eric."

Eric nodded his agreement. "Now you see why I hesitated to play the tape. Maybe I shouldn't have."

"No, I'm glad you did. Believe me, it's for the best. Do you have any idea who the man is that Edward talked about blowing up with the warehouse?"

"I haven't a clue. You heard the tape. All I know is what's recorded there."

Lisa gave Eric a thoughtful look as a plan began to formulate in her mind. She knew the tape had to be played for her father, and it had to be done quickly while there was still time for him to back out of the deal with Ed Reeves. Her father's reputation depended on it. And even worse than losing his money and his reputation, he was about to be framed for a murder.

Lisa foresaw another problem, too. Evidently, her little sister had gone to great lengths to keep Eric away from their father. After what J.T. had done with Rob, Lisa thought that was perfectly understandable. But Lisa was sure that after she played the tape for her father, he would most certainly have a change of heart. Even if he didn't, Lisa was pretty sure that her sister would never let J.T. treat her and Eric as he had Lisa and Rob. So Lisa made a decision. She would take both Eric and the tape home to her father and her little sister.

Just then, Lisa had a mischievous thought. In the past, Julie had always been quick to play pranks on Lisa, whenever an opportunity had presented itself. *Why not turn the tables on her for once?* Julie thought with a grin. *After all, she did use my name as a part of her little ploy to keep Eric from knowing who she really is. I can understand why she kept Eric tucked away from Dad—but she didn't even tell me!* The old Lisa would never have dared to pull a stunt like this, but the new Lisa that gave Greg Reeves the old heave-ho found the idea quite intriguing.

"I've changed my mind, Eric," she said. "I'd like to take you to your Lisa tonight. Right now, in fact. But only if you agree to play out a little gag with me."

In the last twenty-four hours, Eric had agreed to do a lot of things he never could have imagined he'd do willingly. Now he felt he was up to anything. "What do you want me to do?" he asked eagerly.

"All right," Lisa said. "Let me give you a little background on what you've gotten yourself into, then I'll lay out my plan."

For the next several minutes, Lisa described her situation to Eric. She told him about Rob and how her father had maneuvered him out of her life, and how her father was determined for her to marry Greg. She explained the contract for the super mall, and even before she was finished, Eric realized he had stumbled onto a much more complicated plot than he had supposed.

For the moment, Lisa was careful not to mention her sister, Julie. For this bit of news, Eric would just have to wait a little longer. Then, after she had finished explaining, she laid out her plan. Although Eric had been quick to agree to help with her prank, once he learned what she had in mind, he wished he had taken more time to think it over.

"You want me . . . to marry you?" he asked slowly. "You're proposing to me right here at Benny's Pizza Parlor?"

Lisa shook her head. "Not a real marriage, silly. Just a pretend marriage, so I can prove a point to my father, and to my—uh . . . that is, to another person who's involved."

"But I don't get it. Why would you want to make your father think we're married?"

"Because I think he needs to learn a lesson about tinkering with my life. It may also shake him up a bit so he'll be more receptive when we play the tape for him. So, are you game?"

Eric sighed and brushed back his hair with his hand. "You leave me little choice, Lisa. I guess I'll just have to marry you. But I insist on a prenuptial agreement. All rights to Little Blue are off in the deal."

"You drive a hard bargain, Eric, but I agree. Now I need to make a quick phone call. Does your friend Benny have a phone?"

* * *

Julie set the popcorn bowl aside and turned down the stereo to answer the phone next to the sofa where she sat. "Hello?"

"Julie? It's me, Lisa."

"Lisa? What's wrong?" Julie asked anxiously.

"Everything's okay," Lisa assured her. "I had some problems earlier, but I'm fine now. Where's Father? He's not where he can hear, is he?"

"Are you kidding? He's the same place he always is—in his study."

"Listen, Julie, I've hit on a gold mine of information tonight that's guaranteed to change Father's mind on a few things. And more than this, I met this guy—"

"You met a guy?" Julie interrupted, suddenly more interested in the conversation. "Who is he? How did you meet him? What about Greg? What about Rob, for goodness' sake?"

"Julie, will you be still a minute and let me finish what I'm trying to tell you? This guy has a tape recording that will knock your socks off, not to mention what it will do to Father."

"A tape recording? What sort of tape recording?"

"You'll just have to wait and see. I'll let you hear the tape at the same time Father hears it. Only I don't want him to know you're listening."

"What do you want me to do, hide outside the door?"

"That's exactly what I want you to do. I'm going to bring this guy by the house and put on a little show for Father. Then after I get him softened up for the big punch, I'll play the tape."

"What about this guy you mentioned?" Julie asked, curious. "How long have you been seeing him? Are you serious enough about him to forget about Rob?"

Lisa's laughter filled Julie's ear. "I haven't known him long at all," she said. "But this much I can truthfully say—this guy thinks Lisa MacGregor walks on water. And I don't mean Lake Michigan in December, either. I've never seen anyone more in love. There's no way—and I do mean no way—Father could ever get to this guy."

"Lisa, no! You're not going to bring him home to meet Dad?"

"Oh yes I am! And if you don't like the idea now, you're really going to hate it when you see him. But honest, I think everything's going to work out just fine for both of us. Will you trust me on this one? I know what I'm doing."

"Lisa, this is crazy. I can't stand the thought of you setting yourself up to be hurt again."

"Believe me, Julie. The difference this time is the tape. Once Father hears this tape, everything is going to change. My only fear is his reaction when he hears it. He could have a heart attack."

"No need to worry about that, big sister. When it comes to bringing home the guy *we* like, Dad has no heart."

"Well, things are going to be different after tonight, I promise. Now I need a promise from you. I need you to promise me that regardless of what you may see or hear when I come in with this guy, you won't interfere. I want you out of sight and quiet, but don't you dare miss one detail of what goes on in Father's study. Do I have your promise?"

"I don't like this, Lisa. I don't like it one bit."

You have no idea how much you're going to dislike it later, Lisa thought but only said, "I know what I'm doing. Please, give me your promise."

"Okay, you have my promise. I won't interfere," Julie said reluctantly.

"Now don't you dare go back on your word. If you've ever trusted me in your life, little sister, trust me now."

CHAPTER 17

It was nearly nine o'clock when Eric brought his car to a stop in front of the MacGregor home. This time, however, he parked in the driveway instead of across the street, as he had done earlier that evening. "Boy, do I feel out of place here," he complained.

Lisa gave him a sympathetic look. "Much as I hate to admit it, my father would think you're out of place here, too, Eric. But he's about to have a change of heart—once he hears your tape, that is. Now, do you think you're a good enough actor to pull off this little show I've set up?"

Eric switched off the ignition. "I'll play my role okay, but I hope you're planning to keep your part of the bargain, too."

Lisa smiled. "Not to worry, Eric. Your Lisa will be in your arms before the nightly news hits Channel 5. Trust me."

The two of them left the car and started toward the house. "Remember," Lisa reminded him. "Don't mention the tape until I bring it up. In fact, let me have the recorder. I'll keep it in my purse."

Eric handed her the recorder. "You got it. This is your show; we'll do it your way."

As they neared the house, Lisa glanced around for signs of Greg's Porsche. "Good," she said. "There's no sign of Greg. I was hoping we'd get here ahead of him."

"Are you kidding me?" Eric asked in surprise. "You think Greg will show up here after the way we humiliated him?"

"The minute he figures out a way to get here," Lisa assured him. When Eric looked at her questioningly, she added, "I threw his car keys away back on the mountain."

"You did what?" Eric laughed. "I'd sure hate to get you mad at me. Just for your information, I tossed his shoes away."

"You did what? All right, Eric!" As Lisa inserted the key in the door and twisted the lock, she took a deep breath. *I think my sister has fallen in love with the right guy. And speaking of Julie, I wonder where she is? I don't see a sign of her. I sure hope she doesn't blow this whole thing when she realizes I have Eric with me.*

* * *

At the sound of a car pulling up to the house, Julie hurried to the living room where she parted the drapes and peered outside at the two approaching figures. In less than a heartbeat, she understood why Lisa had been so persistent about getting her to promise not to interfere. The guy she was bringing home was Eric. "No!" she gasped. "Lisa, how could you?"

In two bounds she was at the door, ready to fling it open.

"No!" Samantha cried out. "Don't do it, Julie. Listen to what I've been trying to tell you. Trust your sister. She knows what she's doing."

"I'd sure like to know what she's doing," Julie grumbled to herself. *That's the guy I'm in love with out there. She's bringing him here to meet Dad. After all my efforts to prevent this very disaster from occurring, now my own sister is ruining everything!*

"The coat closet!" Samantha said. "Hide in the closet NOW!"

Julie could hear the key in the lock. Gathering up more courage than she thought possible, she darted into the coat closet and pulled the door closed except for a small crack. From there she watched as her sister and Eric stepped inside.

"So help me, Lisa MacGregor," she threatened. "If you make a mess of things, I'll kill you. No, I'll do worse than that. I'll burn everything in your closet."

* * *

"Let me do the talking," Lisa whispered as she led Eric toward her father's study. "You just go along with my story, okay?" Eric nodded silently.

As she had supposed, J.T. was inside, although she was a little disconcerted to see him watching TV instead of perusing contracts and business proposals. "Hello, Father," she said, catching his attention. "You look tired. Have you had a bad evening?"

"You're darn right I have," J.T. grumbled. He added to himself, *And it's all because of this hardheaded niece of mine who thinks she's an angel.*

Then J.T. noticed Eric. Switching off the set, he stood and approached the two of them.

"I don't believe we've met, young man," he said coldly. "Are you a friend of Greg's?"

Lisa slid her arm through Eric's and smiled sweetly. "No, Father," she said, enjoying every second of her newfound courage. "This is Eric Roberts, your new son-in-law. Isn't he cute? Especially his eyes. Ahhhh—" she sighed. "It was those dreamy eyes that first won my heart."

"Is this your idea of a joke, Lisa?" J.T. choked.

"A joke? You accuse me of making a joke? I'm Lisa, Father, not Julie. I just decided that if I couldn't marry Rob, I might as well find someone else just as good. This time I was smart enough to keep him from you until it was too late. And you know one of the best things about it? I won't ever have to go out with Greg Reeves again. What do you think about that, Father?"

J.T. went suddenly pale. "Are you saying you've eloped?"

"Yes, Father. Isn't it romantic? Sort of like you and Mother."

"I wish I could take your picture, Uncle Mac," Samantha added. "If ever there was a Kodak moment, this is it. The look on your face is priceless. And Lisa's right, don't you think? Eric does have nice eyes."

"I won't put up with this!" J.T. shouted at Lisa. "I won't have you bringing some young fool into my house telling me you've eloped with him. I'll have it annulled. And while we're at it, where's Greg?"

"Greg? Oh yes, I almost forgot about him. The last I saw of him he was having a little car trouble up on Hillview Road. But that's his problem now. After all, I'm a married woman. I can't be fooling around with single guys anymore."

At that moment Lisa caught a glimpse of Julie's astonished face peering around the corner of the open door. This was the moment she was waiting for. After a smile and a wink at Julie, she turned to Eric and kissed him. She had fully expected him to pull away, but she was ready for him and pulled him into a tight squeeze. Then she released him and gazed happily into his eyes. "That, Eric Roberts, is for being a great guy. You kept your part of the bargain, now it's my turn to keep mine. Okay, little sister, you can come in now."

"What are you doing kissing my guy!?" Julie cried, rushing to Eric and pulling him away from her sister. "And what's all this nonsense about your being married?"

Lisa giggled. "Relax, little sister. He's all yours. I just had to make sure he was a good enough kisser for you, that's all. And believe me, he passed the test."

Eric's jaw dropped. "Lisa? Is it really you?" he gasped. "But this is Lisa, and if she's your sister . . . ?"

"Confusing, isn't it?" the real Lisa spoke up. "It would seem my little sister has been borrowing more than my best clothes lately, Eric. She borrowed my name, as well. You'd better get used to calling her Julie, because I want my name back. I've grown very accustomed to it over the years."

"Will someone please tell me what's going on around here?!" J.T. stormed. "Who's supposed to be in love with who? And who's married to who? And what happened to Greg Reeves?"

"Oh, be quiet, Uncle Mac," Samantha scolded, "and let these kids enjoy their moment."

"This guy is all mine, Dad," Julie said, pulling Eric to her and giving him a kiss of her own. "And you might just as well get used to him being around because I plan to hang onto him pretty darn tight from here on out. And as for you, Eric," she added with a finger waving under his nose. "Don't you ever let me catch you kissing my pushy sister again. Do you hear me?"

"I didn't kiss her," Eric stammered. "She kissed me."

"Well, you enjoyed it! I was watching, remember. Go ahead, I dare you to deny that you enjoyed it."

Samantha could see that J.T. was ready to blow up, so she decided to take control of the situation quickly. "You don't know yet how glad you should be to have such a great prospective son-in-law as Eric," she said to J.T. "But you're going to realize it in just a few minutes. Jason," she turned to her husband. "Let's get on with the show, so my Uncle Mac can finally get his priorities in line. Why don't you get Eric to play the tape for Uncle Mac?"

"Who are you talking to?" J.T. asked Samantha, before he remembered that the others in the room didn't know she was there.

"I'm talking to my husband, Jason," Samantha explained. "You can't see him, of course, but he's right here beside me."

"Who are *we* talking to, Father?" Lisa asked, staring at J.T. in surprise. "I think the better question would be who are *you* talking to?"

J.T. glanced around to see everyone in the room staring at him. "Oh, what's the difference?" he grumbled. "You might as well know. I'm being haunted by a stubborn angel. I have been for a few weeks now."

"You can see Jason, too?" Eric burst in. "I thought I was the only one he showed himself to."

J.T. wasn't ready to accept Eric as his prospective son-in-law just yet, and Eric's question didn't endear him to J.T. "What are you talking about, young man? I didn't say anything about a Jason."

"No, sir, you didn't. But when you mentioned an angel, I just—"

"J.T. can't see or hear me, Eric," Jason hurriedly explained. "He's referring to my wife, Sam. She's the angel who's been working with him."

"Oh," Eric responded, his confusion clearing. "You can't see Jason, Mr. MacGregor, but you've been working with his wife, Sam."

"How do you know my angel's name?" J.T. asked suspiciously. "I didn't mention her name."

Lisa stared first at her father and then at the young man she had brought home this evening. "What on earth are the two of you talking about?" she asked pointedly. "Who's Jason? And who's Sam?" When the two men didn't answer right away, Lisa had a peculiar thought. "You aren't talking about Cousin Sam, are you, Father?"

Since J.T. seemed to be having difficulty speaking, Eric was the one who answered Lisa. "Jason is an angel," he said with a sheepish smile. "He's been working with me most of today. He's the one who put me up to recording the meeting between Greg and his father."

Julie stared at Eric. "First it's car gremlins, now it's angels?"

"The car gremlins were strictly imaginary," Eric explained. "Jason is real. And he led me here to you."

"He did?"

"Yes, and he's standing right over there."

Julie looked in the direction Eric was pointing, but she saw nothing. "And my dad sees an angel, too?" she asked, looking at both men in disbelief.

"Jason tells me his wife, Sam, has been working with J.T. I can't see her, though."

"Sam?" Julie turned to her father. "You've been working with an angel named Sam?" she asked. "She wouldn't by chance be—"

"Yes, by thunder." J.T. bellowed, who had been struggling to contain his frustration ever since Lisa first came through his door with Eric. "Your Cousin Sam has been haunting the socks off me, and I'm getting pretty tired of it!"

"Cousin Sam is here?" Lisa burst out. "Then that explains it." She looked at Julie. "We really have been feeling her near us, Julie."

"I've had enough of this!" J.T. shouted. "I want some answers, and I want them now! And you all might as well get it through your heads that I'm not accepting this young pup into the family. So he might as well go on home."

"Oh," Lisa responded. "With me it was Rob, with Julie it's Eric. You really do have your hands full trying to run our lives, don't you, Father?"

"Young lady, I will not—"

Samantha stepped directly in front of J.T. "Be quiet," she said. "There's a tape you need to listen to before we go any further. Jason, get your boy to play the tape."

"Stay out of this, Sam!" J.T. warned. "This is between my daughters and me."

"It's time to play the tape, Eric," Jason directed him.

Eric turned to Lisa. "I know I agreed not to mention the tape until you picked the time, but I think the time is here. Your father needs to hear it."

Lisa pulled the recorder from her purse. "You're right, Eric," she agreed. "Here, Father. I think you had better listen to this. And you'd better sit down first."

J.T. stared blankly at the recorder in Lisa's hand, but made no attempt to take it from her.

"Take the recorder and listen to the tape," Samantha persisted. "There are some things recorded there that you need to hear, Uncle Mac. And I agree with your daughter. It would be best if you sit down before listening to it."

"I don't need to hear anything this young pup brings into my house," J.T. grumbled.

Samantha smiled. "You will, unless you want me around for another twenty years, or so. Now be a good little uncle, and listen to the tape."

J.T. reluctantly took the recorder from Lisa, and all eyes in the room were on him as he turned it on. As it began, he remained standing near the desk. The stubborn look on his face quickly changed to one of interest as he realized the voices on the recording were Greg and his father, Big Ed. He gave Eric a questioning glance, obviously wondering how Eric had gained access to this tape, then turned his full attention to Big Ed's words, which were coming across loud and clear.

"What I intend to tell you today is going to come as a shock. This is something I've never told any living person. As I said, I expect you to keep these things to yourself. No one is ever to know any of it."

The corners of J.T.'s lips curled into a sly grin. He evidently assumed he was about to learn some information that might prove to be useful. His grin grew even larger as Big Ed brought the conversation around to a more personal level for J.T.

"Why do you suppose I've navigated the project on the super mall and brought in J.T. MacGregor?"

"I never understood why, because I've never seen you dabble in real estate before. I just figured you had your reasons. To tell you the truth, it didn't bother me that you were helping J.T. make a few bucks. I sort of like the old boy. He's on my side with Lisa, you know."

J.T. glanced at Lisa, who felt almost felt sorry for him, knowing what was coming next. The sound of Big Ed's fist striking Greg's desk came sharply from the tape. Big Ed's voice turned bitter as he chastised his son with words that removed the grin from J.T.'s face.

"Don't ever let me hear you say you like that old fool. If you're a son of mine, you'll learn to hate him the way I hate him."

J.T.'s mouth fell open. Still staring at the recorder, he reached over, pulled his chair from his desk and nearly fell into it, holding the desk as if holding on to a lifeline.

"But—I thought you . . . that is, you sought him out to do business with you. I thought you must like him."

"That's exactly what I wanted you to think. And that's what I wanted MacGregor to think. I learned a long time ago, son, it's always best to profess cooperation. That way you can usually catch the other guy with his guard down, and slit his throat clean through—just as I plan on slitting MacGregor's throat."

Then came the unveiling of the greatest shocker of all.

"When you first started seeing Lisa MacGregor," Ed's voice continued from the tape, "the name MacGregor stirred something long buried in the tunnels of my memory. I couldn't put my finger on where I had heard his name, so I hired a detective to check him out. What I learned astounded me. You had somehow become involved with the daughter of a man who had crossed paths with me years ago. A man I've hated passionately ever since. You see, son, I was once engaged to marry the woman who later became Lisa's mother."

CHAPTER 18

Ed Reeves smiled as he looked over the documents on the mall project one last time in anticipation of his final meeting with J.T. in the morning. He was certain the documents were in order, but one last check couldn't hurt. Page by page he examined them carefully, as if life itself depended on each one. Suddenly, he was interrupted by a strange sound near the door to his office. Glancing up, he was shocked to see that his trusted bodyguard Hank had apparently drifted off to sleep and had fallen to the floor. Even before Big Ed had time to react to this, he saw that Lou, the other bodyguard on duty, was also lying on the floor as if asleep.

If this wasn't bad enough, Big Ed also realized that an intruder had apparently entered his office, having somehow managed to avoid being detected by the numerous alarms in the building. As if oblivious to the personal danger of approaching Edward Reeves in this manner, the man was smiling like he owned the world. Ed had no way of knowing it, but he was about to cross paths with someone far different than anyone he had ever encountered before.

"In case yer wonderin' what happened ta yer stooges," Gus said matter-of-factly. "I just sorta gave 'em a nudge. They looked like they could use a little nap, and I figured—what the heck?"

Ed quickly pulled a nine millimeter automatic pistol from his upper right-hand desk drawer and pointed it at Gus. "I have no idea who you are or how you got in my office," he said menacingly. "But I think you'll find it was the greatest mistake of your life." Ed stood and, while pointing the gun at Gus, moved around the desk to face him. "On the floor," he demanded, "and spread 'em wide."

"Sorry, pal," Gus responded. "I'm not in the mood fer a nap myself. And besides, we have things ta talk about. I'd rather remain standin', if ya don't mind."

"I do mind," Ed bellowed. "Now get on the floor or you'll get a taste of lead."

Gus's smile grew even larger. "A taste of lead?" he asked with a touch of humor. "I think ya must mean a taste of Hershey's chocolate. That is what yer holdin', isn't it? A gun made of Hershey's chocolate?"

Ed wasn't worried as he gave a quick glance at the gun in his hand, but to his absolute astonishment, he discovered Gus was right. It was made of chocolate. "What . . . how . . . this is impossible!"

"Nah, it was simple really. You should see me turn a shotgun into a banana. That's a neat trick, too. Now listen, pal, we got some business ta take care of here, so if ya don't mind—I'd sorta like ta get on with it. Oh, and if ya think yer friends might still be packin' a piece, ya can ferget that one, too. I gave 'em both plastic squirt guns. Plastic is cheap. I slipped in yer chocolate model just fer effect, but they don't give chocolate away, ya know. And since the whole thing comes out of my budget . . ."

Ed paid no heed to what Gus was saying. Rushing first to Hank, he was aghast to discover his shoulder holster actually did contain nothing more than a red plastic squirt gun. Next, he checked for Lou's gun, which he found to be an orange water gun. Looking back at Gus, he growled, "You won't get away with this! Cheap magic acts belong on the stage, not in my office." He reached into his blazer pocket and grabbed what he thought was his specially designed cellular phone. Holding it up for Gus to see, he said, "One push of this red button, and I'll have a dozen men in here with guns that shoot something more than water or jelly beans. Now do as I say— face down on the floor in a spread-eagle."

Gus didn't bat an eye. "That phone yer holdin'? Take a close look at it, pal. I think yer gonna be in fer a bit of a shock. I'd especially suggest ya look at the name engraved on the little brass plate on the back."

Ed glanced at the phone. To his chagrin, he discovered it wasn't his own special cell phone at all. It was—but no, that was impossible. He had sent J.T.'s phone with the boys to be planted at the scene of the planned warehouse explosion.

"Sorta upsettin' isn't it?" Gus grinned. "I mean, after all the plannin' ya did ta get that phone where it could be used as evidence against my good friend J.T., there it is right inside yer own coat pocket. Isn't it great when all the details of a plan come together? Now think about it, pal. If the phone yer holdin' is the one that's supposed ta be at the warehouse, where do ya suppose yer phone is right about now? Ya don't suppose . . . ?"

"My phone?!" Ed gasped in horror. "It must have been taken to the warehouse by mistake." Ed went suddenly silent as he realized what he was saying in front of a potentially dangerous witness.

Gus shrugged. "Hey, pal, ya don't hafta clam up on my account. I know all about yer plan ta blow up the warehouse with Rob Jensen inside. And yes, yer right in assumin' the phone that got planted at the scene was yours. What do ya suppose the cops will think when it's your phone they find there?"

Great beads of perspiration formed on Ed's forehead as he contemplated the situation. "Here," Gus said, tossing a set of keys across the room to him. "You can take the limousine, but ya'll hafta drive yerself, pal. It seems the rest of yer crew are just as laid out as these two guys here. I'd think long and hard about handin' out any bonuses the next time their personnel reviews come up."

Just as suddenly as he had appeared, Gus was gone. Ed was completely stunned, but his naturally strong sense of self-preservation asserted itself. One quick glance at his sleeping body guards told him he couldn't rely on them for any help. He looked in disgust at the chocolate gun on the floor, then at the phone in one hand, and the set of keys in the other. He had little doubt that the slippery intruder had been telling the truth about the others being asleep, too.

This whole impossible scene would have been ludicrous if it hadn't been for the threatening possibility that his personal phone might well be at the warehouse. The only thing Ed Reeves was sure about following his encounter with the mysterious intruder was that he had to retrieve his phone at all costs. Even if that meant driving the car himself—something he hadn't done in more years than he cared to admit.

CHAPTER 19

J.T.'s hand shook noticeably as he reached for the recorder to shut it off. His face was drawn and colorless. For a very long time he sat in silence, staring at the machine. Then, after a deep breath, his pain-filled eyes rose to meet those of his daughters'. He spoke with great difficulty. "I—don't know what to say. I've been a fool."

Lisa moved around behind her father and placed a hand on his shoulder. "I'm sorry, Father," she said. "I'm sorry you got mixed up with a man like Edward Reeves, and I'm sorry I had to be the one to bring your world crashing down around you. But you're right. You have been a fool. And more than that, you've been dead wrong in some of the things you've been doing lately. I hope you're ready now to take a long hard look at the sort of man Greg Reeves is. Would you really want me spending my life with a man like him?"

J.T. stood and pulled Lisa to him. He didn't speak, but only held her, grateful that he hadn't sold her to a man who didn't deserve her. When he stepped back to look Lisa in the eye, he did something she was totally unprepared for. Opening his center desk drawer, he removed a small diamond ring, a ring Lisa had no trouble recognizing as the one Rob had given her that night on the lake. The one J.T. had taken from her the day he drove a wedge between her and Rob. Still not speaking, J.T. gently lifted Lisa's hand and slid the ring on her finger, then leaned forward and kissed her on the cheek.

"Oh, Father," Lisa cried. "Does this mean . . ."

"Yes, Lisa. It means exactly what you think it does."

"Way to go, Uncle Mac," Samantha congratulated him. "I've never been more proud of you."

J.T.'s attention turned to Samantha. "The man mentioned in the tape," he asked softly. "The one Ed plans to lure to the scene of the explosion . . ."

Samantha understood his question even before he could finish it. "There's no reason to worry. He's in good hands. He has two angels on his side, plus Gus Winkelbury, who you met earlier in your car. And in case you're concerned about Ed Reeves, don't be. Where he's going, he'll never be a threat to anyone ever again."

Slowly, J.T. walked over to where Julie and Eric were standing. He spoke to Eric. "Just two things, young man," he said soberly.

"No, you don't, Dad," Julie said, quickly stepping between the two men.

"It's all right, Julie," J.T. assured her, gently easing her aside so he was again facing Eric. "First of all, young man, I'd like to know if you can accept the apology of a stubborn old fool. And next, I'd like to ask if you'll tell me how you managed to acquire this recording."

Eric smiled and extended his hand toward J.T. "No apology needed, sir."

As the two men shook hands, J.T. said, "I seem to have been blind to a lot of things lately. But your tape had a way of convincing me. And speaking of the tape, did your angel by chance have anything to do with you recording it?"

"Jason had everything to do with me recording the tape," Eric explained "You see, I didn't know where Julie lived. I didn't know her last name." Then with a glance in Julie's direction he added, "I didn't even know her *first* name."

J.T. looked embarrassed. "I understand completely. She couldn't trust letting you meet her father. Ashamed as I am to admit it, she was right. But I'd like to say, Eric, you're a man after my own heart. You were very brave making that tape, however you did it. When you walked into my office, I thought you were just another young pup trying to get at my money through my daughter. I was wrong about you, Eric. If it makes any difference, you have my permission to properly court my daughter. Not that you haven't been doing it anyway," J.T. added with a chuckle.

"Oh Daddy," Julie cried, throwing her arms around J.T.'s neck. "Do you mean it?"

"Yes, Julie. I mean every word of it. I've been a blind old fool, and it took an angel named Sam to help me recognize that. Can you forgive me?"

Julie kissed him on the cheek. "Yes, Dad. I can gladly forgive you, if you just stay the way you are now. But if you ever fall back into your old ways . . ."

J.T. squeezed Julie's hand. "I've learned my lesson," he said. "You can count on it."

Lisa stepped up next to them. "Father, does this mean Rob and I have your blessings, too?" she asked.

"Yes, Lisa," J.T. assured her. "You and Rob do have my blessings. Is he still in town?"

"He is, Father. He's staying at—"

In mid-sentence, Lisa was cut off by a familiar and furious voice as Greg Reeves entered the room. "I'm glad to see you're here, J.T.," he said angrily. "I think you'll find this stubborn daughter of yours has some explaining to do. And personally, I doubt if you're going to like what she has to say."

J.T. eyed Greg, who looked a mess. His suit looked like it had survived a tornado, and as he wore no shoes, his stockings were torn and covered with mud. His face was coated with what appeared to be road sludge.

"What do you want here?" J.T. asked curtly.

"What do I want?" Greg snapped. "I want to know once and for all where I stand with your daughter. She embarrassed me badly tonight, J.T., and I see no reason why I should tolerate her childish actions any longer. If you still want me to marry her, then I suggest you have a serious talk with her about her inappropriate behavior."

J.T. drew a deep breath and spoke in a cold, but controlled voice. "You've obviously been drinking, Greg. Haven't I made it clear I don't want you drinking when you have my daughter in your car?"

"Oh come on, J.T., don't make a big deal out of a couple of drinks when the real problem is your daughter."

"Get rid of him, Uncle Mac," Samantha ordered. "You and Lisa can do much better than him."

J.T. nodded in agreement, then very deliberately said, "Get out of my house, young man."

"What did you say?" Greg stared in surprise at J.T.

"I said—get out of my house."

"Listen, you old fool," Greg spluttered furiously. "If you want to see one dime of my father's money invested in the mall deal, you had better start treating me a little more civilly."

J.T. took a step closer to Greg, leaving them only inches apart. "Do me a favor, Greg," he said, emphasizing each word very carefully. "Give your father a message for me. Tell him our business association is finished. He can take his money and shove it up his nose for all I care."

The anger in Greg's eyes gave way to anxiety. "What? Have you lost your sanity, J.T.?"

J.T. shook his head. "No, Greg. As a matter of fact, I've just regained it."

Greg nervously ran his fingers through his hair. Blowing the deal for his father would bring serious retribution, and he knew it. "You can't do this! Too much depends on your deal with my father— more than you can possibly know."

"I know everything, Greg. I know about your father's plans to blow up the building and his intentions to murder an innocent man. I know who the victim is supposed to be, and I'm aware that your father intends to lay the blame at my door. Well, you can tell him his plan has backfired. I won't be signing any of his papers, and if he so much as looks at the man we both know he wants killed, I'll have the police down his throat so fast he won't be able to swallow for a year. And you can tell him one more thing for me, Greg. Tell him even if Katherine Allen hadn't walked out on him to marry me, she would have found another reason to leave. Katherine was much too intelligent to put up with the life your father would have given her."

"But—this is impossible," Greg stammered. "How could you . . . ?"

"How do I know?" J.T. laughed. "An angel told me, Greg. No, come to think of it, there were two angels. And they were assisted by a man I'm happy to announce will soon be my son-in-law."

Greg lunged forward, gripping J.T. by the lapels. "You can't do this to me!" he shouted.

Grabbing J.T. was a mistake, Greg quickly found, as he landed in a limp heap on the floor. It took several seconds before his eyes could focus enough to see J.T. standing over him ominously.

Greg put a hand to his aching head. "You can't get away with this, MacGregor," he growled. "My father is a powerful man."

"Your father may be a powerful man," he responded. "But not as powerful as the people I have on my side. Now are you going to leave, or do I have to throw you out?"

Julie glanced over at her sister. "Shall we?" she asked.

"Let's," Lisa answered with a nod.

Before Greg realized what was happening, Lisa had grabbed his left arm and Julie his right. Together they escorted him to the front door and ushered him through it. "I'll see to it you live to regret this," Greg said angrily to Lisa.

"The only thing I regret is not doing it a lot sooner," Lisa said firmly. "My mother once turned her back on your father, and now it's my turn to do the same to you, Greg. I wonder if it felt as good to her as it feels for me." And with that, Lisa closed the door in Greg's face.

"That's the most fun I've had in years!" Julie exclaimed.

"It did feel good, didn't it?" Lisa agreed as the two of them enjoyed a sisterly hug.

"Well, it didn't feel all that good to me," J.T. grumbled, as he joined them. "I'm getting a little old for that sort of thing. You were about to tell me about Rob when we were so rudely interrupted, Lisa. I'd like to see him, if I could. I owe him an apology, and I'd just as soon not put it off."

Lisa smiled. "I'll take you to him, Father. I wasn't sure I'd ever see the day I'd be glad to hear myself say those words, but—"

"Hey," Julie cried. "Eric and I are coming, too. There's no way I'm missing this show. We can all go in Little Blue. So get ready for the ride of your life, Dad!"

* * *

Rob sat alone in his apartment, picking at the strings of his guitar while quietly singing the words to a song he had written after first meeting Lisa. He missed her deeply, and he wondered if she missed him, too. He hated the idea of her going out with that Greg fellow. But if Rob interfered in any way, it would be his father who would suffer. His father was already starting to walk with his new legs, and Rob knew his father would continue to need therapy for quite some time. Which meant Rob would have to wait out the year before contacting Lisa.

At least things were going well in his career. The tour he'd just completed had been a great success. It had given him the chance to present several of his songs to a live audience, and the fans had gone wild. He felt sure his songs were good enough to go to the top, if he could only find someone who would record them and put them out on the airwaves. Heaven knows he had sent out enough demos.

A knock came at the door, and Rob wondered who it could be. He seldom had visitors these days. Setting his guitar aside, he walked to the door, remembering the times he had opened the door to Lisa's knock and seen her beautiful, smiling face. How he wished it would be her face waiting on the other side of the door now. But he knew that was impossible.

He sighed and reached for the doorknob, then opened the door to the most wonderful surprise of his life. There was Lisa's beautiful, smiling face, and even before he could catch his breath, she was in his arms, kissing him like never before.

It was no less than a full minute before Rob realized Lisa was not alone. When he saw that one of them was J.T. MacGregor, his heart leapt into his throat. Sensing his concern, Lisa stroked his hair and kissed him once more. "It's all right," she said, handing him the gold chain he had given her at their last good-bye. "I won't be needing this anymore. I'm wearing your ring again, and it was my father who put it back on my finger. He has something to say to you, Rob. May we come in?"

Rob could hardly speak. "Uh—yes. Please come in, all of you."

With no warning at all, Julie slipped ahead of everyone and pushed her sister aside. Planting a kiss soundly on Rob's lips, she greeted him warmly, "Welcome to the family, Rob."

Lisa grabbed her sister by the arm. "Julie MacGregor!" she hissed. "What are you doing?"

Julie laughed. "Fair is fair, big sister. Now maybe you'll think twice before you kiss my guy again. And I'm happy to say that Rob seems to be a good enough kisser for my big sister. He's almost as good as Eric."

Lisa pulled Rob away from Julie. "Eric," she called out. "Will you come over here and get this crazy woman of yours before I forget she's my little sister?"

J.T.'s apology was brief, but heartfelt. "I won't welcome you to the family the way my daughter Julie did, but I assure you, my welcome is just as sincere."

"Way to go, Uncle Mac," Samantha responded happily. "I think you'll be glad to know you're about to get your wish. I'll be going home now, since I'm no longer needed here. It's been fun haunting you. And don't worry about Edward Reeves. I give you my word, he won't be bothering you ever again." She turned and took a step toward the door.

"Wait!" J.T. called to her. She stopped and faced him once more. "I just want you to know . . ." J.T.'s voice fell silent as the lump in his throat grew tighter.

Samantha smiled. "I know, Uncle Mac," she said understandingly. "I'm proud of you. I always knew you'd come through in the end. You're still my favorite uncle, and you always will be. I love you Uncle Mac. Now get on with the rest of your life, will you? And make it a little happier than it's been the last few years, okay?"

"Okay, Sam," J.T. managed to say. "You take care, now."

She smiled at him once again, then stepping directly into the closed door, she disappeared from sight.

"What is it, Dad?" Julie asked. "You look like you're about to cry. Are you all right?"

"I'm fine, Julie," he answered. "I just watched your cousin Sam walk away. I never thought I'd say this, but I'm going to miss her. I'm going to miss her."

CHAPTER 20

Ed Reeves brought the big limo to a stop in the alley behind the old warehouse at 707 Waterfront Drive. It was here that he'd had the faulty building materials stashed away until he could make them appear to be J.T.'s property. Ed was glad traffic had been light, and that he'd encountered no police along the way. Not only was his driving experience well beyond the rusty stage, he didn't even have a valid license. Wouldn't that have been something? Edward Reeves stopped by a cop for a traffic ticket. He had lawyers who had gotten him off various charges ranging from drug dealing to murder. Wouldn't it be something if he got a traffic ticket he couldn't beat in court? That would be humiliating to say the least. No matter, he was here now and there was work to be done.

Stepping from the car, he slid the key into the lock of the only unbolted door to the building. Slipping inside, he fumbled for the light switch, which he finally located on the wall near the door, and flipped on the switch. Out of the twenty overhead fixtures, a meager three lights came on. The rest remained dark, their lamps having long ago burned out. The faint, scattered light left eerie shadows on the stacks of boxes and materials stored throughout the large warehouse. The building was a far cry from the settings of luxury Ed was more accustomed to. He wished his bodyguards were with him.

Ed made his way purposely to the desk in the center of the room where he had instructed that the explosives be placed. Just as he expected, he found the job had in fact been carried out just as he had ordered. And, as he had feared, his own personal cellular phone lay in plain sight on top of the desk. Just as he was about to pick it up, he was interrupted by the unexpected sound of a voice. Whirling to see who had spoken, he was mortified to see the same strange little man he had encountered earlier in his office.

"The place sorta gives ya the creeps, don't it, pal? I'll bet there's enough spiders in here ta eat a ton of flies."

"You again?" Ed snorted. "Who are you? And what do you want? If it's money, you've come to the wrong man."

"Name's Gus. And yer money's got nothin' ta do with it. I'm here ta be yer escort into the next dimension. Not that I'm a regular at this sort of thing, ya understand. I'm just fillin' in for my friend, Gabe. He has some other things goin' on right now, and I sorta wanted ta do this anyhow. This may come as a shock to ya, pal, but yer not one of my favorite people."

Ed stared at Gus as though his eyes could burn the unwelcome visitor to stubble. "Do you have any idea who you're dealing with?" he said belligerently. "With one call on that phone, I could have you buried so deep so fast you'd never know what hit you. You had better do some fast talking, and you had better come up with the right answers."

Gus paid no attention to Ed's idle threat. "I gotta say, pal. It was darn human of you ta rearrange yer affairs so yer money goes ta help all those homeless fellows and gals. Of course, most of them are homeless in the first place because you made them that way. Shuttin' down apartments ta make more enterprisin' use of the buildings was a great pastime of yours. But then, every big-shot crook should have places ta store his contraband, right? So what if it messed up a few lives? I'll tell ya this much, though. Old Greg ain't gonna like yer little surprise. He was sorta countin' on havin' those big bucks fer himself."

"What are you raving about? I wouldn't leave one rusty dime to those bums on the streets."

Gus shrugged. "I suppose Maggie's computer had somethin' ta do with changin' yer will, but it got changed, nevertheless. Now, pal, I hope yer about ready for yer little trip. In your case, it won't be as pleasant a trip as most folks I deal with. But I'll leave the bulk of the explainin' to a fellow you're about ta meet. Not a likeable sort, but one who has a way of gettin' his point across."

Ed shook his finger at Gus. "You're a cop!" he shouted. "You think you can pin something on me here, don't you? Ha! A lot of cops have tried, but not one has ever succeeded. Buying off a judge is a lot easier than you can imagine. You may think I'll end up in prison, but I have news for you—it's not going to happen. There's no prison built that can hold Big Ed Reeves."

"Humph," Gus responded. "I know one that can. And whether you like it or not, yer about to get a good look at the one I have in mind. Ya know, fer a fellow who thinks of himself as such a bright sort, you sure pulled a dumb one on yerself. After goin' ta all the trouble ta have the door on this place rigged so's it couldn't be opened from the inside, you walked right into yer own trap. Personally, I wouldn't put much stock in you bein' all that smart."

Ed shot a quick look at the door he had come through. Gus was right; Big Ed had managed to trap himself inside. He had been so interested in retrieving the phone that he had completely forgotten about the door being rigged. The phone! Yes, at least he had the phone. He could make a call, and help would be here within minutes. He turned back to the desk, and felt the pulse of his heart quicken when he realized the phone wasn't where he had seen it only minutes earlier. His attention shifted to Gus. Who was this man, and how did he manage all these crazy things? None of this made any sense. First his bodyguards falling asleep, his own chocolate gun, and their plastic guns. No doubt about it, this guy was good. And now he had managed to conceal Ed's phone. The hair on the back of Ed's neck stood up, and for the first time he felt a hint of apprehension. This was something he was completely unaccustomed to. "What have you done with my phone?" he shouted at Gus.

Gus smiled and pointed toward the ceiling over the desk. Ed looked up and spotted the phone. It was hanging in mid-air—barely out of reach, although Ed couldn't see the wire that had to be there suspending it.

"Like I said," Gus went on. "I'm here as yer escort. Just as soon as that phone rings, the fireworks will begin. You'll get a bang out of it, pal. But then you already know that, don't ya? I mean, yer the one who masterminded this whole setup in the first place."

Ed's heart was pounding. "No!" he cried out. "That can't happen. The detonator is set to trigger only at the sound of MacGregor's phone, and I left that one in the limo."

Gus laughed. "Fer a fellow who made it a habit of not trustin' people, you sure got yerself caught up in this one. Sure, George Weathersby was smart enough ta steal the idea from Eric Roberts, but that don't mean he was smart enough ta make it work. George was lucky ta get a detonator workin' off the sound of any phone. But that's just what he did. He figured you'd never know the difference, anyway."

Ed looked at the phone again. "You mean," he gasped. "If someone calls me on that phone . . ."

"Ya got it, pal. And I have it on good authority that ya got a call coming through in the next few minutes. By the way, do the names Ralph Richmond, Carl Sanders, and Frank Albertson mean anythin' to ya?"

Ed was sweating heavily now. The names Gus had mentioned were among those Ed had put contracts out on in the past, to have them wiped out.

"I can tell by the look on yer face ya know the names," Gus went on to say with a great deal of pleasure. "Well, pal, let me tell ya—they're all three waitin' to greet ya. Won't that be a reunion ta write home about?"

* * *

Greg stared at the reflection of himself in his bathroom mirror. He was a mess. His clothes were tattered, there were bruise marks on his head from being scraped on the asphalt on Hillview Road, and his shoulder ached from having his arm twisted behind his back. But if he hurt on the outside, it was nothing compared to the way he felt on the inside. It was bad enough he had lost all hopes of ever marrying Lisa, but now he had to face his father, too.

After applying a skin-tone Band-Aid to the bruise on his forehead, he stepped back into his bedroom where he stood for a long time looking at the phone next to his bed. At last, he picked it up. There was no use putting off the inevitable. One digit at a time, he pressed in the number to his father's personal cellular phone. Pushing the last button, he heard the "click" as the connection was made. At that moment, the sound of a distant explosion drew him to the window for a look. Staring into the darkness of the night, he saw what appeared to be a fire in the direction of the waterfront.

"What in the world could have caused that?" he wondered as he waited for his father to pick up the phone. However, instead of his father's voice, Greg heard only a recorded message.

"We are sorry, but the cellular phone you are trying to reach is not in service at this time."

CHAPTER 21

J.T. leaned against the railing as he stared out across the serenity of Dove Park Lake. A soft evening breeze ruffled through the overhead branches, lulling him into a world of thoughtful contemplation. There was a definite autumn chill in the air. Of all the seasons, J.T. loved autumn the best. It had been an autumn day when he had first met Katherine. It had been autumn when both Lisa and Julie were born. Now, another occasion could be added to the list—the double wedding of his beautiful daughters had taken place less than seven hours earlier.

J.T. had to laugh at himself. He couldn't believe how he had come to love and admire the two men who were now his sons-in-law. Was it only last year when they were "the enemy"? One thing he couldn't figure, though, was how Lisa had ended up with Rob and Julie with Eric. J.T. thought Julie's personality seemed better fitted for the part of a musician's fast life while Lisa's personality would seem to be more suited to the laid-back routine of an electrical engineer. *Maybe the old adage is true, after all*, J.T. mused. *Opposites do attract.*

Another thing J.T. had found hard to believe was the change in his relationship with Lisa and Julie. In the past few months, both had shown an increased willingness to open up and share the tender feelings of their hearts. Lisa had shared with him the story of how Rob proposed to her on this very lake. J.T. chuckled as he wondered if the ukulele was still out there somewhere on the bottom of the lake.

I have to admit, J.T. said to himself, *Rob has more class than Greg ever could have had. I'm not sure if Greg ever actually proposed to Lisa. If he did, I imagine he would have done it by fax. I'm glad that stubborn*

Sam came along when she did. I'd never admit that to her, of course. But she did help me make some good changes in my life. Not that I couldn't have done it without her, he told himself quickly.

Spotting a small, flat rock next to his foot, J.T. bent down and picked it up. With a flip of his wrist, he sent it skipping across the surface of the lake. He was pleased to note that it skipped seven times. He was sure that must be some kind of record. *Is this what you've come down to, J.T.?* he chuckled to himself. *Coming alone to the park to skip rocks?*

The truth was, he just couldn't bring himself to go home to his big lonely house. Being alone was something J.T. never could handle well. When Katherine went away, he at least had the girls to keep him company. Now they had left to go on their separate honeymoons, and when they did return it would be to homes of their own. Not that he wouldn't be welcome in their homes, and they in his. But it just wouldn't be the same.

With a deep sigh, J.T. began walking along the narrow sidewalk that circled the edge of the lake. As he walked, he smiled to himself. *Won't the kids be surprised when they each learn what I've given them for their wedding presents?* As both Lisa and Julie had been preparing to leave after the reception, J.T. had handed them each an envelope with instructions not to open it until the next morning. That way, he figured they could wake to an even better first day of their new lives.

J.T. drew in a deep breath of the crisp autumn air and paused to look out across the lake once more. He smiled as he remembered how shocked George Weathersby had been when the judge ruled in favor of returning the patent for the voice-control device to its rightful owner, Eric Roberts. It had been a relatively simple matter for a professional lawyer, along with his private investigator, to prove that the device had belonged to Eric, and not to George. Much of it had been due to their past records with similar college projects. Testimony after testimony showed how capable Eric was of the design, whereas George couldn't figure out the workings of the most simple electronic circuitry. The lawyer had even set up a test to be conducted in the presence of the judge. It was a test that required only the most basic design skills, and George failed it miserably. The clincher had come when a handwriting expert testified that the project notes matched

Eric's handwriting, and not George's. After the verdict, George had accused J.T. of everything from fraud to thievery. But in the end, justice had been served.

Naturally, J.T. had kept all this a secret from Eric and Julie. When they opened their envelope tomorrow morning, they would find the ruling. J.T. was proud of himself for thinking of such a great wedding gift.

He figured he had done as well with Rob and Lisa. *Won't they be surprised when they open their envelope to find a contract for the recording and release of Rob's last five songs?* J.T. thought with satisfaction. The only thing left to make the contract legal and binding was Rob's own signature. J.T. had used Rob's demos to secure the deal. No question about it, Rob was good. And with J.T.'s contacts, the deal wasn't all that hard to negotiate. The songs would be released one at a time over the next year. *That's the advantage to having friends in the right places,* J.T. boasted to himself.

Shoving his hands in his pockets, J.T. began walking again. As he walked, he kicked at a dry leaf and watched it flutter a few inches before falling motionless back to the sidewalk. *Life is a lot like the flight of that leaf,* he observed somberly. *An instant after its flight began, it was over. Everything good seems to pass away just that fast in real life. One minute I had my wonderful Katie, the next she was gone. Then I had the girls, and now they're going away to lives of their own. Wouldn't it be nice to have something wonderful that could last forever? But I suppose that's just not how real life works.*

Feeling a bit tired, J.T. took a seat on an empty park bench not far from the lake's edge. Glancing up at the big moon, he brushed back his hair and released a heavy sigh. "I wish you could have been there today, Katie," he said aloud, as though this might help her to actually hear. "You would have loved seeing your daughters so happy. Happier than I've ever seen them, and more beautiful, too. Oh how I wish you could have been there."

"Aunt Katie was there, Uncle Mac," came a familiar, but completely unexpected voice. "She saw the whole thing. And you're right, she did love every minute of it."

J.T. glanced up. "Sam?" he asked in surprise. "I don't understand. I thought I'd seen the last of you."

"Well, that's a nice way to greet the angel who almost single-handedly turned your life around. I'd think you'd be a little more glad to see me," Samantha said.

"Glad to see you? Why in heaven's name would I be glad to see you, Sam? What more can you possibly want from me? I've done everything you expected of me, haven't I? Even Ebenezer Scrooge had it better than this. Once his tormenters managed to get their message across, they went away and left him alone."

Samantha smiled at his grumbling. "You, Uncle Mac MacGregor, are beyond a doubt the most stubborn and ungrateful man I've ever met. I'll never understand what Aunt Katie sees in you. Come on, admit it—you're glad to see me again and you know it."

J.T. laughed. "Some things never change. I see you're still the same old Sam. I admit it wasn't too bad having you around. And you do deserve some credit for helping me out of a bad situation—not that I couldn't have worked everything out myself, mind you."

"Oh sure you could, Uncle Mac. About as well as you could turn Godzilla into a lovable house pet."

"So what's it going to be, Sam? Are you going to stand there trading insults with me, or do you want to tell me why you're here this time?"

"Why am I here?" Samantha asked. "I'm here to finish the job I started the day I first met with you in your office. My assignment was to secure three contracts," she explained. "You probably don't understand what I mean when I refer to Gus' typo, but suffice it to say that it caused some pretty big problems. Part of those problems concerned you and my cousins."

"You used the word 'contracts,'" J.T. observed. "You used the same word on that morning you first came to me in my office. At the time, I thought you meant the contract between Ed Reeves and me. But that wasn't it at all, was it, Sam? You were referring to something else altogether, weren't you?"

Samantha nodded. "I was referring to three specific contracts. One between Lisa and Rob, another between Julie and Eric, and the third—"

"Between Katie and me?" J.T. broke in.

"That's right. You see, if I'd lived, like destiny originally planned for me to do, I'd have been there to make sure you didn't blow everything with that strange attitude you developed over the years. But since I didn't live to do my part in the flesh, I had to come back as an angel to get the job done. I'd say two of the contracts are well on their way to being sealed in stone. But there's still one contract left open, and that's why I'm here, Uncle Mac. Actually, I didn't have to come back personally this time. This part of the plan could have been handled in a more routine way. But Aunt Katie asked me to finish the job—so here I am."

"You've seen my Katie?" J.T. asked excitedly.

"Hey!" Samantha suddenly cried out, completely ignoring J.T.'s question. "I just realized something. The bench you're sitting on is the same bench I sat on with Jason when I came to this park to feed the ducks one afternoon. It was on this very bench I first began to realize he was more than just a trick of my imagination."

J.T. was more interested in hearing about Katie than about Jason. "Tell me about Katie, Sam. How does she look? Does she miss me? You said she was at the wedding. Was she satisfied with how things went?"

Samantha didn't seem to hear him. "I remember it like it just happened," Samantha rambled on. "Jason and I had been talking. He came over to this bench and sat down, right where you're sitting now. I don't know what possessed me to do it, but I sat down next to him." She paused to let the memory wash over her. "Jason was shocked," she laughed. "'Do you know what you just did, Sam?' he asked me. 'You just broke your own ground rule.' I did break my own rule, too, Uncle Mac. You see, when I first met Jason, I had made up this ground rule that he couldn't come near me, him being a ghost and all. Anyway, when I sat next to him, I broke my own rule. I think that was when I began to realize he was more than just a trick of my imagination."

"Blast you, Sam!" J.T. complained loudly. "Just once I'd like to see you stick to a subject. You said you saw Katie. Is it asking too much for you to tell me what she had to say?"

"I'll get back to Aunt Katie in a minute," Samantha said, brushing off J.T.'s anxiousness. "Right now I want to tell you something. After I tried to touch Jason's face and found I couldn't feel him at all, he called me beautiful. He even said he loved me. Can you imagine how I felt, Uncle Mac? How many women ever have a ghost in love with them?"

"How would I know how many women have a ghost in love with them?" he grumped. "And for that matter, what do I care?"

"What's with you?" Samantha scolded. "You came to the park tonight so you could remember some of the good times. Is it so bad if I want to do the same?"

"Hogwash! I came to the park because I wanted to be alone. Now you've come along and spoiled my quiet evening. You're the one who brought up the subject of Katie in the first place."

"All right," Samantha sighed heavily. "If you're in such an all-fired hurry that we can't even take a minute to enjoy a few fond memories, then let's get on with what I came here to do."

What Samantha did next caught J.T. completely off guard. "Here," she said, offering him her hand. "Let me help you up."

J.T. stared at her hand. "What, do you think I was born yesterday?" he scowled. "I can't touch your hand. You yourself told me it's part of the rules."

Samantha grew impatient. "The rules have changed," she snapped. "Take my hand."

"What do you mean the rules have changed?" J.T. asked, still not moving.

"Uncle Mac! Haven't you learned by now not to argue with me? Take my hand!"

J.T. reached for her hand, expecting his own hand to slide through it as it had before. To his amazement, it didn't. Instead, he felt the touch of her soft hand in his own. Not knowing what to expect next, he let her pull him to his feet. For the first time, he noticed someone standing a few feet away. "Who's your friend, Sam?" he asked, still astonished he could feel her hand.

"This, Uncle Mac," she said, "is my favorite ghost and my husband, Jason Hackett."

"Jason?" came J.T.'s confused reply. "I'm—happy to meet you. But I must say, I never expected to see you firsthand. You've got yourself a great little woman here. A bit strong-minded at times, but a great little woman, nevertheless."

Jason reached out and took Samantha by the hand. "You're right about that, J.T." he agreed. "And you're pretty lucky yourself. Your Katherine is certainly a very special lady."

"You know my Katie, too?"

"You bet I know her. I know her very well after helping out with your assignment. She was there giving me advice every step of the way."

J.T. was angry at himself for the lump that suddenly formed in his throat. That wasn't supposed to happen to a man. He swallowed hard. "Do me a favor will you, Jason? The next time you see my Katie, tell her I love her. And tell her I miss her, too. I miss her most of all when I lie down at night and find her pillow cold and empty. We used to have these little nighttime chats and . . ." It was no use. By this time J.T.'s voice had choked off completely.

Jason smiled. "I don't think I could do you justice with Katherine. So it might be better if you tell her yourself."

"Tell her myself?" J.T. asked. "How am I supposed to do . . . ?"

Before he could finish his own question, she was suddenly there, right in front of him. She was wearing a beautiful white dress, the same one she wore in his favorite picture of her. She looked more beautiful than he remembered. "Katie?" he choked out. "Is it . . ."

"It's me," Katherine said, smiling.

J.T. wanted to rush to her, but his feet refused to move. "How is this possible?" he stammered. "Am I dreaming?"

"Are you going to stand there asking questions all night?" she whispered. "Or do I get the kiss I've been waiting for—for more than eleven years now?"

J.T. still couldn't move, but it didn't matter. Katherine came to him. After he gazed into her eyes for a moment, he felt a new strength. He, too, had waited eleven years for this kiss, and it proved to be worth every second of the wait. It was a kiss that erased all the pain and loneliness he had felt over the long years. It was also a kiss that offered a promise. A promise of a love that would be his throughout the decades of forever.

Still cradled in her arms, J.T. marveled at her beauty. "You're so young," he whispered. "And so beautiful. I've never seen you this beautiful."

Her reply caught him by surprise. "And you're so young and handsome, J.T. More handsome than I've ever seen you."

He laughed. "No, Katie. I'm not young and handsome. Not any more. The years without you have taken their toll, I'm afraid."

"Look," Katherine said, pointing to the water's surface near where they were standing. "See for yourself how young and handsome you are."

J.T. looked, and there in the light of the full moon he caught a glimpse of a man in the reflection who was much younger than the one he had faced when he shaved that morning. And then a thought struck him. "Wait a minute," he said, thinking aloud. "When Sam offered her hand, I could feel it in my own. That's not supposed to happen. And I can see Jason. That's not supposed to happen, either. And now I find myself in your arms, Katie. Good heavens—I must be—"

J.T. looked back to the bench where he had been sitting only moments earlier. Just as he suspected, the old J.T. was there slumped over as if asleep. "But it was so easy," he whispered. "I never felt a thing."

"That's because you did it the natural way," Samantha laughed. "Not like choking on a chicken bone, or something."

"Very funny," Jason grumbled. "You never will give up on that, will you, Sam?"

"Probably not," she teased, with a quick kiss to let him know it was all in fun.

Katherine spoke up. "Not five minutes ago you were wishing to be with me forever, Mr. MacGregor. Well, you've just been granted your wish. You have my word, there will be no more empty pillows ever again."

A mixture of emotion flooded J.T.'s mind as he thought about Lisa and Julie. "But Katie," he gasped. "What about our daughters? They still need me."

"To use one of your favorite words," Katherine laughed, "'hogwash.' Lisa and Julie will do just fine without you. You should know what strong young women they are. I'm the one who needs you now. It's been a little lonely on my side these last years, too, you know."

"Tell you what, Uncle Mac," Samantha offered. "Since Jason and I plan to volunteer for another assignment anyway, we'll look in on your daughters once in a while. Just to be sure they're all right."

"We plan on doing what?" Jason choked. "Over my dead—well, you know what I mean."

"Would you do that for me, Sam?" J.T. asked. "It would mean a lot. Much as it pains me to admit it, I'd trust you with most anything. Even watching out for my daughters."

"Well, thank you, Uncle Mac. That was a nice thing to say. And yes, I give you my word I'll keep a close check on Lisa and Julie, although they're both in pretty good hands with those guys I convinced you they should marry."

"Okay, Sam. I can't argue with that. Not in good conscience anyway."

Suddenly, a tiny light burst into sight against the blackness of the velvet sky. It soon outshone the luster of the full moon, and grew even brighter until it rivaled a noontime sun. Within the light a tunnel gradually appeared that led into the distance as far as the eye could see. J.T. stared at the spectacle with silent wonderment.

"It's our passageway home," Katherine whispered, smiling. "You're about to see the wonder of the far side of forever."

J.T. glanced at Samantha, as if wondering what to do next. "Go on," she said, motioning toward the light. "Jason and I won't be far behind."

Drawing in a deep breath, J.T. took Katherine by the arm and stepped forward. Soon, they were engulfed by the light.

Once they could no longer be seen, Samantha lay her head on Jason's shoulder. "Does this remind you of anything?" she purred.

"You bet it does," Jason was quick to respond. "It reminds me of the happiest day of my life."

"The happiest day of your life?" she asked. "Does that mean you're satisfied with me being your forever wife?"

Jason pulled her to himself, and kissed her. "That, my cute little lady ghost, is a question that needn't be asked. You're everything I've ever wanted a wife to be."

"Oh yeah?" she asked, with a playful poke to his ribs. "I saw the way you drooled over Lisa and Julie's long gorgeous hair. Admit it. You're disappointed that mine is short, aren't you?"

"Sam," Jason said, as the two of them stepped into the light. "How many times do I have to tell you? I love your hair just the way it is."

The light dimmed and the tunnel closed, leaving the beauty of the autumn night to a lone owl in the branches of a nearby tree.

Reflections from the big round moon shimmered brightly off the calm surface of Dove Park Lake, and all was at peace with the world.

P.S. Lisa kept her word. Scarcely a month passed that she didn't visit the cemetery with flowers for Katherine's grave—and for J.T.'s, as well. She always bought her flowers at Jan's Floral, the same shop where Greg worked as night janitor. True, this was a step down from state governor, but as luck would have it, it was the only job he could get.

ABOUT THE AUTHOR

Dan Yates has always enjoyed writing. "I love storytelling," he says. "It's my belief that using a story for teaching is the best way possible to get a point across. A good story will always hold the student's attention and turn the work of learning into fun. I learned this principle from the greatest teacher who ever lived. He taught the same way, but he called them parables."

Dan's previous writing efforts have resulted in Church productions and local publications, as well as the two best-selling novels *Angels Don't Knock* and *Just Call Me an Angel*.

A former bishop and high councilman, Dan and his wife, Shelby Jean, live in Phoenix, Arizona. They have six children and sixteen grandchildren. He loves to hear from his readers, who can write to him at yates@swlink.net.